CHAPTER 1 ~ THE BET

Louis' POV

I was standing by my locker at school when one of my two best friends, Zayn, walked over to me. I was just about to slam the locker shut when he opened his mouth.

"Ey, Louis? I've got a bet for ya, mate," he smirked at me.

He was wearing a black t-shirt along with some skinny, black jeans. He also had his nose and lip ring, while his eyes were framed by long eyelashes and a pretty thick layer of eyeliner.

According to us and our friend Liam, we were the school's most popular lads, but according to some other people, the more 'posh' ones, Harry and his best friend Niall were. I hated them for that. Especially Harry, the curly-haired one. He looked so cute that I wanted to vomit. Those pretty curls were just too much, and those piercing green eyes... ugh. Okay, he was cute, but absolutely not my type. Niall, on the other hand, was a bit cooler. He was a little bit of a man-whore like us lads but didn't have any piercings. Honestly, I quite enjoyed being the so-called 'man-whore', or 'womanizer' at school. Every girl practically threw themselves at me all the time.

However, Harry and Niall did exist as well. They had all the cute girls, which I - of course - also wanted. Harry had a girlfriend though, Sarah Hamilton. They'd been together for almost a year now. She had blonde, wavy hair with blue eyes, and was one of those jealous girls that got upset if someone else just held his hand. She did seem like a nice girl, though. Not that I'd been keeping an eye on them or anything...

"What is it this time?" I asked, shaking my head while grinning.

I actually liked Zayn's bets. Once, he'd bet me that I couldn't ask Tarah, one of Danielle Peazer's best friends, for a fuck without getting a slap in the face. You see, she wasn't that girl who would sleep around with different people all the time. Danielle and her two best friends, Eleanor and Tarah were the ones I called 'ordinary' at our school. They were somewhere in between me and Harry. However, I had won the bet. It turned out Tarah had wanted to fuck me for two years.

We never had a price, though. When one of us won, we just laughed about it, nothing more. It was all just fun and games, after all.

"I bet you can't kiss Harry without getting caught by his girl-friend. And, I bet he won't kiss you back," he said, tilting his head to the side with a smug look on his face. It was probably thanks to the fact that he was sure he was going to win.

I rolled my eyes. "Two bets in one, I see. You don't think I'm going to accomplish it?" I wondered, wiggling my eyebrows challengingly at him.

So, I would have to kiss Harry to win the bet? I didn't know whether to be disgusted or happy about it. I mean, Harry was just too much. I don't know, but I had never liked him, and the fact that I had to kiss someone I didn't really like disgusted me somehow.

However, I had never kissed a boy before. Yeah, I know, weird. I'd probably fucked more than half of the girls at our school, but I had never kissed a lad. I had always wanted to, though, just to feel what the difference was between a guy's and a girl's lips. And, I had to admit that Harry's lips looked quite delicious and plump. Not that I'd been checking his lips out, though. Pfft...

"We'll see about it."

"Easy," I said, stomping away.

I caught sight of Harry in a matter of seconds. He was leaning against his locker, facing Niall who was standing in front of him with his books in his arms. A smirk was playing on my lips as I walked over to them. Without a word, I grabbed the collar of Harry's shirt and backed him up against the wall of lockers behind him. Before he could open his mouth or even register what was happening, I pulled him down to crash my lips to his.

It took a while until he reacted, and when he did, he placed his hands on my chest in an attempt to push me off. However, it didn't take too long until a moan escaped his lips, and he started kissing me back. I almost fell to the floor by that moan. I mean, shit. It was so goddamn sexy!

My eyes fluttered closed as I felt myself leaning in even more to kiss him deeper. His pouty lips moved in sync with mine, my lip ring pressing against the skin of his bottom lip. Sparks were running up and down my spine and-- Wait, what the hell?!

I continued kissing him, biting his bottom lip harshly, asking for entrance, which he gladly granted. As soon as my tongue found his, butterflies erupted in my stomach. It felt like my entire body was on fire.

I let out a moan, pressing him even harder against the lockers behind his back. I then let my arms go around his neck and started tugging at the curls at the end of his neck with my fingers. His fingers dug into the skin at my waist, pressing me impossibly closer to him.

His lips felt soft, but not as soft as a girl's. They were a little rougher, which was just so perfect.

It wasn't until then everything suddenly hit me like a slap in the face. What was I doing?! It was supposed to be a kiss, not a full-blown make-out session!

I pulled away, opening my eyes. His were still closed, and a smile was slowly making its way to his lips. Seconds later, they fluttered open, and the sight in front of him caused his mouth to drop. He suddenly looked at me as if I was a murderer.

I lifted my hand to slap his cheek rather harshly. His hand instantly reached up to clutch it as his face showed nothing but pure fright.

I leaned in close to his ear. "This never happened, okay?" I breathed.

He nodded, tensing up at my proximity.

I smirked at that and pulled away, but not before giving him one last peck on the lips. I lingered a bit too long, but oh well, his lips were just perfect.

"You're a great kisser," I winked, turning around only to see that half of the school was staring at us with wide eyes.

Inwardly groaning, I shoved through the crowd until I found Zayn, still standing by my locker.

I hadn't even reached him until I could hear a loud voice shout behind me. "HARRY, WHAT THE HELL?! HOW COULD YOU?!"

I couldn't help but smile smugly to myself. I was probably the cause of a breakup today.

Zayn tilted his head to the side with an amused look on his face when he saw me. He opened his mouth to say something, but I beat him to it. "Don't ask. It just kind of happened," I said, scratching the back of my neck.

He burst out laughing. "I won."

I pulled my eyebrows together. How did he win? Harry reciprocated my kiss. However, right then, I could hear a loud smack, and that reminded me of something. I turned my head in the direction of the sound.

Harry was clutching both of his cheeks now, and his girlfriend - or now probably ex-girlfriend - was stomping away from him angrily.

I chuckled. "I guess you did," I said, turning back to Zayn.

CHAPTER 2 ~ GAME ON

Harry's POV

What the hell was that? Louis, the Louis Tomlinson actually kissed me? But why? Last time I checked, he would be someone who usually beat the shit out of me, so what the hell was going on?

I clutched my throbbing cheek in my hand, wincing at the pain that shot through it. God, why did he slap me? You couldn't just kiss someone then slap them afterward. That was just wrong on so many levels. It seemed like Louis was one of those people who could do just that, though.

"HARRY, WHAT THE HELL?! HOW COULD YOU?!"

Oh, shit. I was so dead. Out of all people, my girlfriend was suddenly heading towards me with quick strides, an angry look on her face. "Please, Sarah. Let me explain. I... I didn't want this. He kissed me first, and I tried to push him off, but he wouldn't budge! Please, you have to believe me! You know I love you," I pleaded, feeling close to tears.

I wasn't gay. I had never had feelings for a guy, and I had never even thought of being with one. Sure, maybe I had always found Louis attractive, but I had never felt the desire to kiss him! But those lips... They had felt so good against mine.

What are you talking about Harry?! That kiss was far from good!

"Bullshit. Do you really think I would believe that?! I saw you two, Harry, and what you did was far from pushing him off!" She huffed, and with that, she slapped the cheek that wasn't already aching.

I winced at the impact, pressing my other hand to the cheek she'd just hit so I was now clutching both of them. What was it with people slapping me today? And what had I ever done to deserve all this? Okay, so maybe I had kissed a guy when I was already in a relationship with a girl, but I didn't do it intentionally, at least. Fine, maybe I did... sort of, but it didn't mean anything!

"You're disgusting, Harry. And if you didn't know it already, we're over," she snapped, stomping away through the crowd that was watching everything take place.

I closed my eyes, letting out a sigh. I didn't want this to happen. Why did Louis have to kiss me? I didn't want to lose my girlfriend. I loved Sarah, and I had done so for an entire year.

I felt tears brimming my eyes both due to the throbbing in my cheeks and the fact that Sarah wasn't mine anymore. I slumped down to the floor and pushed my back against the lockers behind me. I then brought my knees to my chest while burying my face in my hands.

I couldn't care less about the fact that half of the school was watching me. They knew the reason I was crying at least.

"Okay, there's nothing's left to see. The show's over!" Niall called out to the crowd.

A few seconds later, I could feel a presence beside me. I didn't bother to look up and see who it was, though, because I already knew.

"Why are you still here, N-Niall? You should tell me how d-disgusting I am and leave me like everybody else," I sniffled behind my hands.

Niall grabbed both of them so he could look into my eyes. "You know I would never do that to you," he said, looking at me in concern.

I took a deep breath. He was right. He would never leave me. We had been best friends for as long as I could remember, and we had always been there for each other. So, why would that change now? But, I kissed a guy...

"Come on, Ni. You saw everything that happened. I fucking kissed a guy. Everyone should be disgusted," I muttered against my knee.

I looked around and noticed that the hallway was now empty. Wait, when did the bell ring? Eh, whatever, I didn't care anyway.

"Harry, I would never be disgusted with you, whether you were to like guys or not. You're my best mate. I could never hate you no matter who you like or what you do," he assured me, patting my shoulder softly.

I breathed out a sigh of relief. Niall didn't hate me. "Thank you, Nialler. You're the best."

He flashed me a smile before getting up to his feet. He reached out a hand for me to take, which I gladly did. Once I had dusted off my clothes, Niall spoke up again. "So, how was it to kiss a lad?" he asked, a hint of humor lacing his voice. He was clearly trying to lighten the mood.

"Horrible," I muttered.

He snorted. "You want me to believe that?"

Of course he didn't. Louis and I didn't just kiss, we made out, which definitely meant that I kissed him back. Honestly, it had been one of the best kisses I had ever experienced. His thin, pink lips had worked magic against mine, and the way his lip ring had pressed against my bottom lip... God, I got shivers just thinking about it. It was too good. "Fine, it was better than it should've been," I mumbled.

There was no reason to lie to Niall. He would find out the truth somehow anyway.

He bent down to pick up his books from the floor that he had apparently placed there when he decided to sit down beside me. "I knew it," he chuckled. "Now, let's go to class. We don't need to be later than we already are."

I nodded, unlocking my locker to grab my own books.

That was when I realized that I shared all my lessons with Louis. What was this? Some kind of joke?

Louis' POV

My head snapped up from the desk when I heard the classroom door open. In came none other than Harry and his best friend, Niall. Harry's eyes literally sparkled from the lights in the room, and I could feel my breath hitch at the sight but decided to ignore it. My gaze continued down to his plump lips that were now a darker shade of red than they had been an hour ago. I smirked to myself as I realized I was the one who had caused that.

To top that off, his curls looked like a mess, as if he had just had sex. I knew the cause of that was my hands, though, and that fact made me smile even wider.

Why was I so happy that I had caused all of that? I should be disgusted and think 'how could I do that to a guy?' But I wasn't. I was rather the opposite, actually.

As soon as Harry's eyes found mine, a blush crept to his cheeks, making me flash him a wink.

If only he knew how much trouble he was in... I had bullied him for the last couple of few years, though, so he might already know. I was not going to stop bullying him just because of that kiss if that was what he thought. He was still just... too much and in the way for me to rule the school together with my two best friends. That kiss meant nothing, and I was going to prove it.

Harry and Niall sat down at the desk in front of me and Liam, while Zayn was already sitting behind us with his legs propped on the chair beside him.

I leaned over the desk to Harry's right ear, brushing my lips and lip ring against it. "You know that kiss meant nothing and that I'm still your bully, right?" I breathed into the shell of his ear, causing him to shudder involuntarily.

He nodded curtly, flinching a bit at the touch.

I leaned back with a satisfied look on my face. Game on, Styles.

CHAPTER 3 ~ CONFUSING THOUGHTS

Harry's POV

So, the kiss meant nothing to him? Well, okay. I could play this game with him because that sure as hell wasn't a kiss you experienced every day.

I walked out of the classroom and headed towards my locker as fast as possible with Niall by my side. If there was someone I didn't want to see right now, it was Louis. I knew he would probably only beat me up like he always did when he caught sight of me, and I was not exactly in the mood for that.

Once we were at my locker, Niall turned to me. "Dude, you really have to gain some confidence around Louis. He treats you like you're some part of his game," he told me.

I nodded my head with a sigh, biting my lip. I knew I had to be more confident around him, but it was hard. If you were constantly bullied by someone, how could you possibly stand up to them? It wasn't weird to get weak when your bully was around. "I know, Niall, but it's not as easy as it sounds. I wish I could stand up to him, but I find it really hard."

He sighed, giving me a sympathetic look. "I'll help you, yeah? I promise you'll be the most confident guy at this school once I'm

13

finished with you," he smiled, patting me on the shoulder.

"Yeah, you can always hope," I muttered under my breath. I was thankful he wanted to help me, though. I could definitely use it.

"Sorry, mate, I didn't get that," Niall said.

"Nothing," I mumbled and opened my locker. I shoved my English books into it and grabbed the ones I needed for Civics instead.

"Aren't you mad at him, though?" Niall asked once I had shut my locker and turned back around to him.

I pulled my eyebrows together. "What do you mean?"

He raised his eyebrows in disbelief. "Wait, you mean you don't remember that he was the reason Sarah broke up with you?"

Oh, that. How come that thought had kind of slipped my mind? Obviously, I was devastated that she had broken up with me, but it wasn't like I didn't understand her. If she had kissed a girl, I would probably have broken up with her too. I couldn't blame it all on Louis either because if I didn't kiss him back, she probably wouldn't have broken up with me.

Hang on for a second… Was I defending Louis? Nope, I definitely wasn't. "Of course I do. It just… it kind of slipped my mind?" I grimaced.

Niall burst out laughing. "Man, you've got it bad," he chuckled, slapping a hand against his thigh.

"What do you mean?" I frowned, looking at him in confusion.

"You have feelings for him, don't ya?" he said, still laughing while looking at me.

The crease deepened between my eyebrows. I didn't have feelings for him. How did he even come across that possibility? "Of course I don't! Where the hell did you get that from?" I snapped, feeling anger well up within me all of a sudden.

He raised his hands in surrender, shaking his head while trying to stop laughing. "I'm sorry, but you're acting as you do."

"I do not!" I hissed, turning on my heel to stomp away from him.

I was boiling with anger now. How could he even say those words? I wasn't gay. I had no feelings for Louis whatsoever. Sure, that kiss was one of the best kisses I ever had, but that was obviously only because he was a great kisser, nothing more, nothing less. Letting out a frustrated groan, I ran my hand over my face.

"Oh, babe, easy there," I heard someone chuckle slightly.

I snapped my head to my right only to see Louis pressed against a locker by some girl I didn't know. He was smiling at her cheekily, his hands wrapped around her waist while she was very close to his face, her hands squeezing his ass.

I looked away without a second glance at them and continued walking to Civics. I didn't know why he was acting like this. Like a slut, I mean. Did he enjoy having sex with different girls every night? Or was it because he had some kind of family issues that he wanted to get his mind off of? Or was it maybe something else?

Ugh, why did I even care?

Sighing, I walked into the classroom. I didn't care that there wasn't anyone there yet, I just sat down at an empty desk and looked out the window, deep in thought.

The anger was slowly leaving my body, which made it easier to think about what Niall had said just a few minutes ago. Did I have feelings for Louis? He was really attractive, I couldn't deny that. With his piercing blue eyes, his black dyed hair, his piercings, and oh, his tattoos. Don't even get me started on his body, especially his ass. I wasn't sure I had even seen a girl with such an amazing ass before.

Oh my God. What was I even thinking? Louis, attractive? Pfft, like he would ever be.

God, I really did have it bad, didn't I?

———-

Louis' POV

I was pressed to my locker by Laura when Harry suddenly showed up out of nowhere. Where did he even come from? Didn't he stand by his own locker across the hallway with Niall just a few seconds ago? Not that I was keeping an eye on him though.

Suddenly, I felt someone squeeze my butt, and I instantly knew it was Laura, which made me chuckle. "Oh, babe, easy there," I said, smiling at her.

She looked at me hungrily, pressing herself even closer against me, still with her hands on my arse.

I looked away just in time to see Harry walking away, probably towards our next lesson. Guess he didn't even catch sight of us...

Fuck, why was I disappointed that he hadn't seen me? I should be thinking about beating the shit out of him, not feel down be-cause he hadn't acknowledged me.

Out of nowhere, Laura leaned in to crash our lips together, catching me off guard completely. It took a while until I started moving mine against hers, but when I did, I deepened the kiss by pressing her body flush against me, grabbing a firm hold of her hips. For some reason, however, the adrenaline from kissing her suddenly died down, and I found myself pulling away from her before she could slip her tongue inside my mouth.

A frown made its way between her eyebrows as she stared at me suspiciously."Why did you pull away?"

I shrugged my shoulders, not really knowing myself. "I didn't feel anything," was all I said because that was true, right?

Wait a second. I didn't feel anything? I always felt something when kissing girls, so what was so different about this time?

She looked hurt as if I had just rejected her, and I couldn't blame her. I would probably feel the same thing if I were in her situation.

She was just about to walk away when I reached out to grab her hand and pull her back. "God, I'm so sorry. So much has been going on and..." I trailed off. Where was I even going with this?

She shook her head. "No, I get it. You didn't feel anything because you kissed Harry this morning and you obviously like him, I saw it myself," she muttered before snatching her hand out of my hold and walking away.

She did not just say that, did she? I swear I could've followed behind her just to knock her down to the floor. However, she was a girl, and I didn't hit girls. But I did not like the kiss I had shared with Harry this morning. That was just absurd. Sure, he was a great kisser, but there had been no feelings involved in that stupid kiss. I kicked my locker in frustration.

"Ey, easy there, mate. What's wrong?" Zayn asked as he walked over to me.

"Everything's wrong, Zayn! I just kissed Laura, and I felt nothing. N-o-t-h-i-n-g. Her pink, soft lips just sickened me, and I wanted to fucking pull away," I groaned, running a hand over my face.

Everyone in the hallway was staring at me by now, but I couldn't care less. There were just too many things going on right now for me to do so.

Zayn sighed, placing a hand on my shoulder. "This is about

17

Harry, isn't it?"

I looked up at him, clenching my hands into tight fists. "This has nothing to do with Harry, okay?!" I snapped, shrugging off his hand from my shoulder.

"Chill man, I was just—" he started, but I cut him off.

"No! Don't even mention his name around me," I hissed, turning around to open my locker and grab books before walking away from him.

I was so furious I could probably punch a wall, but I didn't want to face the consequences that would follow if I broke something or hurt myself, so I pushed the thought to the side. Instead, I made my way to Civics even though the bell hadn't rung yet.

Once I stepped into the classroom, I noticed there were just five people in there yet, and one of them was Harry. He looked up at me when I walked by him to sit down at an empty desk, sending him a glare.

He gulped, and instantly turned around to look out the window again, just like he had done when I stepped into the classroom.

During the lesson, I avoided him when he tried getting my attention by staring at me, keeping my eyes on the whiteboard ahead of me instead. Halfway through the lesson, however, he seemed to give up and let out a sigh before looking down at his books.

Once the bell rang, Harry gathered his stuff and tried to leave the room as fast as possible, practically running out of there. I smiled to myself as I followed him out of the classroom, walking just a few feet behind him.

I could tell he wasn't aware I was walking right behind him because he let out a sigh of relief a few seconds later and slowed down the rapid pace.

We were just about to walk by the toilets when I made my move and reached out to grab a hold of his shoulder, pulling him inside the said room. Shutting the door behind us, I pinned him to the nearest wall and knocked the books out of his hands. I let my own books drop to the floor as well, so I could easily grab a hold of his collar with both of my hands.

"Why the hell does my friend think I have feelings for you?" I hissed, shaking him slightly.

He flinched at my closeness and whimpered; "I-I don't know."

I raised my hand to slap him across the face. "Well, I sure as hell don't! Who the hell would want to be together with someone like you?"

I threw another punch at his face, seeing how his cheek started getting red from the impact of my hand. My heart told me to stop punching him while my brain told me to go on. I was so torn between the two that I let out a cry and dropped him to the floor. Without looking at him, I bent down to pick my books up before storming out of there, leaving him with tears running down his cheeks.

I felt my heart break a little at the sight. He looked so innocent and so hurt that I almost wanted to go back and hug him. Almost.

With my head hung low, I went back to my locker, where surprisingly both Liam and Zayn were standing. "Eh, what are you two doing here? Shouldn't you be at your own lockers?" I asked, raising an eyebrow.

Zayn turned to me. "Well, yeah, but I wanted to apologize for what hap—"

"Forget about it. Just don't mention his name again, okay?" I mumbled, looking down at the floor.

"Sure," he smiled before returning to his conversation with Liam, which I eventually joined in on as well.

CHAPTER 4 ~ AT THE BAKERY

Harry's POV

That day I drove home to a silent house. Mum worked late every weekday, just like Robin, my step-dad, and my sister went to uni. That was why I worked in a small bakery in town, to have something to do when I was alone. I worked there every Monday, Wednesday and Thursday, so on Tuesdays and Fridays, I had the house all to myself.

I usually called Niall over those days, or I would just go over to his because I didn't really like to be home all by myself. I knew it sounded childish, but that's the way I was.

Obviously, Sarah would come over as well during those days, but since she broke up with me today, I didn't expect her to do so anymore. It was weird how easily I could forget about her. I mean, I didn't even think of being mad at Louis for making Sarah break up with me. I should be yelling and screaming at him for ruining my life, but since he somehow didn't ruin it, there was no need to.

If I was being honest with myself, I hadn't thought about her since Niall asked me why I wasn't mad at Louis. I didn't know why, though. I knew I loved her, but ever since that kiss I shared with Louis, I just felt... nothing? Well, it was extremely hard to explain.

Since it was Monday, I walked into the kitchen to make a sandwich and gulp down a glass of milk before exiting the front door again to head to work. I ate the sandwich while I drove there, which wasn't a very good idea, but I was in a hurry, okay? My shift started in five minutes and it took me at least three minutes to drive there if I drove quickly.

Three minutes later, I parked my car into an empty parking space and slid out of the car. After locking it, I headed straight for the door.

"Barbara!" I yelled as I stepped into the small bakery.

"Harry!" she called back. She came out of the room where she baked everything with a wide smile on her face.

Barbara was like my second mother. I had worked here for three years now, and she had always been there for me whenever something happened at school or at home. I could always go to her when something was wrong, and she would listen to whatever I had to say. I really loved having her there since my life was kind of always upside down.

I walked over to her and gave her a tight hug. "How has your day been?" she mumbled against my shoulder.

I released her and looked down at my shoes. "Eh, well..." I trailed off.

How had my day been? First off, Louis had kissed me, then Sarah had broken up with me, and to finish it off, Louis had beaten me up in the toilets. Well, what could I say?

She noticed that something wasn't right, and she instantly got worried. "Shall we talk later, Harry, when you've finished your shift?"

I thought for a while before I nodded my head. I needed to tell someone about my eventful day.

After I had pulled my red apron over my head, I walked over to the cash register. My shift lasted from four to seven, so I didn't have to work for too long, which was just perfect.

Usually, no one I knew would come here to buy anything, only Niall occasionally. I guess they didn't know about this bakery. It wasn't that big or well known, after all. Usually, younger people just walked by, while the older people were the ones who would notice it and sometimes enter.

I didn't know for how long I worked the cash register until an all too familiar boy was suddenly standing right in front of me.

Louis' POV

~30 minutes earlier~

"I'm home!" I called out as I stepped into the flat I shared with my mum and four younger sisters. Since neither of my mom or I worked, we couldn't afford anything but this small flat that only had three bedrooms, a kitchen, a toilet and a small living room. The only money we had was what we got from our granny and granddad.

Ever since Mark, my sisters' dad, died in a car accident three years ago, mom had done nothing but lying in her bed while being drunk off her ass. My sisters had taken his death a lot better. Obviously, they had been sad that their dad passed away, but not at the same level as mom. Her reaction was beyond okay. I mean, she couldn't just stop living just because her husband had passed away. She still had five children to take care of.

However, since she wasn't able to do that, our grandparents usually took care of my sisters when I was at school and when I was out with my friends and different girls.

I loved my sisters more than anything else, though, and I always made sure to be there for them if they needed me. I was kind of their mom. I always tried to act like my mom did throughout my childhood. She was so caring and loving that I never thought she would be able to this to any of her other children later on in life. I had been her entire world as if nothing else on earth mattered but me. That was how I looked at my sisters now. Of course I cared about other stuff like music and girls too, but my sisters were extremely important to me.

"Louiiis!"

The twins, Daisy and Phoebe came out of the room they shared with their older sisters, Lottie and Fizzy.

They ran over to me and hugged my legs. "You're home!" They squealed in unison.

I chuckled softly at them as I bent down to their level. "I am. Where do you guys have your sisters and grandparents?" I smiled at both of them. I picked them up in my arms and carried them to the couch.

"Lottie and Fizzy are at some friends', granny is in the bathroom, and granddad is at his and granny's house," Daisy explained.

"I see," I said, sitting down on the couch with them on my lap.

I felt a tug on my lip ring, making me turn to my right. It was Phoebe who had taken my lip ring between her tiny fingers. "I like your piercings, Lou," she giggled, nuzzling her face in my chest.

I smiled brightly at her before looking at Daisy. "What do you think about them, love?" I asked her when I felt her staring at me.

A frown formed between her eyebrows, and she reached up to touch the stud in my eyebrow with her index finger. I looked her in the eyes as her finger moved down to my right eye where my eyeliner was. I tried to understand her facial expression, but it was hard since she didn't show any emotion.

Her eyes trailed down to my chest, where you could see one of my many tattoos while her hand found its way to my black, dyed hair.

"I remember three years ago when you didn't look like this," was the only thing she said before letting go of me and turning around in my lap.

Although she couldn't see me, I stared at the back of her head while swallowing hard. The only reason I dressed like this was to hide my feelings, to hide the real me. Mark's death had turned my life upside down. Now, I hid behind some badass that didn't care about a shit in the world but his sisters. The real me was still not 'ordinary', though. I mean, I had bullied Harry for as long as I could remember, and I still loved being with girls, but the real me cared about other stuff too, like school and other people's feelings (except for Harry's, I guess). The real me didn't have tattoos, piercings, eyeliner, dyed hair or black clothes.

Phoebe was still nuzzling her face in my chest, but I felt her tensing up by the words her twin spoke. She moved her head up to my right ear. "We'll always love you, though, no matter how you decide to look," she whispered.

I smiled and mouthed a 'thank you' to her.

Right then, our granny decided to come out of the bathroom. "Hi there, Louis," she greeted.

"Good afternoon, granny" I nodded in return.

She walked to the hallway and slipped on her shoes. "Is it okay that I leave now that you're home, son?" She wondered, even though she was already halfway out of the flat.

I nodded my head with a look of amusement on my face. "Of course."

She shrugged on her jacket and turned to us again. "Goodbye girls, see ya tomorrow! Bye, Lou!"

The twins said their goodbyes, as well as me before she walked out of the flat and shut the door behind her.

I turned to the girls with raised eyebrows. "So, what do you guys want to do?"

Daisy had turned back on my lap and was facing me again, but she had her eyes on Phoebe. They thought for a while until Phoebe suddenly exclaimed, "Can't we go to that bakery in town that granny showed us last week?"

Daisy nodded excitedly, turning to me. "Please, please, please, Lou" she pleaded, jumping up and down on my lap.

I nodded my head. "Of course, anything for you, guys" I smiled, putting down them on the floor.

We walked to the hallway together. "Have you checked on mom today?" I asked hesitantly. I didn't want them to see what condition she was in. What if they would start crying and break down?

"Eh, no, but granny did," Daisy replied.

"Good," I was all I said before slipping on my TOMS and shrugging on my jacket.

I helped the girls tie their shoes and zipping up their jackets as well. Once we were ready to leave, I went to the living room to grab the key to the flat before walking back to the girls. I shut the door behind us and locked it.

We went out of the apartment building and started making our way to the bakery. I had never been to this bakery before. Well, I hadn't been to any bakery in my entire life, so they had to show me the way to it.

About ten minutes later, we were standing outside a small

building. If you walked by, I wouldn't be surprised if you missed it. It was really small and it didn't even look like a bakery. More like an abandoned candy shop.

"So, this is it?" I asked, raising an eyebrow.

They nodded eagerly, tugging at both of my hands to pull me towards the door. As soon as we were inside, Daisy and Phoebe pulled me to where all the cakes were.

"Look at that one, Louis!" Daisy exclaimed, pointing at a huge chocolate cake.

I knew for sure that I could not afford that. "Daisy, I'm not sure if I can buy th--"

"No, I mean, it's pretty, isn't it?" she gushed, cutting me off.

I let out a sigh of relief. I hated to disappoint my sisters, and I knew I would if I told them I couldn't buy something they wanted. "Yeah," I agreed.

Suddenly, I heard a familiar voice say; "Goodbye!" in a polite tone.

My entire body froze to ice, and when I turned to my right, I saw none other than Harry Styles standing in front of the cash register smiling at the customer who was about to leave. Did he work here? Shit, this could be awkward.

"Have you guys decided what you want to have yet?" I wondered, turning back to my sisters.

I wanted this to be over as quickly as possible.

They nodded their heads, and we made our way to the cash register... or to Harry, to be more specific. He didn't notice us at first since he was busy counting the money in the cash register.

"You're not planning on stealing anything, are you?" I asked cheekily.

He instantly stopped moving and looked up at me slowly. "L-Louis? What are y-you doing here?"

Maybe this wouldn't be so awkward after all...

I turned my gaze to my sisters who looked a little confused. "First off, you didn't answer my question, and secondly, I'm here because my sisters wanted to visit this place," I said, ruffling the twins' hair.

"Oh," he mumbled awkwardly, playing with the hairs at the back of his neck. "And, uh, I wasn't g-going to steal anything."

I rolled my eyes. "Of course. Forgot you are Mr. Perfect."

Something suddenly flashed in his eyes. Was that anger?

"I'm not perfect, Louis. No one is," he snapped.

My eyes widened at his sudden confidence. Where the hell did that come from?

"Easy there, mate," I said, trying to calm him down.

"I'm not your mate! If anything, I'm your fucking enemy!" He shouted, slamming his fist against the surface of the counter beside the cash register.

To say I was shocked would be an understatement. I was gaping with my mouth hanging open. Harry had never acted like this before. I mean, he had never stood up for himself before, so how come he was suddenly doing so now?

I looked down at my sisters again. "Right... Uh, shall we pay for what you guys wanted then, girls?" I coughed awkwardly.

The anger in his eyes suddenly disappeared and was replaced by a dark blush on his cheeks. "Oh... uh, yeah. Um, sorry," he mumbled awkwardly.

Once I had paid for what Daisy and Phoebe wanted to have, we exited the bakery and started walking home in silence.

"Why were you and that boy arguing?" Daisy suddenly asked, so low it was barely audible.

I let out a sigh. "Well, let's just say Harry and I don't really get along."

CHAPTER 5 ~ BACK TO NORMAL?

Harry's POV

~One week later~

It was now a week ago Louis visited the bakery. Everything was pretty much back to normal. I seriously had no idea where my sudden confidence had come from that day. He'd just made me so angry. I wasn't perfect. I mean, I made mistakes as everybody else did, and my life certainly wasn't perfect either. My family was barely home when I was, and most of the time I was all by myself. Sure, I wasn't that guy who liked being in trouble and fuck things up - like Louis - but that didn't automatically mean I was 'perfect'.

Currently, I was sitting at my desk in English class with Niall beside me. I felt someone staring at me from behind, and I tried my best to ignore it because I knew it was Louis. He had been staring at me every time he caught sight of me ever since that day at the bakery. I mean, fine, I had been acting weird that day, but there was no reason to stare at me like that, right?

I felt someone pinch my arm, and when I turned to my right, I found Niall looking at me. "Why is Louis staring holes in your head?" he whispered so no one could hear but me.

I glanced at Louis to see that he had a frown on his face while staring intently at me. I gulped and turned back to Niall. "I...

I have no idea what you're talking about," I replied, playing dumb. You would have been blind not to notice the way he was looking at me.

Niall shook his head while laughing. "Yeah, sure."

He turned back to focusing on his schoolwork after speaking those words. He obviously knew that something was off, but I didn't feel like this was the best time to tell him what had happened a week ago.

I sighed heavily, leaning into his ear again. "I'll tell you after this class, alright?"

Niall nodded his head. "You'd better," he winked.

I rolled my eyes before picking up my pencil to continue working myself.

Riiiing!

I got up from my seat and gathered my books before exiting the classroom with Niall by my side. It wasn't until we were standing at my locker when he first started talking.

"Alright, tell me," he demanded, looking at me eagerly.

Okay, hold on. What did he think happened? Because to me, it seemed like he thought it was something huge and exciting.

"Well," I started hesitantly, looking around me to make sure that nobody was listening. "On Monday last week when I was at work, Louis visited the bakery."

Niall's eyes widened in surprise. "Louis was at the bakery? What? Why?" He wondered.

I shrugged my shoulders. "He told me his sisters wanted to go there. However, he wouldn't stop getting on my nerves, so I got angry and stood up for myself against him."

"You what?!" He gasped.

I looked at my surroundings, noticing that a few people were looking at us. "Shh, Niall!" I hushed him.

I actually didn't know why I was so scared that people could hear about what had happened last week at work, but maybe it was because I was embarrassed by my actions? I mean, I knew I hadn't been exactly nice to Louis, but then again, he hadn't been nice to me either...

"You defended yourself against him? But, how did you manage to do that? I mean, you've never done it before," he asked, now talking in a more hushed tone.

"Well, I don't know. I guess it was out of anger or something," I said, grimacing a little.

Niall sighed and looked at something behind my back. "He's still staring at you, you know?"

I smacked him on the arm. "Stop looking at him!"

He chuckled. "Do you still want to come over after school today so I can help you with your confidence, or have you already learned enough on your own?" He winked.

I let out a snort. "Honestly, I still think I could use some help because believe me when I say that I had no idea what I was doing that day."

Niall tilted his head to the side, giving me a bright smile. "See you after school then," he chirped before walking off towards his own locker.

Louis' POV

Why did I keep staring at him? It wasn't like he had become a

PAULINE ADOLFSSON

pop star that no one could keep their eyes off over the weekend. He was just the same, normal Harry, the Harry he'd always been. So, why was I staring at him every time I caught sight of him?

Ever since that day at the bakery, something literally snapped inside me. He hadn't left my mind for a second. I mean, it was the first time he stood up for himself against me, and I remembered not knowing how to react. I had been so shocked that I actually wasn't able to sleep that night.

Despite what happened, however, I had refused to stop bullying him. It wasn't like he would have the courage to talk back at me again, right?

I was currently sitting in the cafeteria with Liam and Zayn on each side. Zayn was rambling about some chick he had slept with the other night. I was too busy staring at a certain some-one to pay attention to him, though. Harry was sitting across the room with his blonde friend, Niall, just like usual.

"Guys! You're not even listening to me!" Zayn suddenly whined.

I turned to Zayn, muttering a 'sorry'.

Right then, I noticed that Liam was looking in the same direction that I just did. A sudden feeling of anger welled up inside of me for some reason. But why? Why did I feel like punching Liam in the face just because he was staring at Harry's table?

"Liam?!" Zayn hissed when he noticed that Liam was still dazing off.

The brown-haired boy snapped his head towards Zayn. "Yeah?" He wondered, biting his bottom lip.

"Why are you both so caught up with yourselves? Like, what the hell?" Zayn whined.

Liam looked at me quickly before turning his gaze back to Zayn. "I'm uh... I'm sorry Zayn. Now, what did you say?"

32

Zayn sighed heavily and started explaining what had happened last night once again. I couldn't say that I paid my entire attention to him, but I was positive I picked up the most important parts at least. I managed to hear that he had met a girl that went to our school - but he refused to tell us who - and that during the time they had sex, he had felt his heart fluttering in his chest. It was pretty big news, to be honest. I mean, Zayn had never been in love before, just like me and Liam. We had just gone from girl to girl during our entire youth.

"So, what you're saying is that you're in love?" Liam asked, raising an eyebrow at him.

Zayn looked at him as if he were an idiot. "Of course not. Why would you think that?" He snorted, shaking his head in disbelief.

I laughed quietly under my breath while looking at him, making him glare at me. "What?" I winked.

"What the hell are you laughing at?" He grumbled.

I raised my eyebrows while trying to contain my laughter. "Oh, come on, Zayn. By the sounds of it, I would say you're definitely in love with this mysterious girl."

"Alright, let's make this clear, Louis," he started with a dark voice. "I am not in love with this girl. I have never been, and I won't ever be in love with someone, okay?"

I looked over at Liam who had dazed off again. What the hell?

"Sure, Zayn," I chuckled, but it died down in a second and was quickly replaced by a frown on my face. It really bothered me that Liam was staring in the direction of Harry and Niall's table for some reason.

After that, the day past by quite slowly, and I got more and more frustrated about the way Liam couldn't take his eyes off of Harry or Niall. I mean, they were basically our enemies. He should be glaring at them, not staring at them as if they were an interesting movie. But, then again, I hadn't exactly been shooting daggers at Harry these past days either...

I was walking to my last class of the day, P.E. Since I only had two classes with Liam and Zayn, English and Science, I was walking alone. Niall didn't have P.E, so I knew I would get the chance to talk to Harry alone... Wait, what? I was not going to talk to him. If anything, I was going to beat him up. Yep, that was it.

I reached the door to the locker room and opened it. Instantly, I was greeted by the boys in the class with either a nod or a 'hi, Louis'. Well, what can I say? I was quite popular after all.

I found an empty locker and started stripping off my clothes. I had just pulled my shirt over my head when I heard someone say my name behind me.

"L-Louis?"

My muscles froze to ice. Why was he out of all people calling my name?

I turned around to face Harry with confusion written on my face. "Harry, why are you ta... I mean, what do you want?" I wondered, snapping out the last part.

Harry fidgeted before reaching his hand out to me. He was holding a book. "Um, you forgot your book in Science, and I-I just wanted to give it back. I mean, you'll probably n-need it some time," he mumbled, blushing furiously.

I took it from his hand harshly, although he was being kind of adorable. Wait, adorable? No, no. I did not just say that. "Thanks," I muttered.

I thought Harry would leave after that, but to my surprise, he remained on his spot, staring intently at me. I cocked an eyebrow at him as I followed his gaze down to my bare stomach, or in this case, my abs.

I chuckled to myself before looking up into his green eyes. "Like what you see, eh?"

Harry snapped his eyes up to meet mine, and his cheeks turned even redder if that was possible. "O-of course n-not," he stuttered, staring at me with wide eyes.

I took a step towards him and leaned into his ear, causing him to shudder involuntarily. I smiled brightly as I brought my lips up to his ear. "Oh, but I think you do," I whispered, breathing into the shell of his ear.

He gasped loudly and tried to pull away, but I kept him in place. My hands found their way around his waist, and I dug my fingernails into his skin through his white V-neck as I pressed my chest against his.

"You miss my lips on yours, don't you?" I whispered, chuckling softly.

He shook his head curtly, causing his curls to brush against my face. God, they were so soft!

"Too bad you can't have them," I breathed, pulling back with a smirk on my face.

He shuddered and tried his best to get back to normal. It took a few seconds until he was able to storm off, leaving me to chuckle to myself.

There was one thing that bothered me, though, and it was that I was afraid that I wanted Harry's lips on mine more than he wanted mine on his.

CHAPTER 6 ~ I DON'T LIKE HIM!

Harry's POV

I waited for Niall to come back from his last class at his locker. I was fiddling with my fingers, having nothing better to do. Students passed by, but I couldn't care less about them. My mind wandered back to my last class of the day, P.E, where Louis had been acting really weird. It wasn't just the situation in the locker room I was talking about, but during the lesson as well. He had been watching me intensely every now and then, and it had really crept me out.

Okay, so about the situation in the locker room. What even was that? Did he suffer from bipolar disorder or something? Because that guy surely had mood swings. One moment, all he intended to do was beat me up, while in the other, he acted as if he had feelings for me or something. I had no idea which of these options was the real him, but I really wanted to know.

If I was totally honest with myself, I liked the Louis who fancied me most. I didn't like to get beat up, okay? It wasn't like I had feelings for him, even if I felt kind of flustered after that incident in the locker room. It was just because he had been so close, alright?

"Harry!" Niall shouted through the hallway as he came running towards me.

I chuckled at his actions and nudged him in the side once he was standing beside me. "No need to shout at me. I'm standing right here and wasn't planning on moving until you came."

Niall shrugged. "I guess I just felt like it," he smiled.

I rolled my eyes, watching as he shrugged on his jacket. We then walked out of the building together, heading towards his car in silence.

When he had hopped into the car, I heard a honk coming from my left. I turned around to see a red car that looked slightly familiar. That was when I could see the driver's face through the window. The sight of that boy made me freeze.

It was Louis, and as if that wasn't enough, he blew me a kiss at that second. I didn't have enough time to think of anything else until he flashed me a wink and drove off.

All I could do was stand there, trying to take in what just happened. To say I was shocked would be an understatement. I was gaping at the spot the car had just been.

"Harry, what are you doing?"

I turned around to see Niall leaning over the passenger seat, sticking his head out the open window with a confused look on his face.

"Eh, nothing," I said, nearly falling over as I walked to the other side of the car. I hopped in and took a deep breath.

"Seriously, Harry. What happened? All I could hear was a honk, then nothing."

I nodded. "It was Louis. He's been acting weird the whole day, and now he just fucking blew me a kiss!" I groaned, throwing my head back.

Niall turned to me, his mouth hanging wide open. "He what? I thought he hated you?"

"Well, so did I! But then he came up to me in the locker room and started saying things about kissing me while I just stood there, not knowing how to react." I placed my hands over my face and let out another groan.

Niall gasped but tried to contain himself. "Well, I guess we have to work on your confidence quickly, so you can tell him to back off. Because that's what you want, right?" Niall asked, looking at me suspiciously.

Did I want Louis to stop acting like he was around me? Well, I had no idea, but I couldn't tell Niall that. He would think I liked Louis, which I obviously didn't. However, I still liked this side of Louis better than the violent one.

"Of course," I said a little hesitantly.

Niall looked me up and down before nodding his head. He believed me, I assumed. He then turned on the engine and pulled out of the parking space.

We drove the first five minutes in silence until 1 decided to turn on the radio. A song I hadn't heard before started playing through the speakers. However, it seemed like Niall knew it since he started humming along to it.

Five minutes later, we pulled into his driveway. He turned off the engine and turned to me. "Alright, let's do this," he smiled.

I nodded my head, a small smile creeping to my lips. Even though I might not want Louis to back off me, I wanted to be able to defend myself if he decided to go back to beating me again.

We walked into the huge house I had been in so many times before that I had lost count. Niall's house was my second home after all, so I was practically considered as one in his family.

"Mum? I'm home!" Niall called out through the house.

I slipped off my shoes and shrugged off my jacket. Niall did the same thing before we both walked into the kitchen, where Maura was sitting at the kitchen table with a coffee cup in her hands. She turned her gaze to us when we entered the room, a smile breaking out on her face.

"Hi, boys. How was school?"

One thing that I liked about Maura was that she cared, something my own mom didn't. I was sure that my mom didn't even know that I had a girlfriend for an entire year.

"Same old, I guess," Niall shrugged, looking at me.

I nodded my head in agreement, although 'same old' was far from true. 'Strange' would be a better word to describe my day.

"Great! So, do you want anything to eat? I presume you must be hungry," she smiled.

Niall looked at her as if she were an idiot. "Mum, I don't know why you're even asking me. I'm always hungry."

She chuckled at him. "You're right. What about you, Harry?"

I smiled brightly at her. "Well, I won't say no to that offer, thanks."

Maura shook her head, but a smile played on her lips. "You don't have to thank me, Harry. You're family."

Those words made my smile grow even wider. I really liked to feel welcomed and loved, and there was no other place I felt just that but here.

Maura made pancakes for us, while Niall and I just sat at the kitchen, talking about everything and nothing. Once the pancakes were ready, we ate them in silence before walking up to Niall's room.

I sat down on his bed while he decided to sit down in his armchair that was placed beside the bed.

"So," he started. "What you want is to be able to defend yourself against Louis, right?"

I nodded. "Right."

"Well, I have been thinking about it, and you explained that you actually did stand up to him when you got mad at him, right?"

I raised an eyebrow, looking at him in confusion. "You mean I defended myself against him just because I was mad at him?"

Niall nodded. "Yeah, that's exactly what I mean."

"So, the only thing I have to do to be able to stand up to Louis is to find something about him that makes my blood boil?"

"That's exactly what I'm saying," he said, smirking.

I pulled my eyebrows together. "I don't know if I can do that, though. I mean, sure, if he beats me up, then fine, but if he's going to approach me and make me all flustered like he did today, it's going to be a whole different story."

"Hold on for a second. He makes you feel flustered?" Niall asked, shocked.

I felt my eyes widen in realization. Oh, shit. Did I really say that out loud? He was going to think that I actually liked him now. "Uh, no. Not like that. It's just... He makes me nervous when he's close to me. It's the same feeling I get when he's about to beat me up," I tried to lie, although I was sure I didn't do well.

"O-kay, I don't believe you. I can read you like an open book, and that was obviously a lie. So, he makes you feel flustered when he's close to you? Do you like him?" I could hear the panic building up in his voice.

During the next couple of minutes I tried to explain to him that no, I didn't like him because it was the truth. I didn't have any feelings for Louis. I just got a little shy and nervous around him, okay? Louis was my bully, after all, it should be illegal to have feelings for him, which I obviously didn't anyway. Why did it feel like I was going nowhere with this?

However, Niall eventually believed me, sort of, at least.

"Alright, shall we continue the 'gain confidence' mission?" he asked after a while, raising his eyebrows at me.

I breathed out a sigh of relief as I nodded my head.

Niall got up from his seat and walked over to stand in front of me. "Pretend that I'm Louis and try to stand up for yourself, okay?"

I got up to my feet as well. "I don't think that'll wo--"

I was interrupted by Niall pushing me against the wall. "Don't question me, just do what I say, okay?" He snapped in my ear.

I nodded my head curtly, feeling my heart pick up its pace in my chest.

He punched me in my stomach lightly, but since I wasn't prepared for it, I fell to the floor.

"Oh my God, Harry! Shit, are you okay? You weren't supposed to fall," he gasped, his voice back to normal. It made me relax, even if my back hurt a little from the fall. At least he was back to his normal self.

The pain faded away in a few seconds, so I sat up against the wall to run my hands over my face. "Thanks a lot for that," I muttered, rolling my eyes.

Niall let out a chuckle as he helped me sit down on his bed. "I think we need to work on this again, another time. Because if that is how you react I'm threatening you, then I don't want to see how you react when it's Louis."

I nodded my head, agreeing with him. I didn't even know if these 'lessons' were going help, though. I mean, look at what happened this time. I accidentally told Niall I got flustered around Louis, and then I got a punch to the stomach, even if that wasn't what had hurt me.

The only thing we had really come up with was that I was hopefully going to be able to defend myself against Louis if I just found a way to get mad at him.

CHAPTER 7 ~ CONFESSIONS

Harry's POV

The next following days, I hung out with Niall at his place after school. Well, those days I didn't have to work. It would be a lie to say that we were making progress with our 'mission, though. I was still very bad at defending myself, even against Niall, and that really sucked.

Louis kept winking at me every time we walked by each other in the hallway, and whenever it happened, I would always dart my eyes to the floor with a blush on my cheeks.

What surprised me, though, was that he actually didn't beat me once that week. It was as if something had snapped inside him that had caused him to change his mind about me. I still liked this Louis better than the one that used to beat me up every time he saw me, even though he freaked me out with his actions. It wasn't even healthy nervous he made me. I just wanted to dig a hole in the ground and bury myself alive in it, just to get away from the looks he gave me.

One thing that was weird, though, was that he hadn't tried to talk to me. He hadn't even approached me like he did that day in the locker room. I knew I should be happy about it, but I couldn't help but be a little disappointed about it...

I knew that was really wrong. I mean, he used to bully me all the time, and the fact that he was a guy didn't make this any better. I had never been with a guy before. That kiss with Louis was the first kiss I had experienced with a boy and the fact that I had actually liked it scared the hell out of me.

"Harry? Do you think Liam likes me?" Niall asked out of nowhere when we were sitting in the cafeteria on Monday during our lunch break.

I turned to him in surprise, my mouth falling open. "Um, what?"

"Do you think Liam li--"

I cut him off by covering his mouth with my hand. "I know what you said, silly. It just surprised me, is all. I mean, where did you get that from?"

Niall turned to where Liam was sitting across the room with Louis by his side. I felt a shiver run down my spine when the thoughts of Louis suddenly came flooding back.

Niall shrugged his shoulders, keeping his eyes on Liam, who was laughing at some joke Louis had just made.

"Ni, I'm sorry to say this, but Liam's into girls."

He turned back to me. "I know, it's just... he's been looking at me a lot lately, and I just jumped to the possibility that he might-- Eh, whatever. It's not like I have feelings for him anyway," he said, waving a hand in dismissal before picking up his fork to continue eating.

I just shook my head, a smile playing on my lips. I had no idea what was going on inside that boy's head. I mean, last time I checked, Niall was straight, so where did this suddenly come from? But let's say Liam had been looking at him. Did that automatically mean he liked Niall in a romantic way? No. So, something else must have happened if the thought of Liam liking him had entered his brain, or he simply had feelings for Liam and wanted him to like him back. But then again, why would Niall lie to me?

Once we had finished eating, we went to my locker so I could grab my Math books before we walked to Niall's.

"Niall?" A voice behind us asked.

We both spun around to see a nervous-looking Liam. Niall's eyes widened in surprise and his cheeks reddened by the second.

My gaze flicked back and forth between them. *Did* something happen?

"Can I uh... Can I talk to you?"

Niall turned to me. "Haz, would you mind if I...?"

"Of course not. Go with him. I can walk to Math class by myself," I smiled.

He nodded his head, flashing me a small smile in return before they walked off towards the exits.

I could see from across the hallway how Louis and Zayn followed the two figures' backs closely. Right then, Louis' gaze found mine, and he looked at me with a frown on his face. Suddenly, he started walking towards me with firm steps.

I felt my eyes widen in fear, and my knees started weakening as he got closer and closer to me. What was I going to do? He was going to beat the shit out of me for some reason I didn't quite understand, but I could tell by the look on his face. If there was one thing I had learned throughout the years he had bullied me, it was that the look he was wearing on his face right now meant nothing but trouble.

All I wanted to do was run, but I knew I couldn't. He would get caught up with me sooner or later, and when he did, he would be even angrier with me, probably give me a few more punches. The fact that I couldn't feel my knees either made it even more impossible for me to run.

"You little piece of-- Explain to me why my best mate is walking out of school with that loser right now!" He snapped right in my face when he stopped in front of me.

I shook my head curtly, looking at him with fear evident in my eyes. "I... I don't know."

He grabbed a hold of the collar of my shirt and pinned me against the lockers behind me, my books falling down to the floor with a thud in the process. By now, there was a circle of students around us, watching us closely.

I squeezed my eyes shut as I saw his fist reach up in the air. "Tell me, or I'll beat you up until you won't be able to see the light with your gorgeous green eyes."

I heard the crowd around us let out loud gasps. Well, they weren't the only ones that were surprised by his words. I shot my eyes open only to see that his nose was almost touching mine. His eyes were wide open, clearly surprised by his own words as well as everybody else.

"I- I didn't..." He trailed off, releasing the hold he had on me.

He walked backward, looking at me in shock before turning around to run away.

I remained in my spot for what felt like ages before I started moving. I picked up my books that were lying open on the floor and walked away, still in shock of what had just happened. The crowd that had seen everything dispersed as I walked away, but their mouths were still hanging open.

I went to Math class, thinking about what had just taken place. My head was spinning like crazy, but the only thing I could think of was; What did this mean?

Niall's POV

Liam and I walked out of the school to sit down on a nearby bench. To say I was nervous would be an understatement. I was biting my nails, that was how nervous I was. Liam, on the other hand, seemed to have calmed down as he sat down beside me so close that our legs were touching.

Honestly, I had no idea what he wanted to talk about. Well, I had noticed his glances at me during lunch break the past week. Something with the way he was looking at me made me all flustered, and it sent chills up and down my spine. It was a weird feeling, though, because I had only got it when a hot girl was looking at me before.

"Niall, I... I don't know how to say this but...uh, I guess I'll start at the beginning, yeah? He said, fidgeting a little. I guess he was getting nervous again.

I nodded my head although I had no idea what he was talking about.

"And promise me you won't be disgusted," he pleaded.

I looked him deep in the eyes, trying to understand what he meant by that, but he was unreadable. He showed no emotion at all, except for a look of plea.

I nodded my head again, not trusting my voice enough to speak. I then patiently waited for him to start explaining.

He took a deep breath. "Okay, so it all started a few weeks ago. It wasn't until last Monday that I started showing it, though. However, I couldn't help but notice how this feeling would erupt within me every time I saw you. You started making my heart beat faster than usual, and a comfortable warmth started always filling my body. Every time you laughed, I always caught myself smiling, even though I had no idea what you were laughing at. When you walked through the hallways, looking so care-free and innocent, I got this sudden urge that I wanted to pin you to a wall and kiss you right there..." He trailed off with a blush on his cheeks.

Throughout his speech, I looked down at my lap, trying to hide the way my own cheeks we're turning a crimson red. Truth be told, I had no idea how I was supposed to react to all this. I mean, he practically just put his heart out to me. Alright, so maybe I had been wanting him to tell me this for a while now, but I still didn't know exactly what it was that I was feeling for him.

I was aware that I asked Harry if he thought Liam liked me, and well, I had been noticing his intense glances at me, but that wasn't the whole truth. I had kind of lied to Harry. Or, I hadn't told him the entire truth because I knew I had feelings for Liam, although I didn't exactly know what kind of them.

Liam noticed that I wasn't planning on saying anything for a while, so he sighed heavily. "I knew you would be disgusted." He made a movement to get up and walk away, but I pulled him back by grabbing a hold of his wrist.

"Please don't go," I pleaded.

He turned around to look at me, sadness evident in his face. "It's okay Niall. I know you don't feel the same way. I just wanted you to know that I can't really stop thinking about you."

I got up from the bench so I was standing just a few inches away from him. "Would you please let me talk?"

He nodded his head, looking down at his shoes while probably waiting for a rejection.

I took his hand in mine and started playing with his fingers. "First off, I'm not disgusted by you, and secondly, you don't even know if I return the feelings or not yet, so don't jump to conclusions."

He looked up to me with pain in his eyes. "Please just tell me you don't feel the same way as quickly as possible because I don't really want to suffer more than I already am."

I let go of his hand. "See! This is what I mean by jumping to conclusions. Would you please just shut up and listen?"

At first, Liam looked shocked by my words, but he eventually nodded his head.

I took a deep breath before I started speaking. "It would be a lie to say that I don't have any feelings for you at all. I know we have never really talked to each other, but I do feel attracted to you. I have always liked girls, though, so I don't really want to admit to myself that I like a boy. As you said, you started looking at me every now and then last week, and every time you did, you made my heart swell with joy. I still don't want to admit that it's you who are causing it, but deep down I know it is. What I'm trying to say is that I think I might fancy you back, but I'm still very unsure of my feelings" I explained, biting my bottom lip.

"Y-you do?" Liam stuttered, sucking his lip ring into his mouth.

For some reason, that action made me go weak in the knees, so I had to grab the bench beside me not to fall to the ground.

"Yeah, but there's one thing I don't understand, though," I said, frowning a little. "I thought you were into girls?"

Liam shifted on his feet uncomfortably. "I was until I started having feelings for you. Now I'm not so sure anymore. Maybe I'm bi," he shrugged.

I chuckled softly, looking deep into his chocolate brown eyes.

Suddenly, he reached his hand out to touch my cheek. "So, what do you say about us?"

I smiled, placing my hand on top of his. "I want to take it slow. I mean, I don't know you very well yet, so it seems like the right thing to do. If that's okay with you, of course."

He nodded his head with a wide smile on his face. "That would be perfect."

CHAPTER 8 ~ I HAVE A BOYFRIEND?

Louis' POV

Gorgeous green eyes? Why the hell did I say that? I didn't like Harry's eyes, so why did I let that slip my mouth?

I ran my hands over my face as I walked to Math class. I hated the fact that Harry and I had exactly the same schedule. I was aware that I had been staring a little too much at Harry the past week, but I was still in shock by the way he acted at the bakery, which was two weeks ago...

However, I hadn't laid a finger on him since then, except for just minutes ago, that is. But, come on, Liam had walked away with Harry's best friend. Shouldn't that be illegal or something? We, as in Liam, Zayn and I were never seen with people like Harry and Niall. We were too different from each other. We liked tattoos, piercings and being in trouble, while Niall and Harry were just too... posh.

"Louis?"

I turned around to see a girl with brown, wavy hair and hazel eyes. It was Eleanor. I had always found her beautiful, but she was hard to get if you knew what I meant. "Yeah?"

She walked over so she was standing right in front of me. "Would you like to go on a date with me?" she asked, batting her eyelashes flirtatiously.

Date? I didn't date people. I just slept with them, then went on to the next one. I had never thought of actually being in a relationship with someone. "El, you're really beautiful and all, but I don't date," I explained, grimacing.

She clenched her teeth together for a second before leaning in to give it another try. "Are you sure about that?" She whispered in my ear in a seductive way.

I shivered at the feeling of her breath hitting my ear, which caused me to take a step back. "I'm sorry, El," I apologized without sounding very sincere about it before I turned around.

I started walking to Math class again with a smile on my face. I knew what would happen next. Just wait for it...

"Louis!"

Yep, there it was.

I felt someone grab my wrist and turn me around. "El, please just let me go. I have a class to attend," I said, trying to not lose my temper with her.

She pinned me to the wall of lockers behind me and leaned in to practically attack her lips against mine. She moved her mouth forcefully against my lips as she wrapped her arms around my neck. Her tongue tried to pry my mouth open, but I wouldn't let her in. She let out an annoyed groan against my mouth before biting down on my bottom lip quite hard. I gasped, and she instantly took the opportunity to push her tongue into my mouth.

For some reason, I fluttered my eyes open, and the sight before me made my body go rigid. Harry was standing there, his books pressed tightly against his chest with a frown on his face.

When he caught me staring at him, he forced a smile on his kissable lips. Wait, kissable? They were not possible. They were just so plump and pink, and I just wanted to... No. Why was I even thinking about this? I was kissing a girl for crying out loud. I shouldn't be imagining having a boy's lips on my own... which I definitely wasn't. God.

Eleanor noticed that I had tensed up, which resulted in her pulling away. "Lo--" she started but cut herself off as she realized I wasn't paying attention to her.

She turned around and saw Harry standing there. You could practically see her getting riled up by the second. "What the fuck are you staring at? Can't you see Louis' too busy with someone else?" She snapped at him.

His eyes widened in shock, and it didn't take more than a second until he walked away from us. I could feel how my blood started boiling up inside me, and this time, it wasn't because of Harry. It was because of Eleanor.

"Now, where were we?" She whispered in my ear before crashing her lips onto mine again.

I instantly pulled away from her. "You can't just do that, El. He didn't even do anything," I said in a low voice, too afraid that I was going to start yelling in her face if I talked any louder.

Without waiting for an answer, I got out of her hold and stormed off. I wiped my lips with the back of my hand as I walked away from her, trying to get rid of the taste of her lips. I couldn't believe she said that to Harry. He didn't do anything. he was looking at us, being the innocent boy he had always been, even those times I had beaten him up...

Okay, wow. I was an idiot, wasn't I? Did I seriously have to witness someone else being mean to Harry for me to realize how bad I was treating him? I mean, he didn't deserve it. He was just so... precious. God, where did these thoughts come from?

On my way to class, I grabbed my books from my locker. I was just about to open the classroom door when the bell rang.

Right on time, I thought to myself as I turned the handle and walked inside.

I closed the door behind me before walking over to an empty desk. Harry was sitting across the room, staring down at his work. I sucked my lip ring into my mouth. I really wanted to know what was going on inside that boy's head right now.

Right then, the door was pushed open, and in came a blonde boy with crimson cheeks. "Sorry I'm late, Mr. Rogers," Niall apologized before speed-walking over to sit down beside Harry.

Throughout the lesson, I kept an eye on Harry, just as usual nowadays. Harry didn't look back at me once, though, which caused me to get a little disappointed and frustrated. I wanted to know his reaction to my and Eleanor's kiss. Why? I had no idea.

When the bell rang, Harry and Niall gathered their books and made their way out of the classroom. I followed them, making sure I was right behind them. I couldn't hear what they were talking about, but I still felt like a stalker.

Without knowing what I was doing, I cleared my throat. Instantly, they both turned around to face me. Their faces were priceless. I would've laughed if we were in another situation.

"What do you want, Louis?" Niall snapped.

I took a step back and raised my hands in surrender. "Chill, mate. I just wanted to talk to your friend here," I said, looking at Harry with a smirk on my face.

Harry's eyes widened in fear. "Louis, please, don--"

Niall took a step forward and pointed at me. "If you ever touch him again, I swear to God, I am going to kill you," he warned me, cutting Harry off.

I smiled at Niall. "I'm not going to hurt him, I promise."

He clenched his teeth together, looking back and forth between me and Harry. "Harry, this is your decision," he finally sighed.

I rolled my eyes. He made it look like this was some kind of decision between staying alive or die. I wasn't going to hurt him for God's sake.

Harry took a deep breath before nodding his head. "I'll see you later, Niall."

I smiled to myself as Harry and I started walking through the hallway towards a place where we could be alone.

Harry's POV

What was I doing? Why did I say yes? He was obviously going to hurt me because why else would he want to talk to me? It couldn't be about what happened this morning when he called my eyes gorgeous, or about his kiss with Eleanor, now could it? No, why would he want to talk about that?

I bit my lip nervously as we walked through the hallway. Glances that were filled with either shock or disgust were thrown at us, which made me flinch. What was so wrong with me and Louis walking in the hallway together? It wasn't like we were together or something like that.

My mind started replaying the scene that I witnessed only an hour ago. Louis had been pressed against the lockers by Eleanor. Their lips had been moving roughly in a disgusting way, and I'd felt like throwing up. Something inside me told me that it wasn't because the kiss had been disgusting, though, but the mere fact that they had been kissing.

No matter how much I wanted to, I couldn't deny that I missed the feeling of Louis' lips against mine. And yes, I had been kind of jealous. But just because I liked Louis' lips didn't mean I liked him as a person, alright? I was never going to like Louis. He was just... bad, and he always cared too much about his reputation.

I mean, he always did what he thought the people around him wanted him to do. Like being with different girls all the time, for example.

Everyone knew he was like that, and if he would change his image now, he wouldn't be as popular anymore. Then it was the fact that he beat me up. That can be just because he had a reputation to uphold. But then again, I didn't know if he actually enjoyed being with different girls every night and beat me up. Maybe he just hated me and hurt me for that reason? But what had I ever done to him?

I sighed, forcing myself to think about something else instead. I hadn't spoken to Sarah since the day she broke up with me. I knew she was ignoring me, but honestly, I didn't really care about it. I had already stopped thinking about her, which was a little strange. We had been a perfect couple. We always spent time with each other and we really enjoyed each other's company, but I guess I just fell out of love.

"Come on, let's go outside," Louis suggested, grabbing my wrist to start pulling me towards the exit.

I felt shivers running through my body at his touch, but I brushed it off as if it wasn't important, but deep down I knew it actually meant something.

Once we were outside, we started walking slower. "So," he started, sucking his lip ring into his mouth.

I gulped at the action and tried to take my eyes off his lips, but it was impossible. You couldn't blame me because Louis sucking his lip ring was one of the hottest things you could witness. I couldn't even deny that fact.

"About what I said this morning, I..." he trailed off hesitantly.

I couldn't help but love it when he showed nervosity. It actually helped me be more confident around him. "It's fine, Louis.

I know you don't think that way about my eyes. It just slipped, yeah?" I said although it felt like a stab to the heart.

"Right," he frowned.

I raised an eyebrow. "Did I say something wrong, or...?"

Louis shook his head. "No, no. Nothing is wrong," he assured me.

I nodded my head slowly. We walked in silence during the next couple of seconds until I suddenly felt myself being pushed against the brick wall of the school. I closed my eyes and waited for the punches. I knew he was going to hurt me.

I stayed like that and just waited, but nothing happened. The only thing I could feel was someone's breath against my lips. I cracked an eye open to find out what was going on. The sight in front of me made me almost jump in surprise. Louis was standing incredibly close to me, our lips almost touching.

"L-Louis, what are you d-doing?" I stuttered nervously, pressing my back even further against the wall.

Louis gave me a wide smile, his teeth even showing. "I don't know, what am I doing?" he asked, raising an eyebrow.

Before I could say something, he leaned even closer, so our noses were touching. I shivered at the touch, which made a smirk form on his lips. "You like this, don't you?"

I shook my head vigorously, feeling my knees go weak. "Please s-stop, Louis," I pleaded, biting my bottom lip.

Louis looked me deep in the eyes. "Why?"

"B-because," I started, trying to take a deep breath. Because what? Because I didn't like him? Because I didn't want him to kiss me? Because I was afraid he was going to beat me up afterward if he did kiss me?

"Because what?" Louis asked, his eyebrows raised.

"B-because... I already have a boyfriend!" I burst out to my great surprise.

I could feel Louis' body going rigid at my words, and the smile instantly fell from his face. "What?!" He let out, sounding both shocked and irritated at the same time.

My heart started racing in my chest at the tone he was using, afraid that he was going to hit me. "I-I said--"

"No, I know what you said. The question is who is your fucking boyfriend?!" He cut me off.

I felt a lump form in my throat. What was I supposed to say to that? I didn't have a boyfriend for crying out loud! I just told him that to make him back off. "Uh," I started. Think, think, think! "Liam!" I let out, covering my mouth with both my hands.

What did I just say? Liam? Why would I be together with him? I mean, Louis knew I wasn't together with him. Liam was his best friend for crying out loud! They probably told each other everything, just like Niall and I did.

Louis' mouth was hanging open. "You, him, what?!" He gaped, his jaw clenching together by the second.

"I, I--" I tried, but he cut me off again.

"Don't even say a word. I knew that fucker was up to something," he muttered with a dark voice.

If I was being honest with myself, I was scared to death right now. Louis was standing there, his eyes looking like they could kill, and his fists were clenched together along with his jaw.

"Louis, no, I--" I tried again, but he wouldn't hear me out.

"I'm going to exchange a few words with my best friend," he grumbled before running off, leaving me alone to lean against the brick wall.

What the hell had I gotten myself into?

CHAPTER 9 ~ FAKE COUPLE

Louis' POV

I walked through the hallway with quick and firm steps. What the hell? Since when was Liam gay? And since when was he hitting on Harry? Every word Harry had just said went through my mind as I walked by students whose gazes followed me curiously.

Then it hit me. That time in the cafeteria when Liam was staring at Harry and Niall's table... Had he been staring at Harry then? Just because they were together?

I bit down on my bottom lip frustratingly. Why did this even bother me? Why did it bother me that Harry had a boyfriend, who in fact was my best friend? Why did it feel like my heart had burst when Harry said the words 'I already have a boyfriend'?

As soon as I spotted Liam at his locker, I forgot all my previous thoughts and only focused on one thing. I had to find out what he had to say about all this. "Liam!" I yelled, a little too loud.

He was having a deep conversation with his newfound friend, Niall, it seemed, but when he heard my voice, he snapped his head up to meet my gaze. A frown instantly formed between his eyebrows.

I stomped over to them, and just as I was about to start yelling at Liam, Niall's phone buzzed. He fished it out of his pocket and read what the screen said. I decided not to care about him, and turned to Liam again.

"Since when the fuck are you and Harry Styles together?" I snapped at him.

I could see that both Liam and Niall stiffened at the same time. Liam was staring at me with wide, confused eyes, while Niall was looking at his phone in concentration. A second later, Niall shoved his phone in his pocket again and turned to whisper something in Liam's ear.

I couldn't hear what he said, and that got me even more frustrated. I was about to yell at Liam again when his face suddenly softened, and Niall pulled away from him.

"Oh, that. Well, we've been together for what is it now, Niall? Two weeks?" he said, raising his eyebrows at the blonde guy.

Niall nodded, turning to me. "Yeah, that's right."

I felt my eyes widen in shock. He didn't deny it. So, that meant he was actually together with Harry? What?

I stomped my foot angrily before storming away from them. I had no idea what was happening to me, but I sure didn't like it.

Liam's POV

Louis ran off with an angry look on his face. I turned to Niall and raised my eyebrows in confusion. "Why did I have to say that?"

He bit his bottom lip, fishing his phone from his pocket again. "Harry texted me and said it was very necessary. He practically begged me to tell Louis that you guys were together," he shrugged, showing me the text.

Once I had read it, a frown formed between my eyebrows. Why

was it so necessary for Harry to tell Louis we were together? What had even happened between the two of them?

Right then, Harry walked by with his hands stuffed deep in his pockets. I took a step forward, pulling him with me to Niall. "Harry, please explain why I just had to tell Louis that I'm dating you," I demanded, looking into his eyes.

He looked scared as if he was afraid I was going to hurt him. "I... I didn't mean to. I'm s-sorry," he stuttered out.

Niall placed a reassuring hand on his shoulder. "It's okay Harry. Just calm down and tell us what happened."

Harry looked at Niall for a few seconds before nodding his head. "Louis and I were just talking to each other when he suddenly pinned me to the wall. He uh, he got so close, and I panicked. I told him that he had to back off because I already had a boyfriend. He demanded to know who it was, and I just blurted out your name, Liam. I'm so, so sorry. I'll tell him the truth. Just please... don't hate me," he pleaded, looking at me desperately.

I could feel myself relaxing now that I knew the reason behind it all. "It's okay, Harry. I don't hate you. It all just came as a shock," I reassured him, smiling slightly.

Harry sighed of relief. "Thank you. I promise I'll tell him the truth when I see him again."

I bit my bottom lip. Would it actually be a good idea to tell Louis the truth? I mean, Louis was head over hills for Harry - everyone could see it but himself. He needed to realize his feelings for him, and what would be better than a little help from something called jealousy?

I smirked to myself as I started shaking my head. "No, don't say anything to him."

I could feel Niall tense up beside me, and it wasn't hard to tell that Harry did the same thing. "What?" they echoed in unison.

I wrapped an arm around Niall's waist and squeezed his hip. "Well, if it's okay with Niall, of course," I said, kissing the top of his head.

Niall blushed, looking down at the floor while biting his bottom lip sheepishly. Harry frowned at me. "I still have no idea what you're talking about."

I rolled my eyes, smiling slightly at him. "I want to make Louis jealous, Harry. He obviously likes you, but he won't admit it to himself."

His eyes widened in shock. "Louis likes me? B-but.. how? I thought..." he trailed off, his mouth hanging open.

"Whatever you thought, you were wrong. He's looking at you as if you are his world, Harry. He can't take his eyes off you, for crying out loud. I'm sure he likes you," I told him.

He opened his mouth, but nothing came out. He was speechless, just looking at me in utter shock. Niall decided to break the silence. "Harry likes him too, I've seen it," he said with a frown on his face as if it had hit him right now. "He would never have let Louis talk to him earlier if he didn't. He's been hurting him for years now. And I mean, no one is willing to talk to their bully if they don't mean something to them."

"I... I don't like him," Harry attempted, but it wasn't even worth it. It was obvious that both Louis and Harry had a thing for each other.

"Wait for a second," Niall said, turning to Harry. "I'm not sure I'm okay with this. I have always told myself to protect you from him because he's always been so mean to you. I can't just forget that," he frowned.

I placed my hand on his shoulder, my gaze finding Harry who was staring at his shoes. "Niall, you can't protect Harry throughout his whole life. He needs to make his own decisions, and if he wants to be with Louis and he believes that he won't hurt him, then you can't stop him even if you want to," I shrugged.

Niall turned to me, looking desperate. "But things can go so incredibly wrong, Liam! Louis is probably going to hurt him one way or another and treat him like utter shit," he huffed.

My eyes widened at his assumption. "No, Niall. Louis' not really like that. He really cares about the people he loves, and I'm sure he would never do that to Harry if he just realizes he likes him."

It wasn't until then Harry decided to interfere. "Guys, you don't even know if I want to be together with him. And, Niall's right. He has been treating me like shit, and I have told myself that I'm never going to like him in any kind of way. He's hit me, he's harassed me, he's called me worthless, and he has made me feel like I'm not worth living. I can't just forget that, and for all we know, Liam could be wrong. What if Louis doesn't have feelings for me and we are going to fake date for nothing?"

Niall nodded in agreement. "Yeah, Harry's right, Liam. Why do you want them to be together so badly anyway?" He wondered.

I pulled my eyebrows together because I knew the answer. Louis had never had feelings for anyone before, and now that he finally did, I wanted him to get the one he fancied if the person liked him back, that was. "He's never liked anyone before, and now that he does, I just thought it was a great opportunity for him to settle down," I shrugged. "And, if he doesn't react to us being a couple, then we'll know that he doesn't have feelings for you," I continued, smiling gently at Harry.

The curly-haired boy's eyes went from me to Niall, who was biting his fingernail. "Niall, are you okay with this? Me and Liam being a fake couple, I mean?" He mumbled, fiddling with his fingers nervously.

Niall looked at him for a while before nodding his head. "As long as it's only to figure out what Louis' feeling for you and not because you like him, then yeah. It's okay," he smiled softly.

Harry chuckled. "Of course, Ni. You know I'd never do anything to hurt you," he smiled.

"Thank you, Haz, but how did you know I had feelings for Liam? I never told you," he frowned, leaning his head on my shoulder.

I pulled him closer to me by the hold I still had on his hip. Harry smiled sweetly at us. "I could tell," he laughed, causing both my and Niall's cheeks to flush. "On another note, I'm heading to Science. You coming with me?"

I nodded my head, letting go of Niall - much to his dismay, but I had to pretend that I was together with Harry. So instead, I grabbed Harry's hand and entwined our fingers, sending Niall a sad look. He tried to smile back at me, but it didn't reach his eyes. I knew he wouldn't like this idea, but I did it for Louis, and for Harry because I knew he would thank me in the end.

Together, all three of us walked to Science, unaware of how Louis was going to react to all this.

Harry's POV

We walked through the hallway towards the classroom. Liam was holding my hand while Niall was walking a little bit behind us with his gaze glued to the floor.

I felt so bad for doing this to him. I knew he had feelings for Liam. It wasn't hard to tell by the way his eyes lightened up every time he looked at him. I just had to go make the biggest mistake by telling Louis that Liam was my boyfriend so he had to suffer from it. God, I really hated myself.

I knew I could have disagreed with this, though, but I was curious. Did Louis really like me? And if he did, what was I going to do with that fact? Ignore him?

Alright, first off, I needed to find out if he really did have feelings for me, then I could focus on the consequences that would follow.

We stepped into the classroom, and I didn't even look up when I walked over to sit down in an empty seat by the windows. Liam sat down beside me, pulling his chair as close to mine as possible. He wrapped an arm around my waist and started drawing small patterns on my hip.

Niall had sat down at the desk in front of us and was now watching us closely. I shot him a sad smile, knowing that this really hurt him.

Right then, the door swung open, and a second later, Louis was walking in with Zayn by his side. I could feel myself tense in my seat, and I shuffled closer to Liam, wanting nothing more than to just disappear. Louis' jaw was clenched, and I was sure that the look on his face could kill. His gaze was searching for something in the classroom, and when he found what he was looking for, the muscles in his face hardened.

What scared me was that what he was looking at was me, me and Liam. I shuffled even closer to Liam, and he tightened his hold on me. I didn't care that I had practically never talked to Liam before this day because all I could think about was the threatening look on Louis' face, and Liam was the closest person to me right now.

Zayn noticed Louis' sudden anger, and placed a reassuring hand on his shoulder, trying to calm him down. Somehow, he succeeded because Louis let out a huff and plopped down in an empty seat at the back of the classroom.

I sighed of relief, reminding myself to thank Zayn for that later... although I probably wasn't since I had never spoken to him before. I loosened the hold I had on Liam but stayed close to him.

His arm was still resting around my waist loosely, which made me feel a little safer.

Throughout the lesson, I could feel eyes burning holes in the back of my head, and I knew exactly who those eyes belonged to. I didn't dare to turn my head to look at Louis, though. What if he was angry? What if he was going to be glaring at me again?

Then it hit me. Why was Louis even angry in the first place?

CHAPTER 10 ~ REALIZATIONS

Louis' POV

Throughout the whole day, I had to watch Harry being all couply with my best friend. I didn't know why I felt so riled up about it. The only thing I wanted was to hit a brick wall just to let all my anger out. What confused me, though, was why I felt this way. Liam could date whoever he wanted, and so could Harry. Then why did their relationship affect me this much?

My thoughts wandered to the kiss I'd shared with Harry a few weeks ago. It didn't feel like weeks, more like a few days. The feeling of his warm lips wouldn't leave my mind, and much to my dismay, I missed them so badly.

I wanted to hit myself for thinking that, but I knew it was true. I couldn't deny that Harry's lips were quire irresistible, and now I wouldn't be able to feel them against mine again just because he was in a relationship with my best friend.

I was currently standing at my locker, ready to go home when Zayn walked by. I grabbed his arm and pulled him towards me. "Hey, what do you think about Liam and Harry's relationship?" I asked, clenching my jaw together just thinking about it.

He shrugged his shoulders. "I don't know, man. If Liam's happy, then I'm too, I guess."

I let out a groan of frustration. "Am I the only one who has something against it?"

Zayn chuckled at me, causing me to get even more frustrated. "Yeah, I guess so, and I think I know why."

I took a hold of his collar and pushed him against the lockers. "What are you trying to tell me?" I asked, my voice sounding as cold as ice.

Zayn's eyes widened in slight shock, but I could tell that he wasn't scared. He knew I would never hurt him. "Calm down, mate. I'm just saying that I think I know why you're feeling this way about their relationship."

I took a deep breath and let go of him. "I'm sorry Zayn. It's just... It's not normal for me to be this..." I trailed off and scrunched my nose up at the thought of what I was going to say. Jealous. I was never jealous. I was practically immune to it, for fuck's sake. I didn't have a heart, I never fell in love. So, why was it so hard for me to see Harry and Liam together?

"Jealous?" Zayn chuckled, already knowing the answer.

I shook my head. "Please, don't say it."

"Well, it's the truth, Louis. You have to face the fact that you might actually like Harry. I've seen how you can't stop looking at him," he continued.

"Stop it Zayn. Before I really hurt you," I warned him.

He raised his hands in the air in surrender. "Fine, I won't say anything else."

"Good," I muttered.

Did I like Harry? Was I even able to do so? I couldn't find another reason why my heart ached every time I caught sight of him with Liam, though, because I was sure I didn't like Liam as more than a friend.

Let's say I did like Harry. Was there anything I could do about it? I mean, he was with Liam and he seemed pretty happy with him. Liam was my best friend, and the least I wanted was to ruin a relationship for him, but I couldn't *not* do anything about it either. Not that I really wanted to be with Harry, but being this angry whenever I saw them together was not an option.

I shook my head, trying to get rid of my thoughts. "What are your plans for the day?" I asked, changing the topic.

Zayn looked around the hallway. For some reason, he didn't seem to like the subject. "Erm, well, I'm gonna meet up with this girl," he shrugged as if it was nothing, but I knew him, and I could clearly see that he wasn't telling me the whole truth.

"Zayn, is there something you're not telling me?" I asked, raising an eyebrow.

"Pfft, of course not. It's just a girl. I'll sleep with her, then I'll move on to the next one," he said kind of hesitantly, and right then it hit me.

"You like her, don't you?" I smirked knowingly.

His eyes widened as his cheeks turned pink. "N-no, of course not. You should know by now that I don't fall for anyone," he huffed, but I knew he was lying.

"Come on, Zayn. Tell me who the lucky girl is," I smiled.

He shook his head, looking down at the floor, probably trying to hide his red cheeks. "You know her," he mumbled eventually, scratching the back of his neck.

"Just tell me," I pleaded. I wanted to know who had stolen this boy's heart because he had always been so sure that he would never fall in love.

"Um... It's Perrie," he finally managed to say.

My eyes widened slightly. The blonde girl with big, blue eyes who was taking the same English class as us? I remembered that Zayn had talked about a girl in the cafeteria a week ago and that he'd felt something while having sex with her. Could it possibly have been Perrie he had been talking about?

"You mentioned a girl last week during lunch. Was it her?" I asked.

He nodded. "Yeah, uh... I don't know, I just... I thought you guys would laugh at me for falling for someone, so I lied. I do have feelings for her, and I would love to be her boyfriend one day."

I placed a hand on his shoulder, suddenly feeling all my anger leave my body. "I would never laugh at you, mate. Love is love, and I think all people eventually find someone they want to share their life with, although they don't always get them," I shrugged.

Maybe I should let myself love someone just like Zayn? Maybe these years of being a man-whore were over? But then again, was I ready to just let it all go?

Zayn smiled at me in appreciation. "Thank you so much, Louis..." He trailed off as if he wanted to say something else, but hesitated.

"Come on. Spit it out, mate," I chuckled, hitting him on the arm playfully.

"Well, not to be rude or anything, but I never expected you to approve of this, me liking someone, I mean," he admitted, biting his bottom lip.

I looked down at my shoes, thinking of what to say. I probably wouldn't have approved of it if it weren't for the fact that I'd contemplated whether I liked someone or not myself. Harry had just stepped into my life and turned it upside down, without him even knowing about it.

Before I had the chance to answer, Zayn opened his mouth again.

"It's because of Harry, isn't it? He's made you question things, hasn't he?" He smiled, seeming to already know the answer.

Well, he was right. It was Harry. Harry, Harry, Harry. I couldn't even go a day without thinking about his lips on mine for god's sake! What was wrong with me? I was so frustrated that I seriously wanted to pull my hair out of its roots.

Right then, a burst of familiar laughter was heard in the hallway, and I felt my heart skip a beat. I turned to the sound and found Harry with Liam, walking towards the exits. I bit my lip hard. Why? What was the world trying to tell me? That I should have tried getting with Harry when I had the chance? That the chance was now gone? That I would never get to call him mine?

I knew one thing, though, and that was that the world wanted to see me suffer. Suffer from something I never thought I would. I was sure now. I fancied someone, and that someone was a boy. A boy I had been bullying for several years now and that was none other than Harry Styles.

Harry's POV

I was walking through the hallway with Liam by my side. He'd just cracked a joke, and I couldn't help but laugh at it. I never thought Liam could be this funny. He seemed to be one of those guys who never cared about anything or anyone, who loved to play with other people's feelings, but boy I was wrong. Liam was caring and really sweet. I would love to stay friends with him after all this was over.

I turned slightly to my left, only to find Louis staring right back at me. I swallowed hard at the sight, ready to see an angry look on his face, but I never did. The expression on his face was impossible to read. It looked like he was thinking rather hard about something, though. I wondered if it had anything to do with me and Liam?

I mentally hit myself. Of course it didn't. He probably didn't even care that I was 'together' with him. Why did I even want him to think about us in the first place? I didn't like him that. He was just attractive, okay?

Without knowing what I was doing, I let my lips form a smile. To my surprise, Louis smiled back at me, causing me to stop dead in my tracks. He smiled at me. He didn't glare, but he actually freaking smiled.

A sudden warmth filled my heart, and I couldn't help but smile even wider.

"He obviously likes you," a voice whispered in my ear, and I spun around to face Liam.

I shook my head, feeling my cheeks heat up. "No, he doesn't. That was just a one-time thing. He has never smiled at me like that before," I mumbled.

He shook his head with an amused look on his face. "You're both so oblivious. I can't understand why you're not together already."

I frowned at him. "What do you mean? I don't have feelings for him, and he doesn't for me either."

Why did the last thing I just said cause my heart to ache?

"See, you're oblivious," he chuckled. "If it wasn't so ridiculous, I would've been mad at both of you for not admitting your feelings for each other."

"Ridiculous?" I said, my frown growing deeper.

"Yeah, your attraction to each other is so obvious that I find it ridiculous that you're not together," he said, rolling his eyes.

I decided not to care about him, and turned back to Louis again. Only this time, he wasn't standing there anymore.

CHAPTER 11 ~ PAYBACK

Harry's POV

When Liam and I were walking to the parking lot together with Niall, I could hear footsteps behind me. I turned around just to be face to face with Danielle, one of Liam's exes. Liam also turned around, swallowing hard at the sight of her.

"I can't actually believe I was in a relationship with you, you faggot," she spat out with a disgusted look on her face.

I squeezed Liam's hand in an attempt to show him I was there for him. He was really tense, and it looked like he was going to burst into tears at any second.

"Danielle, please I--" He started, but she cut him off.

"Don't you talk to me. How could you turn gay? Was it something I did wrong? Was it my fault?" She asked, her voice getting lower by the second. She almost sounded sad at the end.

Liam shook his head. "No, of course not. You don't decide who you fall for, Danielle. I was born this way. There is nothing you, me or anyone can do about it," he told her.

Danielle looked away into the distance, biting her lip. "I... I'm... sorry," she mumbled before sprinting off.

I followed her figure with wide eyes. What the hell was that? It was as if she were afraid she was the reason Liam turned gay.

"Come on, guys. Let's head to my place," Niall suggested and started walking towards his car.

"How are you feeling?" I asked Liam when we started following Niall.

He shrugged his shoulders. "I have never been insulted because of my sexuality until now, and it was by my ex," he grimaced, looking down at the ground.

"I'm sorry, Liam. I don't want to be mean or anything, but receiving comments concerning your sexuality might happen more frequently now that you're showing it off. I guess you just have to get used to it," I explained, trying to comfort him somehow.

"And you have?"

I looked down at the ground. "I... I'm not gay, Liam," I mumbled, feeling my cheeks heat up.

I could hear Liam smacking the hand that wasn't entwined with mine against his forehead. "Oh, right. I'm sorry, I just... After everything with Louis, and now me... I'm really sorry... Haven't people commented about it, though? I mean, you and Louis even kissed that time in the hallway?" He asked cautiously, probably worried that I would be insulted.

"Um, yeah. I have received some comments, but I try not to take offense at it considering I'm not actually gay," I shrugged.

He raised an eyebrow at me. "But if you aren't gay, or at least bisexual, then why did you agree to be my fake boyfriend to make Louis jealous?"

Well, that was something I couldn't answer myself. Why did I want to make Louis jealous? Because I wanted to know if he had feelings for me? But why did I want to know that?

I shook my head. "I don't know, Liam. I haven't figured that out myself yet."

When we were about to get into the car, I could see Niall staring longingly at us through the window. I still felt really bad for doing this to him. You could see from a mile away that he really liked Liam, and I didn't want to stand in the way of their relationship, but I also knew that what Liam and I were doing wasn't going to last long. I would 'break up' with him within a week or so if Louis hadn't shown any sign of being jealous until then.

Something told me that if Louis actually did have feelings for me, I wouldn't be the one out of the two of us at a disadvantage anymore. I would be able to get back at him for what he had done to me the past couple of weeks, if I only gained more confidence, that is. Feelings made you weak, didn't they?

This fact made a smile break out on my face for some reason.

Be careful, Louis. Otherwise, you don't know what is to come.

We stepped into Niall's house, and as usual, Maura was home. "Hello, boys!" She called from the kitchen.

A second later, she walked into the hallway to greet us properly but stopped in her tracks when she caught sight of Liam standing beside me and Niall. "Oh, I'm positive I haven't seen you around before. What's your name?" she asked politely, extending a hand for him to shake.

Niall looked down at the floor in embarrassment. "Mooom," he whined.

Liam chuckled softly, shaking Maura's hand. "I'm Liam, Niall and Harry's... friend," he explained hesitantly, probably not knowing what to call himself to either of us.

"Liam?" She said, turning to Niall. "Is this the Liam you've been talking about non-stop?" She asked excitedly.

Niall's face turned a crimson red, and he suddenly grabbed both my and Liam's wrists, pulling us towards the stairs. "You're embarrassing me," he complained to Maura, making all of us burst out laughing.

With a slam, Niall shut his bedroom door behind us and hid his face in his hands. "I'm so sorry about that, Li--" he was cut off by Liam who stepped forward to remove Niall's hands from his face so he could press a soft kiss to his lips, causing them both to blush a bright red.

My lips formed a wide smile at the sight. I hadn't seen them kiss before. "Was that your first kiss?" I asked excitedly.

They turned to me, both of them nodding their heads. I clapped my hands together, the smile never leaving my face. "You two are so cute, I swear to God," I said, sitting down on Niall's bed.

The two of them shook their heads, chuckles leaving their mouths. "So, what are we going to do?" Liam asked after a while, and I started fiddling with my hands, looking down at my lap.

Niall noticed this and sat down beside me. "You've got something on your mind, Haz?"

I looked up into his eyes and bit my lip. "Well, I don't want to be a bother or anything, but I would love some help from both of you to gain my confidence," I mumbled.

Liam walked over to us and sat down on the other side of Niall. "Confidence?" He asked in confusion.

Niall nodded, turning to him. "As you might know, Harry here isn't too good at standing up to Louis, so we've been working on his confidence during the past few weeks. Nothing seems to be working, though," he explained.

Liam raised his eyebrows in surprise before he knitted them together as if he was in deep thought. "Hmm, maybe I can help you with that considering I'm one of his best friends and know almost everything about him."

I looked at him in shock. "You would do that?"

He nodded his head. "Of course. Wasn't it me who wanted to put you two together in the first place?" He chuckled.

I looked down at my lap. "I didn't say anything about wanting to be in a relationship with him. I just want to be able to defend myself," I mumbled.

"Yeah yeah, whatever. I'd love to help you," he smiled.

"Perfect!" Niall exclaimed, probably happy that we were finally getting somewhere with this 'mission'.

"First off, you have to get the thought that Louis isn't dangerous in your head," Liam started, and I nodded my head in understanding. "Then if things go as planned, Louis has started having feelings for you and therefore won't hurt you physically because you just don't hurt the person you like, right?"

I raised a hand in the air. "How can you be so sure about that? He has never hesitated to hurt me before," I reminded him.

Liam's lips formed into a smile. "That's what feelings do to you, mate. Believe me on that."

"Fine, but how do we know that Louis has feelings for me for sure?" I wondered.

"I'll ask him tomorrow, and I have a feeling Zayn knows a lot more than I do at the moment, so I'll talk to him as well."

"You're planning something Harry, aren't you?" Niall suddenly asked in suspicion.

I flickered my gaze between the two of them, a smile breaking out on my face. "Maybe."

Liam raised an eyebrow. "What are you planning?"

I told them about my plans on getting back at him for trying to seduce me. Liam's reaction was the best. He literally jumped up and down on the bed in excitement while Niall bit his lip hesitantly.

"What is it, Ni?" I asked, furrowing my eyebrows together.

He shrugged his shoulders. "It's just... I don't want anything bad to happen to you," he mumbled.

I wrapped an arm around his shoulders. "Nothing's going to happen to me. No need to worry," I assured him, looking at Liam for help.

He nodded his head in agreement. I removed my arm from Niall's shoulders so Liam could take his face in his hands. "Look, Niall. Louis isn't a bad person, I promise. All he wants is power. Before Zayn made up the bet about Louis kissing Har--"

"It was a bet?" I interrupted, a frown forming between my eyebrows.

Liam tensed up slightly, turning to me with a look of shock. "Oh, shit," he breathed. "Shit, I shouldn't have said that. No one was supposed to know."

It did make sense, though. Why else would Louis just walk up to me and kiss me? However, did that mean he didn't enjoy the kiss as much as I thought he did?

I suddenly wasn't so sure about this whole thing about him liking me anymore. If that kiss was because of a bet, then he probably didn't feel anything when we kissed. That meant there was no real reason for him to get feelings for me.

"Maybe we should just call everything off after all," I mumbled.

Liam shook his head vigorously. "No. I know something that wasn't supposed to happen," he said, looking at me intently.

"And what would that be?" I asked, not really interested anymore.

"It was meant to be a kiss, not a make out session. No tongues were supposed to be involved," he explained.

I raised my eyebrows at him. "Are you... are you sure about that?"

He nodded his head quickly. "Yes, I am. Please believe me on this, Harry. You have to get back at him."

I thought about it for a while before letting out a sigh. "I'm going to do it if it turns out Louis really has gotten feelings for me."

Liam's face lit up in a smile. "Awesome! Now, back to what I was talking about earlier..." he said, looking at Niall who was still stuck with his face in Liam's hands. "Before the bet, Louis wanted to 'rule' the school, and I think he was willing to do anything to do so. I mean, it was even the reason he bullied Harry," he explained, looking at me.

I swallowed hard at this news. Had Louis seen me as some kind of threat? I mean, all I had done was to be together with Sarah and be best friends with Niall.

"Did uh... did things change after the bet?" Niall wanted to know.

Liam shrugged, letting go of Niall's face. "Yeah, they did. He started acting weird. However, what I wanted to say is that I am sure Louis is not going to hurt Harry more than he's already done, so isn't it all worth a shot? If something bad happens, we'll just call it off, yeah?"

Niall bit his lip, thinking deeply. "I guess it's fine by me, but what are you going to say if Louis asks you why you're cheating on Liam?" He wondered, looking at me.

I looked at Liam who had his eyebrows in a frown. "Um..." I started.

"I think the thought is going to cross his mind, but I don't think he's going to ask you about it. And if he does, just tell him that you don't care about what I think, or something," Liam finished for me with a shrug.

"But then I'll seem like a badass," I mumbled, causing both of them to laugh.

"Well, you'll kind of be a badass if you're going to try to seduce him anyway, Harry," Liam chuckled.

I was sure this was going to be a lot more difficult than I first thought it would, but I was still in on it. All we needed now was to find out whether Louis really did have feelings for me or not. Then it was game on.

Payback is a bitch, Louis.

CHAPTER 12 ~ LET THE GAMES BEGIN

Harry's POV

I drove to school the next day, feeling more nervous than ever. What if Louis didn't like me? What if he wasn't jealous? Then my plan was going right down in the trash. If he didn't like me, there was no need for me to try seducing him. Though, I wondered if he was still going to try seducing me? We would just have to wait and see, I guessed.

I parked my car in an empty parking space before getting out of it. I didn't even have time to take a step towards the doors of the school until someone had grabbed my shoulders and pushed me against my car.

"Morning, Harry," a voice whispered in my ear, breathing hot air against the shell of my ear.

I shuddered at the feeling, knowing very well who that voice belonged to. "S-stop," I said weakly as his lips trailed down to my neck teasingly.

"Why?" Louis mumbled against my skin, causing goosebumps to rise on my body.

He tightened his hold on my shoulders, pulling himself closer to me so our chests were pressed together.

I couldn't get myself to say that I didn't like it. My body enjoyed this more than I wanted it to, but hey, could you blame me? Louis was practically sex on legs... I did not just say that, okay?

There was only one problem, though. I was supposed to be the one trying to seduce him today, not the other way around. "B-because I have a b-boyfriend?" I stuttered. Sadly, it came out more as a question than a statement.

His lips left my neck so he could look into my eyes. "You know what? I don't fucking care about that," he growled, leaning in to start kissing my neck this time.

I had to bit back a loud moan as he started nibbling on my skin. Why was he doing this to me? He knew I couldn't resist him... Wait, what? I didn't like Louis. I knew it was all just a game, and two could play at it.

Without knowing what I was doing, I flipped us around, surprising both of us. "Two can play at this game, Louis," I mumbled, leaning in to start sucking on a spot just below his ear.

What the hell was I doing? I didn't even know if Louis liked me yet, and here I was, practically attacking his neck with my lips... Shit, I was going to hell, wasn't I?

He suddenly let out a loud moan, making me pull back in shock.

Louis looked at me with wide eyes. "I-I... Y-you..." he trailed off, biting his bottom lip. "I've gotta go."

With that said, he pushed me off him completely and sprinted away, leaving me frozen in place. What just happened?

"Well done," a voice suddenly said, and at first, I thought it was Louis who had decided to come back, but when I turned around, Liam was standing there with a smile on his face.

I breathed out a sigh of relief. Thank god, I wasn't sure if I could handle Louis being near me all over again right now.

"I... I don't know what just happened," I said, looking at him with wide eyes.

"Well, whatever you did, it worked. Louis was the one who ran away from you, and not the other way around," he chuckled, taking my hand in his.

Right, we were supposed to be together. I had almost forgotten about that. "B-but I shouldn't have... Not yet... What if he doesn't like me?" I breathed, frowning a little.

Why did the thought of Louis not liking me suddenly hurt so much?

"He does like you. I've talked to Zayn and he said he was sure of it. Louis has feelings for you, and it's so damn obvious that I want to hit you for not realizing it yourself," he said, shaking his head in disbelief.

"But, how? I mean, I'm not even worth liking," I muttered, biting my bottom lip.

Liam placed a hand on my shoulder. "Don't you even dare go that way, Harry. Everyone at this school would be happy if they got the chance to be together with you. You're amazing, both inside and out. You have to trust me on that," he said, looking me deep in the eyes.

I stared at him in shock. Did he actually mean that? But what he said wasn't true, though. Everyone had flaws, especially me. "Stop talking shit, Liam," I muttered, looking down at the ground.

He sighed. "I'm not, Harry," he mumbled. "However, we should probably head inside. Class starts in three minutes."

I nodded my head, lacing my fingers with his.

As we walked through the hallways, some people glared at us while some just smiled slightly. I tried not to care about the ones who glared, and it almost worked. They were just homophobic jerks who refused to realize that love was love regardless of what gender you liked.

Liam and I separated to go to our lockers. As soon as I had taken off my jacket and grabbed my English books, I strode over to his locker so we could walk to class together. I tried not to glance at Louis when I passed by him at his locker, but it was really hard not to. He was standing with his back facing me, slowly taking off his jacket, almost teasingly.

"Where's Niall?" Liam asked me, wrapping an arm around my waist.

I furrowed my eyebrows together. I hadn't seen him when I walked by his locker, so hopefully, he was just a little late. "I don't know. He hasn't said anything about not coming, so I assume he's just late."

He pursed his lips. "You're probably right. Let's head to class, shall we?" He wondered.

I nodded my head, and he started pulling me forward by the hand on my waist.

We walked into the classroom, sitting down at an empty desk. I placed my books on it as I turned my head to look around the room. Louis sat down at the desk behind us, looking everywhere but me.

I knitted my eyebrows together, turning to face the front of the classroom. When Zayn made an entrance, he sat down beside a blonde girl who I knew was named Perrie and took her hand in his. I didn't know they were a thing?

I glanced back at Louis again, just to find him flickering his gaze between Zayn and Perrie's entwined hands and me with a frown on his face. I tried to make eye contact with him, but he didn't notice it at first. When eventually did, a mischievous smirk formed on his lips.

I swallowed hard at the sight, suddenly not feeling the need to look into his eyes anymore. Instead, I turned to Liam. He was biting his lip anxiously, glancing at the door every now and then. I assumed he was concerned about Niall. The bell rang a few minutes ago, and he still wasn't here.

Just as our teacher was about to open his mouth to start talking, the door swung open. "Sorry, Mr. Williams. I overslept," he panted, searching the room for an empty seat.

I looked around and noticed that there was only one seat that wasn't preoccupied, and it was the one next to Louis. I bit down on my lip hard, feeling something twitch in my stomach. What was that? It couldn't be what I thought it was, could it? No, I wasn't jealous just because Niall got the chance to sit beside Louis. There was no way.

Niall swallowed hard as he started walking towards Louis hesitatingly. He glanced at me and Liam almost desperately, but Liam shot him a reassuring smile.

He sat down beside Louis without a word, and Louis didn't say anything either. The lesson began, and I started focusing on my work instead of the strange feeling in the pit of my stomach.

After one half of the hour, I suddenly heard a familiar laugh behind me. I turned around just to notice that Niall was clutching his stomach while Louis was smiling at him.

My eyes widened at the sight, and I instantly looked over at Liam only to see that he was frowning at them. Why did Niall suddenly enjoy being in Louis' company? And how did Louis manage to get Niall to laugh so easily? I thought Niall hated him?

Confused, I turned back to start working again, although Louis and Niall wouldn't leave my mind.

Louis' POV

At first, I was just going to talk to Niall because he was Harry's friend. I wanted his friends to know that I wasn't a bad influence on Harry. I was aware that I wasn't in a relationship with Harry, but it was always a good thing to have their friends on your side, right? And, maybe I wanted us to be in a relationship... even if he was with Liam.

However, after about half of the class hour, I started realizing that Niall was hilarious. He seemed to be that type of guy who found it easy to be friends with everyone just because he liked people in general. Moreover, I realized that I liked him because he laughed at my jokes.

One of the jokes made him laugh louder than he did at the other ones, which instantly resulted in Liam and Harry turning their heads towards us. Harry's face was impossible to read, while Liam had his eyebrows furrowed together.

I smiled at Niall, happy that my plan had succeeded by just being myself.

When the bell rang, I headed to my locker to shove my English books into it and grab my Civics ones instead. I was just about to walk to my next class when someone hesitantly placed their hands on my shoulders. I looked up just to stare right into a pair of green emerald eyes.

"Harry?" I asked in confusion.

He didn't reply. He just looked me up and down with an unreadable look on his face. I suddenly felt nervous. What was he doing? He had never done anything like this to me before, except for this morning, that is.

Suddenly, his face was only inches away from mine, and his hands started traveling down my back. I raised an eyebrow at him, causing his face to break out in an almost cheeky smile. His hands found my butt and squeezed it.

I yelped at the touch, looking at him in shock, which made him wink at me. "Remember, this is a game, Louis," he reminded me. And with that said, he walked away, leaving me more surprised and shocked than ever... don't even mention flustered.

What that boy did to me. God, I couldn't even put it into words. However, I never thought he was capable of doing something like that. What had gotten into him? This was not how he usually acted around me, but I had to admit that it was kind of hot.

Just like he said this morning, two can play at this game, and I was not going to back down. To seduce people was one of my talents, so this was going to be easy... right?

Oh, how I wished I had been.

CHAPTER 13 ~ TELL THE TRUTH

Louis' POV

The day passed by pretty slowly after that. Harry didn't get another chance at seducing me. If that was what he was trying to do, that is.

I really didn't know what to think about everything. I mean, Harry had always been the innocent guy who was scared of me. Okay, maybe not scared, but close to it, and now he was acting like he was some kind of bad boy who thought he could make me weak? Even if he did, I would never let him try to embarrass me in front of the entire school.

I may have confessed my feelings for him to myself, but that didn't mean I thought he liked me back because I was sure he didn't. I had bullied him for three years, after all.

I was currently walking out of the classroom of Science with Zayn by my side. He was the only one I had since Liam left for Harry.

Speaking of Liam, why was Harry doing whatever it was to me when he was already in a relationship with him? Not that I minded, though. I mean, I obviously liked the fact that Harry was paying more attention to me than he was to him, but didn't it count as cheating if you kissed someone else's neck? Well, I wasn't the best person to know about those things.

"So, I saw Harry at your locker this morning. What did he say?" Zayn wondered, smiling knowingly.

"Please Zayn, not this again. I've already told you that I don't like him that way," I groaned.

Even if I had admitted my crush on Harry to myself, I hadn't told anything about it to Zayn, and I wasn't planning on doing so either.

He let out a sigh. "Come on, Louis. You have to realize that you have feelings for him."

"Why do I have to realize something that isn't true?" I mumbled, furrowing my eyebrows together to make it more believable.

He came to a halt, making me stop as well. "Really now? You are impossible, Louis," he said, shaking his head.

"Okay, what do I have to do to make you stop accusing me of having feelings for him?" I asked, feeling sick and tired of this conversation about me liking Harry. I just wanted him to stop talking about it.

He raised his eyebrows in surprise, but he quickly composed himself. "Let me think," he said, a smirk forming on his face as we started walking again.

When we got to my locker, I opened it and shoved my books in before pulling out my bag.

"I have it," Zayn said, flashing me a wide smile.

I turned to him, letting out a sigh. I really didn't want to do whatever he was planning for me.

"You have to kiss any girl at our school on the mouth for at least thirty seconds," he said.

I was about to open my mouth to say something when he put a finger on my lips. "And... it has to be in front of Harry," he finished with a smirk.

If it weren't for the fact that I was hiding my feelings for Harry, I would have gasped. How could he do this to me? Harry was never going to like me back if I did this. Zayn couldn't just force me to make out with a girl right in front of him. It couldn't be his only option.

While I was mentally panicking, my face didn't show any expression whatsoever... I hoped. "Really Zayn? You couldn't have come up with something better?" I laughed almost hysterically.

A few days ago, I would have rolled my eyes, telling him that it would be the easiest thing in the world to do, but since I had developed feelings for Harry in some strange way, my reaction was completely different.

This whole thing with Harry was already stressing me out. I mean, I had never had feelings for a guy before, and I had certainly not wanted to be in a relationship. Not since I caught Harry laughing at Liam's joke yesterday. And now Zayn just had to stress me out even more by forcing me to kiss a girl in front of Harry?

It wasn't like it was a big deal otherwise. I mean, I had kissed plenty of girls before, and I did enjoy it, but I was hoping Harry at least had caught some kind of interest to me since he didn't hesitate to kiss my neck this morning. But I could be wrong, and then he wouldn't react to me kissing a girl at all.

Maybe this wasn't so bad after all? If Harry reacted to me kissing a girl in a bad way, it meant he at least had some kind of feelings for me, right? Well, I could always hope so.

"Nope, I'm very happy with it," he smiled toothily.

I let out a sigh. "Fine, I'll do it. Just tell me when."

He looked around the hallway, probably searching for Harry. "He's standing right over there, so you can do it now," he suggested.

I swallowed hard, looking for a girl I could kiss. It didn't take long until I found a blonde one - her back facing me - a few feet away. I dropped my bag to the floor before making my way over to her. I glanced at Harry, who was talking to Liam and Niall across the hallway with a frown on my face. I really didn't want to do this, but if it was the only way to make Zayn stop talking about me liking Harry, then it was worth it... I think.

I made sure that Harry was looking at me when I grasped the girl's wrist and pulled her around. I didn't even get a look of her face I crashed our lips together. She remained still for a few seconds due to shock, I assumed, until she started moving her lips against mine in a sloppy kiss. She wrapped her arms around my neck and pulled me down a little so she could get better access to my lips.

Her tongue traced my bottom lip, and I just wanted to vomit right there, but I forced myself to continue kissing her because I knew Zayn was watching me right now and if he found out I didn't really enjoy kissing this girl, I was dead.

I started imagining Harry's lips on mine instead of the girl's, and it almost worked. I didn't feel the need to vomit anymore, but I didn't enjoy it either. Her lips were just too soft.

Once I had counted to thirty, I pulled away to get a look at her. What I saw made my mouth drop. It was Sarah, Harry's ex-girl-friend. "Oh, shit, I didn't realize..." I trailed off. How could I have been so stupid? Out of all people, I just had to kiss Harry's ex? Fuck.

I turned my head in the direction of where Harry had been standing earlier just to see him watch me with a hurt look on his face. My eyes widened and I felt this strange feeling erupt in my stomach. Could it be guilt? No, I never felt guilty. It had to be something else.

"I'm sorry, I shouldn't have kissed you. I know you and Harry just br--"

"No, it's fine. I'm still not fond of the fact that it was actually you who caused me and Harry to break up, but I had planned on breaking up with him for a while. I just didn't know how, so you kind of helped me. Thank you, I guess. Oh, and apart from that, I really enjoyed kissing you. Maybe we could do it again sometime?" She winked.

I stared at her in utter shock. I couldn't form any words. She was thankful that I had kissed Harry so she didn't need to feel guilty for breaking up with him? What? I thought she was mad at me for kissing him?

"Uh, we'll see about that. I should probably head to P.E, now. Bye," I said, scratching the back of my head before turning around to walk over to Zayn, who was still standing at my locker. However, this time, his eyes were widened.

"You actually did it, and with his ex!" He let out in shock.

I furrowed my eyebrows together, forcing a smile on my face. "Yeah, why not?"

He shrugged. "I just... I was so sure you had feelings for Harry, but I guess you actually don't."

"That's what I've been trying to tell you the whole time," I told him, knowing I should be pleased about the fact that I had managed to make Zayn believe that I didn't have any feelings for Harry, but I wasn't.

The strange feeling in my stomach only grew bigger when I didn't tell Zayn the truth. I never lied, but I couldn't tell him about Harry. I was kind of embarrassed about it since I had promised myself that I would never get feelings for anyone, but Harry had just stepped into my life and ruined it all. However, Zayn admitted that he fancied Perrie, so why couldn't I admit that I liked Harry?

Because you're embarrassed about liking him.

I wasn't, though. Harry was beautiful. With his brown curly hair, his green emerald eyes, and pink lips. I couldn't believe that I once said that he was posh. He was gorgeous.

Not like that, you idiot. You're embarrassed that it's a guy you like and not a girl. Not to mention, he's the guy you've been bullying for years.

I swallowed hard. Maybe the voice in my head was right? Maybe I was embarrassed that I liked the boy I had been bullying for years? Or, it was because I had just realized that I did have feelings for him. Everything was still so new, after all. Besides, I knew Zayn was just going to tease me about it anyway.

"Yeah, yeah, whatever. I should head to class now. See ya later?" Zayn questioned.

I nodded my head, picking up my bag that was still lying on the floor before making my way to the locker room.

I was just about to open my locker when someone grabbed a hold of my arm and turned me around. I stared wide-eyed at the person who was standing in front of me, my mouth falling open when I noticed it was Harry.

"Why?" He asked softly.

My breath hitched at the look on his face. He looked so vulnerable that I wanted to reach up and cup his cheek. "Look, Harry. I'm sorry I kissed your ex, I just uh... Zayn told--"

"I don't want to hear your excuses. Do you like her?" He asked flatly, cutting me off.

I shook my head vigorously. "No, of course not. Why would you think that?"

He looked at me as if I were an idiot. "I know everything about the bet Louis, and I'm sure Zayn came up with it just because he knew you liked Sarah and wanted her to break up with me so you could have her to yourself."

I stared at him with wide eyes. He knew about the bet? How come he-- Liam. Of course. Fuck. "You've got it all wrong, Harry. I do not like her. But even if I did, why would you care? I thought you were in a happy relationship with Liam?"

He blinked his eyes, not seeming to be able to find any words to say. "I... I don't know," he mumbled, furrowing his eyebrows together.

I just stared at him, waiting for him to say something or make a movement. Eventually, a blush crept to his cheeks and he started walking backward. "I'm sorry, I thought... Never mind." And with that said, he walked to his own locker, leaving me nothing but confused.

It took me a while to comprehend what just happened. Then I realized it had been my and Harry's first real conversation, and maybe that fact caused butterflies to erupt in my stomach But, even if it did, I would never admit it. Not even to myself.

Harry's POV

The second I walked away from Louis, my head started spinning like crazy. He thought I was upset about the fact that he kissed Sarah? Well, I was, but it wasn't because it was Sarah out of all people because I didn't have any feelings for her anymore. No, it was because Louis had kissed any girl at all.

I didn't know why I was upset about it, though. I just was...

CHAPTER 14 ~ SECRETS

Harry's POV

It had now been a week since Louis kissed Sarah in the hallway, and I hadn't made any attempt at trying to seduce him since then. I didn't feel the need to because he didn't like me, and if he didn't like me, I would just do it for nothing. I couldn't believe I actually thought he had feelings for me, though. He was into girls and kissing me had only been part of a bet.

I told Liam that we didn't have to be 'together' anymore, but he refused to let us 'break up', saying that Louis could've kissed Sarah only to make me jealous. I didn't believe him, though, and neither did Niall.

Niall was still against Louis, although he didn't dislike him anymore. During that class he was sitting next to Louis a week ago, he got to know Louis and it changed his mind about him.

However, I could tell Niall wanted me and Liam to 'break up', so he could finally be with him for real, and I understood him. I never wanted to be the cause of why Liam and Niall couldn't be together officially, and since I was now certain Louis didn't like me, there was no use for me and Liam to be together anymore anyway.

Liam, Niall and I were currently sitting on Niall's bed, Niall doing his homework while Liam and I were deep in our thoughts. I opened my mouth in an attempt to tell Liam that we didn't have to act like a couple anymore once again, but he stopped me by putting a finger on my lips.

"Don't, Harry. I know what you're going to say and it's not going to happen."

"But why, Liam? Don't you want to be together with Niall officially? There's no reason to continue acting like a couple anymore. Louis doesn't like me, and he made that very clear by kissing my ex in front of me," I grumbled.

He let out a deep sigh. "Harry, how many times do I have to tell you? That kiss with Sarah didn't change anything. I haven't talked to Zayn yet, but I'm sure there's a reason why Louis kissed her. There must be."

I shook my head. "I'm tired of assuming Liam. I want to know, and right now all I know is that Louis kissed my ex, which means he doesn't like me. End of story."

Liam closed his eyes, clenching his jaw together, obviously trying to control the frustration that was building up inside of him. "I can't believe you're giving up. I thought you wanted to get back at Louis just as much as I wanted you to?"

I looked down at my lap, fiddling with my fingers. "I do, Liam. It's just... I'm sick and tired of not knowing things. It just makes me so frustrated."

He nodded his head. "I understand that. I just wish you weren't doubting everything."

"Yeah, me too," I muttered.

We stayed silent for a while until Niall suddenly spoke up out of nowhere. "Do you like him?" He asked, looking at me. "Louis, I mean."

I stared at him in shock. "What? Of course I don't," I said, but it didn't sound convincing, and I cursed under my breath because of that. I didn't like Louis, so why did my voice let me down like that?

"You sure about that?" Liam asked, smiling slightly at me.

I let out a grunt, furrowing my eyebrows while looking at the two of them. "I don't like Louis, okay?"

Liam shrugged his shoulders. "If you say so," he chuckled, causing me to get frustrated.

"I do say so. Now, I have to go. My shift starts in ten minutes," I muttered, getting up from the bed.

"Harry we didn't mean to--" Niall started, but I cut him off.

"It doesn't matter Niall. Bye." And with that said, I exited the room and headed downstairs to the entryway. I was just about to open the front door when Maura showed up and stopped me.

"Harry, honey, where are you going?"

I looked down at my feet before looking up to meet her gaze. "Work," I mumbled.

"Oh, I see. Goodbye then, love," she smiled.

"Bye," I said before finally exiting the house.

I slid into my car and put the car key in the ignition before driving off towards the bakery. A few minutes later, I parked my car in the parking lot and got out of the vehicle.

I entered the small building and greeted my workmates. "Harry!" someone exclaimed, and I knew exactly who that voice belonged to.

Before I knew it, Barbara showed up with my apron in her hands. "Glad to see you, honey. Ready to sell some pastries?" She wondered, handing me the red material.

I put on the apron and nodded at her. "Yeah."

Once my shift started, my brain started spinning again. How could Liam and Niall still think I had feelings for Louis? I had told them so many times that I had lost count that I didn't, and yet here they were, still accusing me of it. All I had ever wanted was to know whether Louis had feelings for me or not, which was the only reason I had agreed to fake date Liam. So, now that I had found out that he didn't, I should let it all go and go back to how it was before, shouldn't I?

Then why did the thought of going back to get bullied by Louis cause my heart to ache? It had to be because I didn't want to get hurt again, right?

I was snapped out of my thoughts by someone clearing their throat. I looked up just to be met by a pair of ocean blue eyes.

My breath hitched in my throat as I examined the person standing in front of me. He was wearing a black v-neck with a print of some band I didn't know, a pair of black, skinny jeans that showed off that amazing bum of his and a black leather jacket. He had his lip ring in and damn, it was so tempting to take a step forward and take it between my lips-- Um, he also had a thick layer of eyeliner around his eyes that framed his beautiful eyes.

"Fancy seeing you here, Harry," Louis smiled, showing off his teeth.

I gulped, looking away from him. "What are you doing here?" I murmured.

I could see him shrugging out of the corner of my eye. "I just felt like seeing you, I guess."

To say that didn't cause my heart to flutter would be a definite lie because damn, he came here to see me? "Um, and why exactly would you want to see me?"

He let out a heavy sigh. "I want to apologize, Harry, for what I

THE KISS

did with Sarah. I know I have already apologized once, but I just want you to hear me out before you jump to any conclusions, okay?"

I furrowed my eyebrows together but nodded my head slowly.

"Okay, um... It uh, it was kind of a bet," he finally said, letting out a sigh. "Zayn told me to kiss any girl at our school, and I swear I had no idea it was Sarah until I pulled away."

I turned to him, meeting his eyes. "You know what? I don't care if it was Sarah you kissed, I don't even have feelings for her anymore," I huffed.

Louis looked slightly taken aback by that. "Why were you so upset then?" He wondered.

"Because I don't think it's fair that you can go around and kiss random people and get away with it. In the end, you just hurt them. Why can't you see that?" I snapped.

He seemed deep in thought for a while, until a small smile broke out on his face. "Are you saying that I hurt you?"

I glared at him. "That was not what I meant, and you know it. I can't believe that you're being so heartless. You don't even care about the fact that you hurt them, do you?" I snorted.

When he didn't say anything, I could feel frustration build up inside me. "That's what I thought. Because if you did, you and Zayn would've stopped making those stupid bets a long time ago," I snarled.

Before I had time to even blink, I felt myself being pinned to the nearest wall with a strong grip on my collar. "Our bets are not fucking stupid, Harry," he growled in my ear, causing me to shiver involuntarily.

If it had been a few weeks ago, I would have been scared shitless now, but it wasn't. During these last couple of weeks, I had learned not to be scared of him. Instead, I could feel courage build up inside me. "I say whatever I want and feel like saying."

Louis clenched his jaw together and tightened the grip on my collar, pressing my body even further against the wall. "What happened to you, Harry? You used to never talk back at me."

I avoided his intense stare and looked anywhere but him. The bakery was thankfully empty, and there were no signs of Barbara or my co-workers anywhere. "I built up some courage because I wanted to be able to defend myself against you."

He raised an eyebrow at me. "And how come you all of a sudden managed to do that?"

"I don't know, but what I do know is that I am sick and tired of being pushed around by you. I don't want to be your punching bag, and I certainly don't want to be part of your stupid game," I muttered.

To my surprise, he loosened the hold he had on my collar with one hand and moved it up to my cheek, trailing his fingers against it. "You are not part of a game," he said, his voice sounding softer than ever before.

"Then what am I?" I snapped, feeling sick and tired of the way he was treating me.

He flinched a little at my tone. "I can't tell you. I'm sorry," he mumbled, taking a step back and dropping his hand from my cheek.

"What's that supposed to mean?" I grumbled, breaking free from the hold he still had on my collar.

"It means that I can't tell you what you are to me." And with that said, he turned around and started heading towards the exit.

"You can't just leave like that!" I yelled after him, causing him to come to a halt and turn around.

"Well, there's nothing left to say, so I can't see why not," he shrugged before walking out of the building, leaving me frustrated.

That night, I didn't get much sleep. I couldn't get my and Louis' conversation out of my head. Why was he so secretive? And what was he hiding? Whatever it was, I was going to find it out, whether he wanted me to or not.

The next day, I acted as if the last week never happened, which meant that I was back to trying to seduce Louis. In the morning, I walked by him when he was standing at his locker, and brushed my hand over his bum. He turned around and probably expected some girl to be standing there, but his mouth fell open when he saw me. I had flashed him a wink before walking away, leaving him more confused than ever.

I had to say that it was pretty fun to play with him like this. His reactions to my actions were hilarious. I could honestly do it all day just to see those expressions.

I was currently in Science class, the second to last class of the day. I was in the back, Louis sitting at the desk in front of me. I decided to take advantage of the opportunity and leaned forward to whisper in his ear. "If you don't tell me what you're hiding, I'm not going to stop doing these things to you."

I breathed hot air against the shell of his ear, making sure my lips brushed his skin. I could feel him shiver, and it made a smile break out on my face.

He turned around to face me, his eyes darkened with... lust? No wait, I must have misunderstood that.

"I won't tell you, Harry. Get over it," he muttered.

I pulled back a little to get a better look at him. "Why can't you tell me? I don't care if it's something bad. I'm sure I can take it. I mean, I've taken your punches for years, so I can't see what can be worse than that."

He looked down at my desk, sucking his lip ring into his mouth, and I swear to God, my mouth dropped to the floor at the sight. He couldn't just do that right in front of me.

"Harry, it's not a bad thing. That's where you have gotten it all wrong," he sighed, shaking his head.

"Then tell me," I whined.

"No!"

"Fine, don't, but you know what the consequences will be," I muttered, leaning back in my chair.

He let out a huff, turning around to focus on what the teacher was saying

I took this opportunity to run my fingers up the back of his neck and to his black hair. Honestly, I had wanted to run my fingers through his hair for a long time now, so when I felt it between my fingers, I got this feeling of satisfaction. After a while, I let my hand wander down to the back of his neck again, trailing my fingers along his spine.

A low moan suddenly escaped his lips, making me freeze in my movements. He immediately smacked a hand over his mouth, refusing to turn around and face me.

I withdrew my hand and stared at the back of his head in shock. Did I really have that effect on him?

CHAPTER 15 ~ FRIENDS? OR MAYBE NOT...

Louis POV

I couldn't believe how I could be so stupid to almost admit my feelings for Harry. I could tell he was going to do anything to find out about my 'secret', and that fact scared me. I knew what Harry was capable of doing to me, and it wasn't pretty if I did say so. I had moaned in front of the whole class, for crying out loud. Luckily, they had all been too caught up in their work to notice anything, though.

However, I knew that Harry had heard it because he withdrew his hand right after it happened. I wondered if he did because he had figured out I had feelings for him or because he was shocked. I hoped for the latter because he couldn't find out about my feelings for him. He just couldn't.

It was now Tuesday, the day after the incident in Science class. I was walking towards the cafeteria without Zayn since he was already there. I walked by some girls who flashed me smiles and winks. I rolled my eyes at them, although my lips twitched slightly. If they only knew I preferred someone who wasn't even the same gender as them.

Eventually, I stepped into the noisy cafeteria and bought a

cheese sandwich. I searched the room for Zayn, and to my surprise, he wasn't sitting alone, but with Liam, Niall and Harry.

I swallowed hard, looking for somewhere else to sit because I was sure I couldn't handle sitting with them. Not just that, but the only seat that wasn't occupied was the one next to Harry.

The only other table that had an empty seat was the one where Eleanor, Danielle, Tarah and a few other girls were sitting. I cursed under my breath and headed for the first table I mentioned.

I dropped the sandwich on the hard surface, causing four pairs of eyes to snap at me.

"Why are you sitting here, Zayn?" I asked annoyingly.

I could see Harry tensing up beside me, making a smirk break out on my face. I loved it when he feared me. Why? I didn't know.

Zayn shrugged. "Liam wanted to talk to me about something, so I thought why not?"

"Maybe because you know I didn't want to?" I snarled, noticing that Harry was getting tenser by the second.

Zayn rolled his eyes, chuckling. "Whatever, Lou. We both know that you don't really mind sitting here anyway."

I huffed, plopping down on the chair. Liam was sitting on the other side of Harry while Zayn was sitting beside him. Niall was looking down at his food, frowning a little. It wasn't hard to tell that something was bothering him, but I decided to shrug it off.

Liam and Zayn started talking in hushed voices so no one would be able to hear what they were saying, but I could swear Harry heard everything since he was smiling slightly in places where they laughed.

I picked up my sandwich from the table and started chewing on it. I was just about to swallow when I felt a hand on my thigh. I gulped, choking on the piece in my mouth.

Everyone at the table turned to me with a confused look on their face. I coughed, feeling tears build up in my eyes because the piece of my sandwich literally got stuck in my throat. "You alright, mate?" Niall asked, patting my back.

I eventually managed to swallow it down, and when I did, I nodded my head. "I'm fine," I replied, turning to Harry who now had a smug look on his face. His hand was still on my thigh, that fucker.

He started moving it up and down, causing goosebumps to appear on my skin. I swallowed hard, biting back a moan as his hand moved a little too close to my private area. He wouldn't do it, now would he? But right then, his hand found my growing member and started palming it teasingly.

I felt heat rush to my face as my hands got all clammy. Why did he do this to me?

I grabbed his wrist, stopping him from going even further and pulled his hand away. I clenched my jaw together as I stared at him, shaking my head.

He tried to look innocent as he shrugged his shoulders, causing me to get even more frustrated. "Are you sure you're alright? You look a little... on edge," Niall asked in confusion, causing Harry to burst out laughing.

I glared at him before turning back to Niall. "Yeah, I just... It's a little hot in here," I muttered, taking another bite of my sandwich.

"Okay."

When the painful lunch hour was finally over, I got up and headed towards the exits, hiding my obvious boner the best I could as I did so. Looking down at the floor, I reached the bathroom and opened the door. I was just about to walk into a stall in the empty room when I felt myself being pushed against the door of it, back first.

"Hard for me, are we?" A voice whispered in my ear.

I wriggled out of Harry's hold, refusing to get seduced by him. "No," I muttered, walking into the stall. I was just about to close the door behind me when a foot stopped me from doing so.

"Trying to escape, huh?" He smiled, eyes sparkling.

I furrowed my eyebrows together, feeling a wave of frustration run through my body. "Why are you acting like this, Harry? What the hell happened to you? You used to be the guy who was afraid of me, and now you're acting like you have some kind of power over me," I snarled, glaring at him.

His eyes widened slightly at my tone, and he took a step backward. "I'm sorry, I didn't..." he trailed off, his cheeks reddening a little.

I sighed heavily, taking a step towards him. "It's okay. I just... I kind of miss the old you," I mumbled, looking away from him.

He swallowed hard. "Why? Last time I checked you hated me for being in the way for you to rule the school," he said sarcastically, not seeming embarrassed anymore.

I clenched my teeth together, walking forward so he had no other choice but to walk backward until he was pressed against the sinks. "You still are, but you know what? I've decided not to care about it," I muttered, pressing our chests together.

Harry gulped, looking slightly surprised by my answer. "Why do you want me to go back to being the real me then? So you can bully me again?" He laughed dryly.

I shook my head. "No. I'm not going to hit you again," I said simply, leaning in to skim my lips over his neck, making him shiver involuntarily.

"Th-then what is it?" He stuttered.

I smiled to myself, pulling back to look at him. "I can't tell you."

He groaned in frustration, avoiding my eyes that were trying to meet his. "What's so secretive that you can't tell me? I think I deserve to know since it is about me," he grumbled.

I took a step away from him. "I can't tell you because it's wrong, okay? I wish I didn't feel this way," I said so quietly he almost didn't hear me.

Harry pulled me forward again, so our faces were only inches apart. "What do you feel?" He asked, his eyes widening in curiosity.

I gulped at the proximity and looked anywhere but him when I replied 'I can't tell you' with no emotion on my face.

"Why?"

"I've already told you, Harry. You don't want to know, and you're with Liam now, so it doesn't m--"

"What does Liam have to do with any of this?" He snapped, cutting me off.

The real question was, what did he not have to do with this? He was his boyfriend for crying out loud, and yet Harry was doing this... whatever this was, to me. "You can't be serious," I said, shaking my head.

He took my face in my hands, forcing me to look at him. "Louis."

I swallowed hard and wriggled myself out of his hold. "Don't, Harry. I'm sick and tired of you thinking you have power over me. You have a fucking boyfriend, and yet you do things like kissing my neck? Last time I checked that's classed as cheating," I grumbled, my eyes shooting daggers at him.

For a second he looked like the old, innocent him again, and my heart just wanted to melt. Why did he have to change? His shoulders slumped and he looked down at the floor, biting his bottom lip. "He's not my boyfriend," he mumbled so quietly I almost didn't hear him.

My eyes widened. "What?" I asked in confusion.

He sighed heavily, looking up at me. "Liam's not my boyfriend. I just said his name that day when you had me pinned to the wall because it was the first name I came up with."

I frowned. "But..." I trailed off.

"Let me explain," Harry said emotionlessly, and I nodded. "Um, as I told you, I just said his name out of nowhere that day because I didn't want you to... do anything to me?" He said hesitantly.

I clenched my jaw together but nodded for him to continue.

"As soon as you had stormed off, I sent a text to Niall, asking him to tell Liam to lie to you because I couldn't have you hate me even more than you already did. God knows what you would have done to me then," he chuckled flatly.

I swallowed hard, the same strange feeling I had felt when Harry looked at me after I kissed Sarah that day erupting in my stomach. This time, though, I was sure it was guilt. I didn't want to believe that I had been his bully and had actually hit him because I knew he didn't deserve any of it.

"However, Liam thought it was a great idea for us to fake date because he was sure you had feelings for me. He thought that you would get jealous if we pretended to be a couple," he explained, waving it off as if it wasn't a big deal.

My eyes widened, though, and I felt my cheeks redden, but not enough for him to notice. Liam knew I had feelings for him? Did Harry also know? What if Zayn had known all this time and had told them about it? No, I was sure that was not it, was it? Ugh, what a mess.

"I didn't believe him, though, but I wanted to get back at you for what you did to me, so that's why I have been trying to seduce you lately," he continued, flashing me an innocent smile.

"That's why you suddenly changed?" I asked, feeling how every-thing suddenly fell into place.

He nodded his head. "Yeah."

I took a step towards him, brushing a curl out of his face. "Prom-ise me you'll be yourself for now on, okay?"

He swallowed hard. "Promise me you won't hurt me then?" He mumbled, biting his lip.

I felt my heart drop. How could I have ever even laid a finger on this boy? He was so adorable and vulnerable that I just wanted to kiss those plump lips of his. "I promise," I said, giving him a pained smile.

"Then it's a deal."

I was just about to open my mouth to say something when the bell rang. I looked at Harry, tilting my head to the side. "We should probably head to class."

He nodded his head. "Yeah, just... can I ask you something?"

"Of course."

"Can we be... friends? I mean, I get if you don't want to. I'm not like you with piercing and tattoos and all that stuff, but--" I cut him off by placing a finger on his lips.

"You're rambling," I chuckled, although I felt my heart twist at the word 'friends'. I wanted to be more than just friends...

"Sorry," he smiled, looking away from me.

"To answer your question... Yes, I'd love to be friends," I said as believable as possible, but I could clearly hear the falseness in my voice, and I assumed Harry did too since his face fell.

He turned around to leave the bathroom, mumbling a 'forget it', but I stopped him by grabbing his wrist, spinning him around. "No, Harry please. I do want to be your friend," I tried to reassure him.

He rolled his eyes. "Yeah, sure." And with that said, he broke free and headed towards the door again. "Um, you might want to fix your problem, though," he reminded me, nodding towards the bulge in my pants.

I blushed as I remembered he was the one who had caused me to get hard in the first place. I didn't have a chance to reply to him before he had shut the door behind him, though, leaving me alone.

I walked over to the empty stall I had been about to enter before Harry interrupted me, and pressed my forehead against it.

What had I done?

CHAPTER 16 ~ PROJECT PARTNERS

Louis' POV

I walked out of the bathroom as soon as I had taken care of my problem and headed to my locker as fast as possible to grab my Math books before going to class. I opened the classroom door and stepped into the room.

"Oh, there you are Louis, you can take the seat beside Mr. Styles," Mr. Rogers said before I had even gotten a chance to choose a seat myself.

I swallowed hard and nodded my head, searching the room for the boy with the curls. He was sitting in the back of the classroom, concentrating on his work while biting his bottom lip. To say it wasn't a turn on would be a lie. Damn him! Why did he have to be so irresistible?

I walked over to Harry, making as little noise as possible, and sat down in the seat next to him. He didn't even glance at me as I did so, which hurt. Sure, I told him I didn't want to be friends, but only because I wanted to be more. Why didn't he give me time to explain myself?

I opened my own books to start working, but I couldn't. The thought of Harry hating me because I had practically told him I didn't want to be friends with him made it impossible to focus on anything else, especially school. So, instead, I found myself tearing off a piece of paper from my notebook and scribbling down a message on it.

Harry please, I do want to be your friend, I promise! The question just... shocked me? I don't know, it was only this morning we hated each other, and now you want to be my friend? I'm sorry I reacted the way I did to your question, but I'm willing to give it a try. I don't want to rush anything, though, and I'm sure you don't want to either, so please forgive me?

Louis :)

I passed him the note, hoping he would read it, but he didn't even glance at it. I tried to get his attention by clearing my throat, but that only caused every pair of eyes in the classroom - but Harry's - to look at me. I let out a frustrated sigh and patted him on the thigh. He flinched at the touch, but I could see that he was looking at me through the corners of his eyes now.

"What do you want?" He muttered, looking down at the note that was on the table in front of him.

"Read it," I pleaded, nodding towards the paper although he couldn't see me.

He turned to look at me for a long time before he finally decided to pick up the sheet of paper and read it over. When he was finished, he looked up at me and nodded his head slowly, a small smile forming on his lips.

A warm, fuzzy feeling ran through my body, and I returned the smile. I couldn't believe he forgave me so easily.

Throughout the rest of the lesson, I managed to work although I wasn't convinced that Harry had completely forgiven me after all. He didn't talk to me, and he was sitting on the edge of his seat with his body turned away from me the whole time.

When the bell rang, I gathered my books and left the classroom with a sigh. I started walking towards my locker, thinking about what we were currently working on in Science when I suddenly felt a hand on my shoulder. I turned around to see Harry smiling slightly at me.

"I'm sorry I avoided you during the lesson. I promise I didn't mean to be rude. However, I wanted to tell you that I forgive you, even though I kind of realize that you didn't do anything wrong. I shouldn't have asked you to be my friend so quickly. I mean, just like you said, we couldn't stand each other this morning, so it would've been weird for us to become friends just like that. I guess I just don't want us to have anything against each other anymore," he explained, shrugging.

"I don't want us to either," I mumbled. "So, it's okay that we'll take it slow?"

He nodded his head. "Of course. I wouldn't want it any other way-"

I let out a chuckle. "Great."

"Great."

We just stood there, looking at each other, waiting for the other to say something, but neither of us did. I scratched the back of my neck awkwardly, looking at the students that walked by us with confused looks on their faces when they noticed that Harry and I were standing beside each other. I decided to shrug it off and cleared my throat instead.

"Uhm, shall we...?" I trailed off, motioning towards the direction of our lockers.

"Yeah," he agreed.

We walked in silence, and yes, it was awkward. I really didn't know what to talk about with Harry. Music? No, we probably had different tastes, and then everything would just get even more awkward. Girls? No, of course not. That, if anything, would be extremely awkward considering I preferred him over girls. So, what was there to talk about?

Before I could think more about it, we had to leave each other to get to our separate lockers. "See you later, I guess," Harry smiled slightly.

I nodded my head. "Yeah."

When he had walked away, I closed my eyes and smacked myself on the forehead. Why did I have to be so awkward? Sure, I had a crush on him, and yes, it was the first time we had talked to each other without basically being mat at one another, but dear god, that wasn't a good excuse! If I ever wanted to be friends with Harry - or boyfriends, for that matter - I would have to improve my power of speech around him.

I strode over to my locker and opened it before shoving my books into it.

"Hi mate," I heard a voice say behind me.

I turned around to see Zayn standing there. "Hey," I muttered, grabbing my Science books.

"What's with the bitterness?" he asked, nudging my shoulder with his lightly.

I looked up at him. "Why am I so damn awkward?" I groaned.

He raised a questioning eyebrow at me. "I have no idea what you're talking about. Why would you be awkward?" He asked confusedly.

"Never mind," I mumbled, shutting my locker and starting to walk off, but Zayn stopped me by grabbing my wrist.

"Hey, where did you go after lunch? You just disappeared without telling us where you went," he frowned, loosening the hold he had on my wrist.

I bit my bottom lip, remembering how I had gone to the bathroom as fast as I had gotten out of the cafeteria. "Uhm, I had to use the toilet," I said, cracking a small smile.

"Oh, okay."

The next second, the bell rang, signaling it was time to head to the next class. We walked in silence, but it was far from how awkward it had been with Harry. I still felt mad at myself for not being able to make a casual conversation with him. What if he wouldn't even want to be my friend anymore?

You're overreacting, Tommo, a voice in my head told me.

I sighed heavily. Yeah, the voice was probably right, but I still couldn't get over the fact that he might like me less now after what happened earlier.

We stepped into the almost full classroom and looked for somewhere to sit. Surprisingly, Liam and Niall were sitting beside each other and Harry was sitting by himself, looking down at his lap. I knew now that Harry and Liam weren't together for real, but why wasn't Niall sitting beside Harry then? I thought he was better friends with Harry than with Liam?

Frowning, I started walking towards the back of the classroom to sit down at the only desk that was still unoccupied. When I walked by Harry, he smiled slightly at me, causing my stomach to erupt with butterflies. Maybe he did still want to be my friend after all?

I returned the smile before proceeding to walk over to the desk. Zayn sat down beside me and flashed me a confused look as soon as he caught my attention.

"What?" I mouthed to him.

"Why did you and Harry smile at each other? I thought you didn't like him?" He asked, a small smile forming on his lips.

I shrugged my shoulders, wanting nothing but to drop the topic. I still didn't want Zayn to find out about my feelings for Harry, so the best thing possible was to not talk about him at all.

Zayn didn't question my lack of explanation. Instead, he let out a sigh. He obviously understood that I didn't want to talk about it, and considering he was the good friend he was, he decided to drop it.

Ms. Flack paced the front of the classroom while talking about some lame project we were going to work on. I didn't listen until she started rattling off the pairs we were going to work in.

"Sarah Hamilton and Niall Horan, Tarah Johnson and Tom Lewis, Zayn Malik and Chelsea Moore..." I waited patiently for her to say my name.

It was pretty obvious that she went in alphabetical order, so I started pondering who I could possibly get paired with.

"Harry Styles and Louis Tomlinson."

I gulped as I heard my name being called out after Harry's, and a million thoughts started running through my head. What was the project about in the first place? Where were we going to work on it? What if Harry didn't want to work with me?

I mentally shook my head. One thing at a time. I should listen to what Ms. Flack had to say about it before I did anything else.

"Now, I want you all to switch seats so you're sitting next to your partner," she ordered.

Zayn tapped me on the shoulder, giving me a wink. "Good luck with working together with Harry."

I flashed him a glare before he walked away to sit down beside Chelsea. A second later, Harry plopped down in the seat next to me. "Hey," he greeted, dropping his books on the desk.

"Hi," I said, looking down at my fingers that were laced in my lap.

118

Don't make the same mistake you did before. You should know the consequences now.

I took a deep breath. "So, what is this project about? I wasn't really listening..." I admitted, biting my bottom lip.

Harry chuckled slightly, shaking his head. He told me what it was about before we started working on it. Sometime during the hour, the nerves in my stomach disappeared and I started talking somewhat causally to Harry. Sure, we were a little tense around each other, but that was nothing out of the ordinary.

Just before we left the classroom, we decided to hang out after school at his place on Friday since he had work both tomorrow and Thursday and he was going to hang out with Niall and Liam today. When he mentioned Liam and Niall, he reminded me of something.

"Um, I don't want to seem rude or anything, but why weren't you and Niall sitting next to each other at the beginning of the lesson? I thought you and him were closer than he and Liam."

He scratched the back of his neck. "Yeah, but... remember I said that Liam and I were fake dating?"

I nodded curtly.

"We were, but during the entire time, he and Niall have been dating instead," he explained, flicking his eyes between the two boys.

My mouth formed an 'o', and I could feel how everything suddenly fell into place. Why Niall had been so quiet during lunch, and why he never looked happy nowadays. He was obviously jealous of Harry that he could be with Liam at school and he couldn't.

A crinkle formed between my eyebrows when I couldn't figure out why Harry would do something like that to Niall. I thought they were best friends?

"Harry, uh... I don't mean to be rude, but why would you do something like that to Niall? I mean, didn't he mind?"

He looked down at his lap and nodded. "Yeah, of course he did. I never liked the idea of fake dating Liam because I knew it was going to hurt Niall whenever we pretended to be a couple. Liam told me that it would only be for a short amount of time, though, and that everything would be over as soon as possible, so thought why not? I hated the fact that it hurt Niall, but I guess I don't have to worry about that anymore," he said, smiling slightly.

I looked up to see Liam smiling at Niall from across the room, and you could clearly see the love in his eyes. A feeling of longing erupted in my stomach.

I wanted that, and I wanted it with Harry.

CHAPTER 17 ~ PROBLEMS IN THE SHOWERS

Harry's POV

I told Liam and Niall that Louis knew about Liam and I's fake relationship as soon as Math class ended that day. Niall's reaction was the best. He literally jumped at me, enveloping me in a tight bear hug while repeating the words 'thank you, thank you, thank you' over and over again in my ear.

After that, he had embraced Liam and kissed his lips passionately. At first, I smiled at them happily, but when tongues got involved, I looked away.

I *was* happy for them, though, and it felt good that I wasn't in the way for their relationship anymore.

Louis and I, on the other hand, had developed some sort of friendship during the last three days. It was still awkward at times, like when we were walking in the hallway and there was nothing left to say. But since we were kind of opposites, it didn't come as a surprise that we were acting this way.

Flashbacks from when Louis kissed me in the hallway a few weeks ago suddenly washed over me. I could still remember the feeling of his lips against mine, and to say I didn't miss it would be a lie.

It was weird, though. I had told myself so many times that I didn't have any feelings for Louis, and yet here I was, admitting that I liked kissing him. Nothing was making any sense anymore.

It was now Friday, the day Louis was coming over to my house. I was currently walking towards the last class of the day, P.E. I looked forward to seeing Louis again, but it still felt a little that Louis and I were now somewhat friends. I knew I had been the one to come up with the idea in the first place, but I still couldn't help but think it felt a little strange to be around him and not getting hit by him.

I opened the door to the locker room and stepped inside. There weren't many students here yet, so I silently walked over to my locker and started stripping off my clothes. I had just pulled my t-shirt over my head when I could feel a pair of eyes on me.

I turned to my right to see Louis looking at my naked stomach. I followed his gaze, but couldn't see anything that was wrong. My four nipples were there as always, and so were my abs, although they weren't as visible as they had once been.

My eyes drifted up only to see that Louis was still looking at me. I cleared my throat, feeling slightly self-conscious. Was something wrong?

His eyes snapped up to my face, his cheeks tinting a bright red. "Is something wrong?" I asked, furrowing my eyebrows.

He shook his head abruptly, too abruptly. The frown between my eyebrows only deepened, and I muttered out a quiet 'okay'.

We didn't say anything else to each other after that, so I was left to figure out why he had been looking like that at my body myself.

The bell rang, signaling that we had to exit the locker room and head out to the gym. The class started, and Mr. Ward informed us that we were going to play basketball.

A small smile tugged on my lips when he told Louis and Adam to make the teams. I knew I shouldn't get my hopes up. I mean, Louis and I were barely considered friends, but damn, I really did want him to pick me to play on his team.

People's names were called up, but mine wasn't one of them. I just stood there, watching Louis while biting my lip in slight disappointment. I wasn't that bad at basketball, was I? No, so why didn't Louis want me to be on his team?

"Harry."

My eyes darted to the one who had called my name, and to my disappointment it was Adam. I walked over to him without even glancing at Louis, although I could feel his eyes on me.

Adam held his hand up in the air, indicating a high-five. I smacked it with mine, exaggerating it a little because I wanted to make a point. I know - immature - but I didn't care.

The game was just about to start when I suddenly felt a hand on my shoulder. I spun around on only to come face to face with Louis. "What do you want?" I muttered, staring down at my feet.

"Wow, someone's grumpy," Louis chuckled.

I ignored him and made a move to walk away from him, but he stopped me by grabbing my wrist. "Hey, Harry. Wait."

I turned my head to him. "What?"

He took a step forward and leaned in to my ear. "You know I didn't choose you only because I wanted to be able to beat you in the game, right?" He chuckled, brushing his lips against the shell of my ear.

I took a step backward, furrowing my eyebrows together. "It's not nice to lie, you know?" I muttered, and walked away from him, leaving him dumbfounded.

Well, what did he expect? That I was going to believe that? It was pretty obvious that he didn't want me on his team.

The game finally started, and I played the best I could. I wanted to show Louis that I was good at basketball and that he made a mistake by not choosing me. I scored about ten goals, and Louis only four.

When Mr. Ward blew his whistle, signaling the end of the game, our team had fifty points while Louis' team only had thirty-four. I celebrated with my team for a few seconds before shooting Louis a wink. He avoided my gaze and looked away with a grumpy look on his face.

I walked over to him and raised an eyebrow. "Who's grumpy now, huh?"

I seriously didn't know how I had suddenly managed to become so confident around Louis. He was still the same guy with piercings and tattoos, but I guess I had gotten to know the real him, and the real him was nicer than I had expected. Besides, he wasn't beating me up anymore.

He huffed, walking away from me. The action made me chuckle, and I started following him towards the locker room.

Once there, I made my way to my locker and opened it. I started stripping off my sweaty clothes, pulling the shirt over my head. When I was completely naked, I grabbed my towel and headed for the showers.

I was just about to hang it on a hook when I noticed a slightly familiar voice sing;

"When I see your face, there's not a thing that I would change, 'cuz you're amazing just the way you are"

I stopped dead in my tracks when I heard the beautiful voice. Could it be who I thought it was? When I looked up and found Louis standing there, his back turned to me, I knew that yes, it apparently could.

I didn't know Louis could sing?

"Hey, Louis?" I said, not thinking about what the consequences would be if I talked to him, and I certainly didn't think he was going to turn around and face me.

I blushed a crimson red as his eyes raked my naked body. Without thinking, I sprinted towards one of the showers to make Louis look away from me. Why was he even looking at me in the first place?

However, it turned out to be a bad move when I slipped on the wet floor and almost fell if it weren't for the hand that grabbed my arm. "Th-thank you," I mumbled, knowing it was Louis since he was the only one who was showering at the moment.

I looked up to see a wide smile form on his thin lips. "You're welcome." With that said, he let go of my arm, but he didn't turn around to continue showering. No. He just stood there, looking me deep in the eyes.

Well, this was awkward. I mean, we were standing here, completely naked while just looking into each other's eyes.

I couldn't help but notice the beautiful color of his irises, though. They were as blue as an ocean, and it made my breath hitch in my throat. Honestly, I had never seen so beautiful eyes in my whole life. How come I hadn't noticed it before? I mean, they were just... gorgeous?

The black eyeliner that usually was around his eyes was now running down his cheeks with the water that he had been standing under. You could see that he had been about to wipe it off, but I guess I had stopped him from doing so.

"Ahem."

I pulled away a little to turn my head to where the sound had come from, a blush covering my cheeks.

"If you're going to make out, please don't do it in here," Jack, a boy in our class said in disgust.

I scratched the back of my head, suddenly feeling a little uncomfortable. Make out? Why would we do that? It wasn't like Louis and I had been about to... no, we were just looking into each other's eyes, that was all.

"We were not going to..." Louis started, looking down at the floor.

"Make out," I finished. "I just slipped on the floor and Louis here saved me from falling."

Jack rose an eyebrow and looked at us skeptically. "I don't believe you because you were standing way too close for that, you know?"

I swallowed hard, looking at Louis who was still staring down at the floor, but now had a frown on his face as well. Neither of us said anything, so Jack took that as a sign to drop the subject, but not before muttering a quiet 'gross', though.

I felt my cheeks redden, and I didn't know if it was in embarrassment or anger. I was embarrassed because well, it was kind of an awkward situation, and angry because what if we had been about to make out? He couldn't just stand there and say that it was gross just because we were two boys. It wasn't wrong to kiss someone who was the same sex as yourself.

Alright, but now we hadn't been about to kiss, and I was straight, so this shouldn't even be affecting me... at all.

"Um... I guess I should..." I motioned to the showers. "Shower," I finished, biting my bottom lip.

Louis nodded his head but didn't look up to meet my gaze, which made my heart drop a little. Was something wrong? Was it something I said? God, I sure didn't hope so because I really didn't want him to be upset with me.

Jack had gone back to his friends, so it was just me and Louis in the showers again. I walked over to a showerhead that was quite far from Louis' because I didn't want to make things even more awkward than they already were.

Once I was finished, I turned off the shower and walked over to wrap my towel around my waist. Louis was still showering, his back turned to me so he couldn't see me staring at him. What? Did I say staring? I meant glancing.

The other boys in our class were now showering as well, but they weren't paying attention to me, I hoped. I contemplated whether I should remind Louis that we were supposed to work on the project after school or not. I now knew the consequences that would follow if I talked to him (he would turn around and face me again), but what if he wasn't coming? I didn't want to fail this project because of him...

"Louis, you're coming over after school, right?" I asked him just loud enough for him to hear me.

Fortunately, he just turned his head this time. He nodded his head, his face showing no emotion whatsoever. "Yeah, I'm just going to go home and check on my sisters first," he said.

I was about to leave when he called me again, "What's your address by the way?"

I cracked a small smile and told him it before heading to my locker to get changed.

I didn't know what to think of Louis coming over to my place later on. Was it a good thing or a bad thing?

CHAPTER 18 ~ VIDEO GAMES & MOVIES

Harry's POV

I headed out of the locker room, shaking the water out of my hair like a dog.

Louis left a few minutes ago without as much as glancing at me, and I didn't really know what to feel about that. Was he mad at me? Well, it had been pretty awkward in the showers, but he couldn't be mad at me for that, could he? I mentally shook my head. No, it must be something else that was bothering him.

I walked to my locker and opened it, pulling out the books I needed to do my homework later on. The second I shut my locker again, I could hear laughter coming from across the hallway. I turned my head to the sound only to see Liam and Niall walking towards me, hand in hand. A smile broke out on my face as they approached me with quick steps.

"Hi, mate," Niall beamed.

Liam rolled his eyes and chuckled softly. "Hey, Harry."

"Hi, guys. What are you doing here? I thought you'd already gone home," I asked, slinging my bag over my shoulder.

"Nah, we wouldn't leave without saying goodbye to our best mate," Niall winked, hitting my arm playfully.

I rolled my eyes. "Yea, right."

We started walking towards the exits, chatting about how the day had been. They told me that some new guy at school had broken two boys' ribs because they had been kissing in the hallway. Fortunately, it wasn't Liam and Niall, but what if it had been? They were pretty open with their relationship after all. However, there was a chance that they could be this crazy kid's next victims.

"Please be careful, alright?" I said worriedly as we were standing by my car.

Niall rolled his eyes and stepped a little closer to Liam. "Don't worry. I have a personal bodyguard who won't let any of us get hurt," he smiled, kissing him on the cheek.

Liam blushed as he nodded his head in agreement. "He's right. Well, at least about the fact that I won't let anyone hurt us," he said, scratching the back of his neck. He was most likely referring to the 'personal bodyguard' reference.

I chuckled softly. "Alright, guys. I need to get home before Louis gets there," I said, opening the car door. I slid into the driver's seat and was just about to shut the door behind me when Niall grabbed it.

"Wait. Louis' coming over to your place?" He asked, a small smile playing on his lips.

He had finally gotten over his dislike for Louis. Instead, he now thought he was a genuinely nice guy, so he had no problem with me hanging out with him anymore.

"Yeah, we need to start working on the Science project," I explained, cracking a small smile in return.

I was actually a little excited that Louis was coming over to my place. I mean, I never had people coming over except for Niall and Liam.

"Oh, okay. Have fun," he winked at me.

I raised an eyebrow at him in confusion, but before I could question him about it, he had shut the door for me. I shook my head to myself as I turned on the engine of my car before driving out of the parking space.

A few minutes later, I parked my car in the driveway of my house and took the key out of the ignition. I then grabbed my bag from the passenger seat and slid out of the vehicle. With quick strides, I walked to the front door and unlocked it.

Once inside, I shrugged off my jacket and slipped off my shoes, placing the bag in the hallway, not bothering to unpack it just yet. I went into the kitchen to open the fridge, letting out a sigh when I realized I didn't really feel like cooking anything. So, I just grabbed a carton of milk and strode over to one of the cabinets to pull out a box of cereal.

I ate in silence, tapping my fingers against the wooden surface of the table while secretly wondering when Louis was going to arrive. Before you say anything, no I wasn't desperate. I just hated the fact of being alone in this big house that I lived in.

When I had finished eating, I placed the bowl and spoon in the sink and started rinsing them. I was just about to put them in the dishwasher when the doorbell rang.

My heart skipped a beat at the sound, and I instantly froze on the spot. Shit, he was here.

I quickly grabbed a towel to dry my wet hands before making my way to the entryway. Placing my hand on the door handle, I pushed the door open to reveal Louis. He was dressed in a black leather jacket and the same black t-shirt he had been wearing to school today, but instead of the pair of black skinny jeans, he was now wearing black sweats. He had a grey beanie covering his black-dyed hair except for his fringe. He wasn't wearing any makeup, and I assumed it was due to laziness after P.E.

It would be a lie to say that he didn't look hot because he did.

Yes, I, Harry Styles, just admitted that I found Louis Tomlinson hot, and I didn't regret it.

"Um, hi, Louis. Come in," I said, motioning for him to step inside.

He shut the door behind him and slipped off his grey, worn-out TOMS. "You're home alone?" He wondered, taking off his jacket.

I motioned towards the hangers when he looked for somewhere he could hang it before nodding my head. "Yeah, mum and Robin work late, and my sister is at uni," I explained, stuffing my hands into the pockets of my jeans.

"Oh, I see," he said, cracking a small smile, but it seemed a little forced.

I frowned, thoughts about what happened earlier in the locker room coming back to my mind. Was he actually mad at me? But I hadn't done anything... right?

There was an awkward silence where you could feel tension filling the air. I let out a sigh and decided to take matters into my hands. "Before we start working on the project I want to ask you something. If that's okay with you?"

Louis clenched his jaw together but nodded his head. "Sure."

I took a deep breath. "Are you mad at me?"

His eyes widened slightly in surprise. "Mad? Why would I be mad at you?" He wondered.

I swallowed hard and shrugged my shoulders. "I don't know, I just thought... I mean, you wouldn't talk to me after the um... incident in the showers, and now you seem all tense and I just thought..." I trailed off, scratching the back of my neck awkwardly.

"You thought I was upset with you for that?" He frowned, and I nodded.

131

"Yeah. I mean, I couldn't come up with anything I had done wrong, but I know you've been mad at me for nothing before, so I assumed you were now as well."

He took a step forward and reached up to trace my cheek with his fingers gently, making me blush. "I could never be mad at you, Harry, not anymore. I know I've been acting like an asshole to you the last couple of years, and I'm so sorry about that. The only excuse I have for my actions is that I didn't know you, and I thought you were a spoiled brat, but I know now that you aren't. It wasn't even a good excuse to begin with. I'm so sorry," he apologized, sincerity glimmering in those ocean blue eyes that I had come to like so much.

I shook my head, but not harshly enough for him to drop his hand from my cheek. "You don't have to apologize. The past is the past, and as long as you aren't faking all this and plan on going back treat me the way you did before, I kind of like you," I smiled, reaching up to correct a strand of hair that had fallen out of place from his fringe.

"I like you too," he almost whispered, smiling wide.

Those four words made me all warm and fuzzy inside, and I had no idea why, but I really liked it. I wanted it to stay there forever.

We stood there for a few seconds, just staring into each other's eyes until the reason as to why Louis had come here in the first place hit me.

I pulled away a little, causing Louis' hand to drop to his side, leaving a tingling sensation on my cheek. I frowned at that but decided to drop it. "We should probably uh... start working, shouldn't we?" I mumbled, biting my bottom lip.

Louis nodded, looking down at the floor with furrowed eyebrows. I could tell something was bothering him, but I didn't want to push him, so I decided not to question him about it.

We walked into the living room and settled down on the couch with our school books on our laps. I opened mine and looked over at Louis only to notice that he was doing the same thing. We started working together, but it didn't take long until I noticed that Louis wasn't paying as much attention to the project as I was. I knew he didn't care about school on the same level as me, so it didn't surprise me all too much.

Half an hour later, Louis slammed the Science book on the coffee table with a loud thud. I flinched at the sudden noise and turned to him with wide eyes. "Let's do something else instead. We've been doing this for more than thirty minutes," he complained.

I rolled my eyes, chuckling softly. "Thirty minutes isn't that much, though."

"I don't care. I'm not used to doing my homework for more than fifteen minutes in one sitting, so you have already pushed my limits."

He was acting childish, and for some reason, I found it quite cute. The way his lips were formed into a pout and his arms crossed over his chest... I couldn't help but tilt my head to the side and smile warmly at him. "Okay," I said in defeat. "You win. What do you want to do?"

His lips curled up in a smile as he nodded towards the flat screen in front of us. "You have any video games?"

"Sure."

During the next hour, we played 'Need for Speed', 'FIFA' and... Honestly, I didn't even know all of the names of my own video games. It turned out Louis was really into it because he got really upset when he lost to me.

"Louis, come on. Let's play again!" I said when I had, won for the third time in a row in 'Need for Speed'.

He shook his head grumpily. "No, I don't want to play this stupid game anymore" he muttered, folding his arms over his chest.

I made an attempt to poke him in the ribs, but he immediately swatted my hand away. "Come on, just one more time?" I pleaded, giving him the best puppy eyes I could muster.

Louis pretended as if he didn't see me and stared at the television instead. "Harry, don't try to persuade me. I won't give in," he muttered.

I slumped back against the backrest of the couch and let out a sigh. "Fine. What do you want to do instead?"

He turned his head towards me and shrugged. "Um, I don't know. Can't we just watch a movie or something?" He mumbled.

I nodded my head, walking over to the shelf where I had all of my DVDs. "Which one do you want to watch?" I asked, holding up 'The Avengers', 'The Dark Knight Rises' and 'The Amazing Spider-Man'.

"Um, how about The Avengers? I've never really watched it," he asked, flashing me a small smile.

"Sure," I said, not really caring about which one we watched because all of them were pretty decent. I walked over to the flat screen and put the disk into the DVD player before striding over to sit down beside him again. Reaching for the remote, I pressed play and leaned back against the backrest, trying to make myself comfortable. When I didn't succeed very well, I let out a frustrated sigh.

Louis noticed my lack of comfort and scooted closer to me, wrapping an arm around my shoulders. I sighed in content and snuggled into him, leaning my head on his shoulder.

Sometime during the movie, I felt my eyelids get heavy. I tried my best to stay awake since Louis was here and all, but it was really hard. So, before I knew it, I was drifting off to sleep, and the last thing I remembered was how Louis' head fell down to rest against my own.

CHAPTER 19 ~ DID THAT JUST HAPPEN?

Harry's POV

"Psst, Harry," a voice whispered in my ear, causing my eyes to flutter open.

The first thing I noticed was that Louis was cuddled into my side with his head resting on top of mine while his arm was wrapped around my shoulders. It was nice and warm, and even though I hated to admit it, I kind of enjoyed it.

It wasn't until then I noticed that mom was standing in front of us, a confused look written on her features. She was the one who had called my name. "Yeah?" I mumbled, not wanting to move in case Louis would wake up.

"Who's this?" Mom whispered-shouted, nodding towards Louis.

I bit my lip, trying to avoid her gaze. When she noticed I wasn't going to reply anytime soon, she continued, "He doesn't look like the type of guy you would usually hang out with."

Now that made me frown. Who did she think she was, practically telling me that Louis was someone I shouldn't hang out with? I could hang out with whoever I wanted without her permission.

Let me explain this to you. I didn't like my family very much. They were never at home and therefore didn't know anything about my life. When all three of us happened to be in the house we never spent time together. I was usually up in my room, listening to music or watching TV while mum and Robin occupied themselves with paperwork and stuff like that. They never spent time with me, and that was why I hated that mom was standing here right now, telling me what friends I should hang out with. It was my choice, not hers or anyone else's.

"Mom, there's nothing wrong with him. He's truly a nice guy," I smiled, thinking about the evening we had spent together yesterday. I would love to do that again.

However, after a while, everything suddenly hit me. Louis was here, on a weekday, in my house, in the middle of the night. Shit, did we fall asleep?

Mom didn't look satisfied with my answer, but I couldn't care any less about that right now. "What time is it?" I asked, rubbing the sleep out of my eyes carefully not to wake Louis up.

Although it was night and he was here, I didn't want to wake him. He deserved a good night's sleep, even though we would have a lot of talking to do in the morning.

"It's three am, son."

My mouth formed into an 'o', and I turned my head to look at the sleeping Louis beside me on the couch. He looked so peaceful and dared I say cute? However, there was no way I was going to interrupt his sleep right now.

"Is it okay if Louis stays the rest of the night?" I asked although I wouldn't take no for an answer.

She furrowed her eyebrows together, looking down at the sleeping Louis. "I would rather not have him here, but I guess since it's already three in the morning, I'll let him stay."

I shook my head, avoiding her gaze. "You're unbelievable, mom."

She pressed her lips into a tight line, and before I knew it, she had spun on her heel and walked away like a stubborn girl. I rolled my eyes after her, snuggling closer to Louis, which made him let out a satisfied sigh.

With a wide smile on my lips, I slowly drifted off to sleep again.

I woke up the next time due to the sun shining through the living room windows. I groaned, trying to move in my seat, but I soon realized that was impossible because Louis was still resting his head on top of mine. I turned my face slightly to the left and saw him stirring in his sleep.

Seconds later, his eyelashes fluttered and his ocean blue eyes soon met mine. A wide smile broke out on my face, and much to my joy and surprise, he cracked a small smile himself. "Morning, Harry," he said, lifting his head from my shoulder.

"Morning. Sleep well?" I asked, stretching my arms out while yawning.

He nodded his head thoughtfully. "Yeah. I must admit your curls are pretty damn comfortable to sleep on," he winked, letting out a soft chuckle.

I stood up slowly, shrugging my shoulders. "Well, what can I say? I won an award for having the softest curls in the U.K last year," I joked, but pretended to be serious.

Louis burst out laughing at that, clutching his stomach.

"What? It's true, I can prove it!" I gasped, my lips curling into a smile.

He continued laughing for a while before he suddenly stopped, his eyes widening in what looked like realization.

"What?" I asked worriedly, afraid that I had said something wrong.

He shook his head, his eyebrows knitted together. "What time is it?"

I grabbed my phone from the coffee table and pressed the button. "It's eleven in the morning, why?"

He got up from the couch and hurried to the entryway. I followed him, not knowing what else to do. What was going on? Why was he suddenly so desperate to leave? "Louis, what are you doing?" I asked as I found him slipping his feet into his TOMS.

He looked up, giving me a forced smile. "I'm sorry, I really have to go. See you at school on Monday?"

I nodded, not knowing what to say. He opened the front door and was just about to shut it, when I sprinted forward, grabbing a hold of his arm. He turned around quickly, probably startled at the fact that I had stopped him.

However, I wasn't prepared for how close he was, and I certainly wasn't prepared for what happened next. Louis looked deep into my eyes, muttering out a 'fuck it' before reaching up to curl his arms around my neck, pulling my face down so he could press his lips against mine.

My stomach instantly erupted with butterflies as goosebumps appeared on my skin, but I was too shocked to do anything but just stand there, letting him kiss my lips. My body was numb, and my eyes were wide open. Was Louis, the Louis Tomlinson, the one that had *bullied* me, *kissing* me? *Again*? I could not believe this.

His lips moved slowly, yet passionately against mine, trying to get some kind of reaction out of me. I felt an urge to start moving my lips against his and suck on that lip ring, but I found myself yet again too shocked to do anything about it.

When Louis suddenly realized I wasn't returning the kiss, he pulled away, walking backward. "Oh, shit..." Was the only thing he said before turning around and storming off, leaving me both confused and kind of hurt in the doorway.

What the hell just happened?

Louis' POV

Shit, shit, shit. How could I have let down my guard like that? I was supposed to hide my feelings for him, not go and fucking kiss him! This was not good. This was not good at all. And the fact that he didn't return the kiss made me want to rip my hair out of my scalp. How could I have been so stupid? He was never going to forgive me. I had ruined everything. The friendship we had built up during these past few days had just flown out the window, I was sure of it.

Fuck my life.

I sprinted towards my car, swung the door open, and slid into the driver's seat. I pulled out of the driveway and drove off towards my house, but not before glancing back at Harry's front door. He was still standing there, his mouth wide open while his eyes were widened to the size of two golf bowls.

He would never forgive me.

Once I parked the car in my driveway, I hopped out and locked it. Walking towards the entrance of the apartment building, I tried not to think about what a living hell I was in right now, but it was really hard not to. I had fucked everything up.

I walked into the flat I lived in with my depressed mother and lovely sisters. "Hello?" I called out, slipping off my shoes.

"Louis!" Daisy and Phoebe came running into the entryway, wrapping their tiny arms around my legs. "Where were you all night?" Daisy asked, looking up at me with wide, worried eyes.

I bent down to their level and took them in my arms. "I'm sorry I didn't come home last night. Did granny sleepover, or did Lottie take care of you?"

That was why I'd left Harry's place so urgently. I had pushed the thought of my family to the back of my mind last evening and had lost track of time when Harry and I had started watching that movie. So, when I woke up this morning and all thoughts of my sister came back, it had hit me; who was taking care of them during the night when I wasn't there?

"Granny slept over," Phoebe beamed. "She's gone home now, though since Lottie came back from her friend's place an hour ago."

I made a note to myself that I would remember to thank grandma the next time I would see or talk to her because wow, she was a lifesaver. "Great, so where are Fizzy and Lottie?"

Daisy bit her bottom lip nervously and Phoebe avoided my gaze by looking down at her feet. I furrowed my eyebrows together, brushing a strand of hair out of Phoebe's eyes. "What is it that you're not telling me?" I asked, trying to sound calm, although I was far from calm on the inside.

Had something happened? Had they been in some kind of accident? I should have never gone to Harry's yesterday...

Phoebe grabbed my hand in her tiny one and started pulling me forward. "We think you should see this," Daisy explained as she followed us close behind.

I swallowed hard, letting Phoebe lead me to whatever they wanted to show me. To my surprise, they stopped outside mom's bedroom. "Daisy, Phoebe, I don't think this is a grea--"

"Just open the door, Lou," Daisy said, crossing her arms over her chest.

I raised an eyebrow at her before hesitantly placing my hand on the doorknob. "You sure about this, girls?" I asked, biting my bottom lip.

Phoebe rolled her eyes dramatically and nodded. "Just open it."

I hesitated for a few seconds longer. I hadn't seen my mom in weeks, probably months because I hated to witness what a living mess she had turned into. She no longer cared about anything, and that was thanks to Mark and his death. I knew it was hard for her, but come on, it had been years. She should at least be back on her feet by now.

I flickered my eyes between Daisy and Phoebe once more before I turned the doorknob and cracked the door open, popping my head inside. The sight in front of me made my heart skip a beat, and I was on the verge to fall to the ground in shock. Mum was sitting up in bed, a wide smile on her face as she was talking to Fizzy and Lottie who were sitting on the bed across from her. Was she seriously talking to someone?

The sound of the door cracking open brought mom's attention to me, and she let out a loud gasp. "Louis! Gah, what happened to you?" She suddenly stood up and started walking over to me, making me step backward in slight fright. What was she going to do?

To my relief, she only reached up to run a hand through my hair, pulling my beanie off in the process. "Your hair! It's black! And this, what's this?!" She gasped, tugging at my three piercings. "What have you done to yourself? This is not the way I raised you to become, Louis."

That last part made me go stiff. She had been out of my life for years now and she still had the heart to stand here, telling me she had raised me? I had practically raised myself. "Mom, what are you doing out of bed?" I frowned, pulling her hands away from my face.

She stared at me with wide eyes, probably trying to take everything in. "I-I..." She trailed off.

"Louis, she's finally talking again. Don't be so hard on her," Lottie said in a whisper, still sitting on the bed. The twins had now walked into the room and were now sitting in Fizzy and Lottie's laps.

I clenched my jaw, looking down at the floor. "I don't care whether she's talking again or not. She's missed three years of our lives, and I can't just forgive her for not being there for us after Mark's death. Not after so much trouble she's caused us," I explained, flickering my eyes between my sisters. "Are you all willing to forgive your mother for not being a part of your lives for three years so quickly?"

There was a short silence until I spoke up again, "That's what I thought."

I was about to turn around and walk out of the room when I stopped myself in my movements, facing my mother. "And mom, don't you dare say anything about the way I look. This is what I am and what I feel like being, so whatever you have to say about me won't make any difference." With that said, I spun on my heel and left the room.

I decided to leave the entire apartment, and as I reached the staircase, thoughts about the entire day started filling my mind. I had first fucked everything up with Harry, and now I had probably fucked everything up with my family as well.

Well, what can I say? All I did was to fuck things up.

CHAPTER 20 ~ BETRAYAL OR LOVE?

Harry's POV

I didn't hear from Louis again that weekend. It didn't come as a surprise to me, though, considering what happened just before he left on Saturday morning.

When Monday rolled around and I was driving to school in the morning, I was still shocked by the kiss. It still hadn't registered in my brain that it had actually happened. However, I was nervous too because I was afraid of what was going to happen when Louis caught sight of me. Was he going to act as if the kiss never took place, or was he maybe not even going to talk to me? I didn't dare guess the answer, so instead, I forced myself to think about something else.

However, one thing I knew was that I really needed to talk to Louis.

Parking my car in an empty parking space outside school, I turned off the engine and climbed out. The first thing that caught my eye was Niall's car that was parked a few spaces away from mine. I decided to walk over there when I noticed him sitting in the driver's seat.

I knocked on the car window, startling him. He immediately rolled down the window with wide eyes. "What the hell man. Are you trying to scare the life out of me?"

I chuckled, shaking my head slightly. "Nah, I was just trying to get you to notice me," I winked, earning a glare from him.

"So, where's Liam? Thought he was riding with you nowadays?"

"He usually does yes, but he's going to the nurse later on to check on his kidney, so drove his own car today," Niall explained, giving me a small smile. Apparently, he had already forgotten about me scaring him, which was nothing but a good thing for me.

"Kidney? I thought he had two working kidneys now?" I asked, furrowing my eyebrows together.

"He does. It's just a check-up to see if everything is working as it's supposed to."

My mouth formed the shape of an 'o' in understanding.

"So, what have you been up to this weekend? Haven't heard from you since Friday," he asked me as we started walking towards the entrance.

"Um, Louis came around on Friday," I replied, biting my bottom lip hesitantly because I didn't really want to get into this.

"Right, how was it? Please tell me he didn't hit you. I swear to God, I'm going to--"

"No, Niall. He didn't hit me. He uh... he kind of did the opposite actually," I grimaced, cutting him off.

He furrowed his eyebrows together, looking deep in thought. "The opposite? What do you mean?"

I took a deep breath, preparing myself to tell the truth. Before I could do so, though, the bell rang, and we suddenly had to hurry to get to first class. I jogged to my locker, practically throwing my jacket into it before running off towards English class. Niall met me halfway there, the question I had been about to answer just a minute ago long forgotten... or, Niall had forgotten about it at least.

We sat down at a desk at the back of the classroom, and it just had to be the desk beside Louis and Zayn's. Glancing over at Louis, I noticed he had his head buried in his arms on the surface of the table. I frowned, wondering why he wasn't showing his face.

Deciding not to think more about it, I let out a sigh and slumped back in my chair. I then turned my attention to Mr. Olsen who had started talking.

When the bell rang, signaling the end of first class, Louis got up with lightning speed and sprinted out of the classroom, his books in his hands. I made a move to follow him but stopped myself when I realized that he was gone. "Hey, man. What really happened on Friday?" Niall asked, placing a hand on my shoulder from behind.

I turned around to him, facing the floor. "I was trying to tell you earlier... he um... he kissed me," I mumbled, barely audible.

Niall's hand tightened on my shoulder before he dropped it. "He *what*?"

I looked up at him, biting my bottom lip. "Yeah, but I never kissed back," I continued.

"Y-you... he, *what*?" He gasped, looking from me to the direction Louis had just disappeared in.

I nodded my head slowly. "I don't know what it meant, though. He hasn't spoken to me ever since it happened."

Right then, Liam walked up to us with a smile playing on his lips. "What are you lads up to?" He asked, wrapping an arm around Niall's waist and kissing him on the forehead.

I let out a deep sigh and attempted to walk away from them, but Niall grabbed my arm at the last second. "Louis kissed Harry last

Friday," Niall said, still gaping.

"Louis *what*?" He gasped.

"Actually it was Saturday. He slept over, but excuse me, I really have to go find him so we can sort everything out," I explained, taking Niall's hand off my arm so I could walk away from them, leaving them with their mouths hanging open.

If I was being honest with myself, I was just as shocked as they were by everything that had taken place. I just didn't have time to wait for them to take everything in because I really wanted to go find Louis. I had to know why he had kissed me.

I knew it could be a bet yet again. I mean, it had happened once, so why not twice? But something told me this didn't have to do with some stupid game. I just couldn't put my finger on why he had kissed me.

The first thing that popped into my head about where Louis could be was in the bathroom. It was a usual place to go to if you wanted to be alone, so therefore, I was now walking with quick strides towards the room I had asked Louis to be my friend in a few days ago.

Opening the door, I made my way inside and started checking the stalls for a locked one. I even pressed my ear to the doors in an attempt to hear sounds, but I had no success whatso-ever. After realizing he wasn't in there, I walked out and started thinking about where else he could have gone.

I pushed past people in the hallway, trying to get through the massive crowd that always gathered during breaks. It could get really annoying sometimes, especially when you were in a hurry.

I finally made it through and was just about to climb the stairs to the second floor when I spotted Louis standing at his locker, his back facing me.

Without knowing what I was doing, I walked over to him and cleared my throat, making his head turn in my direction. "Har--"

"Look, Louis, we need to talk about the ki--" I started, but was cut off by him.

"You mean the kiss that you had intended?" He asked, raising his voice so the entire hallway could hear.

I furrowed my eyebrows. "What are you doing?"

"Oh, don't you try telling me I was the one who leaned in to kiss you when we both know it was the other way around," he said monotonously, his face showing no emotion whatsoever.

I swallowed hard, looking at the people surrounding us. "W-what are you talking about? I-I never--"

"I'm sorry, Harry, but I don't swing that way," he winked, patting my head as if I was a little kid.

By now, there was a mini-crowd watching us with wide eyes, and I just wanted to disappear. Why was Louis doing this to me? Why was he lying?

"Hey, Louis. Wasn't it you who kissed him in the hallway a few months ago, though?" An unfamiliar voice asked from the crowd.

Louis' features hardened, and he spat out, "It was all a stupid bet Zayn made me do. Did you seriously think I would want to kiss this loser? Let alone be his friend?"

To say that didn't hurt would be a lie. I could feel tears brimming my eyes, but I forced them back by biting my bottom lip harshly. I thought he liked me? At least to the extent that he didn't have anything against me... but I guess I was wrong. Louis had never wanted to be friends with me.

Despite the anger I suddenly felt inside me, I couldn't help but feel as though my heart had been ripped out of my chest at the same time. If there was something I hated, it was being lied to, especially when it had to do with friendships or any kind of relationship for that matter.

"You know what? If you're being too much of a coward to tell everyone what really happened, I will let you be that. I don't care, and why should I? It seems like you never liked me anyway," I huffed. And with that said, I spun on my heel and started making my way through the crowd that was still watching us, heading towards the exits.

I didn't stop running until I was by my car, opening the car door and climbing in. I put my hands on the steering wheel, leaning my forehead against them. Tears started rolling down my cheeks, and I frantically tried to wipe them away, but it was no use. They just kept on running.

I had never experienced something like that in my life. Louis had humiliated me in front of so many people. How could he have done something like that to me? Oh, right, because he was never my friend. Maybe this was what he had planned all along? To find the perfect moment to humiliate me?

Letting out a sigh of frustration, I reached out to turn on the radio. The first song that came on was an emotional one, and I couldn't stand hearing the meaning behind the singer's words, so I switched to some uptempo song that I didn't even know the name of.

I tried to sing along to the music, but the song barely contained any lyrics, so I started bobbing my head along to it instead. I hummed the melody, doing anything I could to make the thoughts about Louis go away.

About half an hour later, there was a tap on my window. I turned my head to the left abruptly, startled by the sound. A guy with blonde, curly hair and brown eyes was standing there, looking at me with concern. I furrowed my eyebrows together, wondering why a stranger would be concerned about me but decided to roll down the car window anyway.

"Um, hi?"

"Hey, I'm Mike," the boy smiled slightly, extending his hand.

I raised an eyebrow at him, glancing at his outstretched hand. "Who are you, and what are you doing here?" I asked, not bothering to introduce myself.

Mike let out a sigh, withdrawing his hand. "Um, my name's Mike as I just told you, and I go to school here," he said motioning towards the building in front of us. "I was about to walk inside when I couldn't help but notice you sitting here in your car crying. I decided to walk over here to see what was bothering you."

I looked down at my lap, fiddling with my fingers. "Oh," I muttered.

"So, what happened?" He asked, placing his arms on the door, leaning against them.

I shrugged my shoulders. "Nothing. I don't want to talk about it."

Mike looked deep in thought for a while, biting his bottom lip until he let out another sigh. "Could you at least give me your name?" He wondered kind of hopefully.

I quirked an eyebrow at him. "Uh... I'm Harry."

A small smile made its way to his face. "Nice to meet you, Harry, I'm Mike."

I rolled my eyes, trying not to smile. "You've already said that. Twice, actually."

"Oops, sorry," he winked. "So, would you mind telling me what happened to you? I won't judge or anything. I just don't want you to be sad."

I looked down at my lap again. Did this guy really care? Or was there a reason as to why he was here talking to me? What if this guy was like Louis? What if he wanted to become my 'friend' just to humiliate me in front of the entire school a few days later?

I shook my head to myself. No, everyone wasn't like Louis, I had to remind myself that.

I took a deep breath. "A guy I thought was my friend turned out to be a jerk."

A crinkle formed between his eyebrows. "What happened?"

"He said we were friends, but today he told the entire school - while I was there - that he had never wanted to be friends with me," I explained, biting down on my bottom lip harshly to stop myself from start crying all over again.

"You really like this friend, don't you?" he asked, his face full of concern.

I shook my head at first, thinking about when Louis had bullied me. However, thoughts of how nice and sweet Louis could be then entered my mind, and I found myself shrugging. "I don't know, he's bullied me for years. Then it all changed when he one day came up to me and kissed me in the hallway."

I didn't know if it was a good idea to tell Mike about this. He could be homophobic for all I knew, but now it was already done and I couldn't take it back even if I wanted to.

Mike's face suddenly changed, switching between a mix of emotions. Fondness? Disgust? Amusement? Happiness? Sadness? Confusion? Well, I couldn't tell. "So, this so-called 'friend' likes you as more than a friend?" He wondered, raising his eyebrows.

I shook my head and decided to start telling him the entire story because I had already started explaining things, so I felt as though I might as well tell him everything. I started from the kiss that happened a few months ago to when Louis had started trying to seduce me, to when *I* had started trying to seduce *him*, to us becoming friends, and all the way to the kiss that happened on Saturday. Then, at last, I told him about him what happened just a few minutes ago. It felt really weird to vent all these things to a stranger, but I felt as though Mike was a friend I actually could trust. He radiated the vibe to be nice at least.

"Oh, wow, Louis Tomlinson, you say?"

I nodded my head slowly.

"I've heard a lot about him. Never thought that womanizer was into guys, though" he said in shock.

I furrowed my eyebrows together. "That's the thing. I don't think he really is. I'm positive he's played me ever since the beginning."

"But why would he do that?"

"Well, he did bully me for about three years, and he told me it was because I was in the way for him to rule the school. I don't know... it sounds crazy. I mean, how could I be such a huge deal? I'm not even that popular," I mumbled, my face in a scowl.

Mike shook his head in agreement, biting his bottom lip. "I think I know why Louis has done everything he has to you. It kind of makes sense when you have heard the entire story of what you two have been through."

I looked at him in confusion. "What do you mean?"

Mike flashed me a small smile. "I am pretty certain Louis Tomlinson is in love with you."

CHAPTER 21 ~ WHAT IF I LIKE HIM?

Harry's POV

"Wait, what?" I gaped, staring at Mike with wide eyes.

He shrugged his shoulders, still smiling. "Yeah. I mean, think about it, Harry."

And that was exactly what I did. I thought about everything that had happened between me and Louis and what his re-actions to it all had been. There was our first kiss where he had kissed me longer than what he first intended to, according to Liam. Could that mean he liked it?

Then there was when he called my eyes gorgeous. What had that been all about? And his reaction when he had 'found out' Liam and I were in a relationship. He had been so upset. Not to men-tion all those times he had moaned my name when I tried to seduce him, and just the fact that he had kissed me again this Saturday.

Wow, there were so many situations that could be evidence. What if Louis actually did have feelings for me after all? But then again, why would he say that I was the one who had kissed him at my house when we both knew it was him? And why would he even humiliate me in front of all those people in the first place if he liked me?

"I guess there is some evidence that you could mean you are

right, but why would he say that he never wanted to be friends with me in front of all those people if he has feelings for me?"

A wide smile formed on Mike's lips. "That's obvious too, mate. Louis was afraid that you were about to reject him when you walked up to him. That's why he turned the whole thing around and blamed it all on you in front of everyone."

I looked down at my lap again, biting my bottom lip. "Well, if that's the case, he has a strange way of showing his attraction for me."

Mike reached out to pat my shoulder encouragingly. "Yeah, but now you know the truth, and all you have to do now is to forgive him so you can live happily ever after," he winked.

I let out a snort. "Mike, first off, I am not going to forgive him that easily. He really hurt me and I don't know for sure that he didn't mean what he said. Second off, I don't even like him that way."

He raised an eyebrow at me. "Seriously?"

I nodded my head, not daring to look at him. If I was being completely honest with myself, I didn't know anymore, though. I had called Louis good looking, sex on legs and beautiful, hadn't I? And honestly, who did that if they didn't like them? But for some reason, I couldn't bring myself to admit that I had feelings for him. Was it because he was a guy? Or because he had been my bully? I didn't know.

He noticed that I wasn't going to answer him any time soon, so he dropped the topic with a sigh. "Well, I'm gonna head to class. Are you coming with me?"

I finally looked up at him, shrugging my shoulders. "Yeah, I guess. I can't sit here for the rest of my life, even if it's really tempting right now," I said, biting my bottom lip.

Mike shook his head in amusement, opening my car door for me.

"Come on, I'll help you," he winked.

"I don't need any help," I muttered as I slid out of the car, letting him close the door behind me.

We walked into the school and headed to the next class.

For the rest of the day, I did my best to avoid Louis, and there were two reasons why I didn't want to face him. One, because of what he had done to me earlier, and two, because of the fact that he might (most likely) have feelings for me.

Either way, it would have just been plain awkward.

Louis' POV

"You know what? If you're being too much of a coward to tell everyone what really happened, I will let you be that. I don't care, and why should I? It seems like you never liked me anyway." With that said, Harry sprinted off, leaving me alone with the students that were still watching us.

My mouth hung open as I followed his figure until he was completely out of sight.

I couldn't believe I had just done that. Everything I did nowadays was the opposite of the right thing. First off, I had kissed Harry, then I had screwed things up with my mother, and now this?

I liked him so much, and yet here I was, telling him how he didn't mean anything to me. I was such an ass, not to mention a pussy. If only I'd had the guts to stay at his place when I kissed him that day and let him yell at me for practically attacking his lips, I might not be standing here right now, only getting myself in more trouble than I already was in.

"I think you made quite the mistake there, mate," a boy with brown, short hair and dark, brown eyes said, walking over to pat me on the shoulder.

I shrugged his hand off, muttering a quiet 'I know' before turning around to slam my locker shut, leaving the remaining students with confused looks on their faces.

The bell rang on my way to class, but I made no move to pick up my pace whatsoever. I didn't care if I was going to be late. All I cared about was Harry, and how I could possibly make him forgive me. The more I thought about it, though, the more I realized that he would probably never want to even be my friend again. I had most likely lost my chance with him forever.

Letting out a sigh, I forced my legs to move forward, even if they barely carried me anymore. I was just about to round a corner when I heard an all too familiar laugh coming from afar.

I came to an abrupt stop, my eyes widening slightly. No, I wasn't ready to face him yet. I knew he hated me now, and I wasn't sure if I could handle seeing the hatred in his eyes when he would see me. But, the bell had already rung and the only way to get to Civics was this way, so I couldn't do anything but to just keep walking forward.

I finally rounded the corner and was just about to look up when another laugh was heard in the hallway. My eyes snapped up in record time only to see Harry walking with some blonde, curly-haired lad. Thankfully, they were walking in the opposite direction, so they didn't see me walking behind them, but that didn't stop my heart from breaking.

Seeing someone I knew wasn't friends with Harry making him laugh after what I had just done to him broke my heart into a million pieces. Did this mean Harry didn't care about the fact that I had told him I never wanted to be his friend? It was a lie, but still, it didn't even affect him?

I tried to man up and stop the threatening tears from falling, even if all I really wanted was to break down and cry my eyes out.

However, I continued walking forward, keeping quite some distance between me and the two boys in front of me. My eyes were glistening with tears, but I forced them back, knowing I had to if I wanted to keep my image as a bad-boy.

Harry and the other guy stopped outside the classroom of Civics, facing each other. I couldn't make out what they were talking about, but I heard a few words like 'thank you', 'help' and 'appreciate'. It didn't help me at all, so I just watched their actions instead.

The guy made a move to hug Harry, but to my heart's relief, Harry didn't notice this and just turned around to walk into the classroom.

I started making my way over as well and was just about to pass by the blonde guy when he grabbed a hold of my arm. "Listen here, you asshole. If you ever hurt that boy again, I'll make sure you won't be able to see with your damn eyes for the next couple of weeks, you hear me?" He snapped in my ear.

I broke free from him, furrowing my eyebrows. "Who the hell are you, and who do you think you are, telling me what to do?" I snapped back, glaring at him.

His brown eyes darkened as he clenched his jaw together in anger. "Make sure you don't hurt him again, or else I'll fucking punch the shit out of you." With that said, he started walking away.

I raised an eyebrow. "Don't think I am scared of you, you shithead. You would only get disappointed," I yelled after him.

He let out a snigger, not even turning around to face me as he did so. I watched his figure disappear around the corner, making sure he was out of sight when I let out a deep breath.

Who was this guy, and how come I had never seen him before?

What he said didn't even get to me, though. I wasn't afraid of him, and I never would be. His threat didn't matter either because I was sure Harry would never talk to me again, and therefore, it would be quite hard to hurt him, at least with words. Honestly, I never wanted to hurt him again even if I got the chance to. I had already hurt him too many times, and I had made so many mistakes, but it was over now. I would never hurt him again, and that was a promise I was going to keep.

Finally walking into class, I sat down at an empty desk, ignoring everyone and everything. This went on throughout the rest of the day. I went to class, sat down either beside Zayn or at an empty desk, and ignored everyone while staring ahead of me or down at my books.

During lunch break, Liam, Niall, Zayn, Harry and I sat at the same table, considering we always ate together nowadays. The boys noticed that something was going on between me and Harry, but they didn't question it and thank god for that because I didn't want to know how it would have ended if they did.

Harry didn't glance at me once throughout the entire day, and I couldn't blame him. I wouldn't have wanted to look at him either if it was the other way around. What I had said... it was unforgivable, especially when he had no idea that I didn't mean a single word of it.

I did contemplate whether to tell him the truth or not, but I figured he wouldn't have let me explain anyway. He would have just walked off before I even had the chance to open my mouth, I was sure of it.

The last bell of the day eventually went off, and I didn't hesitate to get out of school as quickly as possible, not wanting anything but to go home. I was just about to start the engine of my car and leave when my eyes met a pair of the most beautiful green staring back at me without holding any emotion whatsoever. I swallowed hard, not knowing what to do. It was so intense, yet so emotionless, and I just wanted to break down because I knew why there wasn't a smile on his precious face like it always was nowadays when he looked at me. It was because of me and my stupid mouth.

I eventually broke my and Harry's eye contact, not being able to handle it anymore. I then started driving towards my home.

Not once that day did I stop thinking about the curly-haired boy I liked so much. Not even when my mind wandered to that guy with blonde curls.

I couldn't help but wonder who he was, though, and why Harry was hanging out with him.

CHAPTER 22 ~ BECAUSE I LIKE YOU

Harry's POV

"Honey, wake up!" I heard a voice call from the other side of my bedroom door.

I groaned, rolling over to the other side of the bed, not wanting to wake up. "Okay, mom," I mumbled, but it was barely audible.

Ten minutes later, I found myself standing in front of my closet, going through my clothes. I decided to dress in a black t-shirt and a pair of black, skinny jeans.

When I finally made my way downstairs, I could make out hushed voices in the kitchen. "This boy had piercings and tattoos all over him," a voice I knew belonged to my mom said.

"Are you sure Harry wasn't forced to hang out with him? Those kinds of guys aren't his type. Harry is so innocent. He wouldn't hurt a fly," the other voice, Robin, said.

"I don't know, but I don't like it."

A frown made its way to my face as I listened to what they said. They were talking about Louis and how his appearance didn't fit with mine. Even though the two of us weren't on the best terms right now, I didn't like it when mum and now Robin spoke about him like that.

Louis may have hurt me quite deeply, but I wanted to believe that there was a heart somewhere in that body anyway.

When mom and Robin finally went silent, I stepped into the kitchen, looking down at my feet. "Good morning, sunshine. Sleep well?" Mom wondered, unaware that I had overheard her talking about me and Louis.

I nodded my head curtly, walking over to the fridge to pull out the milk. "Son, why aren't you answering your mother correctly?" Robin asked firmly, causing my body to freeze.

Not this again. First off, he wasn't my dad, and therefore, he didn't get to call me his son. Second off, I hated it when he thought he could tell me what to do with that firm voice. I was eighteen years old, and he couldn't tell me what to do.

During my entire life, I had always been that shy guy who was afraid to defend myself, but that was over now. I'd had enough.

I turned around with lightning speed, my eyes boring into his. "Because I'm sick and tired of how you two think you know me! You just go around here and think I'm still some perfect, innocent kid who is too afraid to defend himself, but guess what? People change, and I'm one of them!" I snapped, causing the room to fall silent.

Mum stared at me with wide eyes while Robin clenched his jaw together in anger. I took a step back as I saw the look on his face, my back hitting the counter behind me. I could feel goosebumps rise on my skin as I watched him approach me with long, quick strides.

"Robin," mom warned, stopping him by placing a hand on his shoulder. "Don't."

He clenched and unclenched his hands, seeming to contemplate whether to hit me or not. Finally, though, he let out a defeated sigh and looked up at me. "If you so much as dare to use that tone with either of us again, you're going to wish you never did. Is that understood?" He spat, glaring at me.

I nodded my head quickly, too scared to open my mouth and answer him with words.

"Great."

With that said, he stormed out of the kitchen, leaving me with my speechless mom in front of me. I avoided her, not wanting to look at her right now, and instead placed the milk on the counter.

I was not hungry anymore.

"H-Harry?" Mom stuttered behind me, making me close my eyes.

"Forget it, mom, I might have deserved that," I muttered without turning around to face her.

"No, sweetheart. You did not. It's just... what you said kind of shocked us, you know? You've never snapped like that before" she reassured me, stepping forward to place a hand on my back from behind.

I didn't open my eyes. Instead, I tensed at her touch because if I was being honest, this was the first time she had touched me since I was a little kid. "I know. I um... I overheard you two talking about Louis and how you thought he was a bad influence on me, and I guess that just kind of made me upset?" I tried to explain, scratching the back of my neck.

I didn't even know what I was talking about. I just spoke what my heart told me to, and it told me to defend Louis. However, my mind was still mad at him for humiliating me.

"Oh," she said hesitantly. "Well, I can't say I like him, Harry, because I really don't. I've never been a fan of tattoos and piercings. Not to mention punks in general."

I finally turned around to face her, but I didn't smile as I could tell she thought I was going to do by the look on her face. Instead, I furrowed my eyebrows together. "I think you should learn not to judge people before you know them," I said in a mutter.

She swallowed hard, keeping a somewhat natural look on her face. "Harry, love. Are you sure you know what you're talking about? If I remember correctly, this so-called 'Louis' was your bully, aren't I right?"

I avoided her intense gaze, looking anywhere but her. "How did you know?" I mumbled, secretly shocked by how she could remember something like that.

I could see her eyebrows knitting together through the corner of my eye. "Am I not supposed to know those kinds of things? I'm your mother, Harry."

"Sometimes it doesn't feel that way," I mumbled so quietly I thought she didn't hear me, but by the look on my her face, I could tell that she did.

Her jaw clenched together, and her eyes darkened with anger. "What did you just say, son?" She asked with a dark voice, stepping forward.

I swallowed hard, looking away from her. "N-nothing," I attempted, but it was too late.

The next second, I could hear a loud smack echoing in the room, and by the blood and pain I felt rushing to my cheek, I knew exactly what had just happened.

Mum had slapped me.

I let out a loud gasp, clutching my now aching cheek in my hand. "W-what the hell?" I croaked, feeling tears well up in my eyes.

The worst thing about the situation wasn't the fact that she had just hit me, but the look on her face. She didn't even have a sign of regret written on her features, and that made my heart shatter into a million pieces.

Before she had time to even open her mouth to say something, I took off towards the front door. I couldn't stay here. Not now, not ever again. If they couldn't respect my choice of friends or the way I was now, I couldn't live here with them.

I slipped my feet into my shoes and shrugged on my jacket before exiting the house, slamming the door shut with a loud banging noise.

I ran to my car, jumped into the driver's seat and sped off towards school. It only took a couple of minutes until I arrived and turned off the engine with a deep sigh. Feeling tears rolling down my cheeks, I desperately tried to wipe them away, but it was no use. They just kept on running.

My cheek was still throbbing by the slap I had received from mom, and the fact that it was from her out of all people didn't exactly stop the tears from escaping my eyes. I couldn't believe she had slapped me. She had actually *hit* me. Out of all things I expected her to do in that situation, I never expected her to do this. It was just uncalled for.

I didn't know how long I sat there, drowning myself in my thoughts until I'd had enough and climbed out of the car. My legs started leading me towards the entrance while my gaze was glued to the ground. I was just about to step into the building when I got this sudden feeling that someone was watching me.

I furrowed my eyebrows, turning my head to the left only to see a pair of bright blue eyes staring at me with concern. I swallowed hard when I noticed that Louis started approaching me, and I instantly reached a hand up to signal him to stop.

He did so instantly, sucking his lip ring into his mouth. I turned back around, continuing my way into school and away from him.

Louis' POV

I watched Harry disappear out of my sight, making me sigh heavily. All I wanted was to ask him what made him cry. I hated to see him sad, it didn't suit him. He was meant to be happy, and if he wasn't, I wanted to make him feel better. Of course I wanted to apologize for what I had done yesterday as well. What I did was just uncalled for, and if I could, I would take it all back.

It wasn't like I had expected him to let me approach him, but I thought it was worth a shot. Not that I had been thinking of the fact that he was mad at me and didn't want me to come over when I first saw the tears rolling down his cheeks because all I had cared about was the sad look on his face.

When the bell rang, I decided to finally make my way into the building and head to my locker to get rid of my jacket and grab my English books. I walked by a few students, nodding my head to the ones I knew and just ignoring the girls that tried to flirt with me.

I was not in the mood. Not now and probably not ever again.

I was just about to walk into English class when I heard someone call my name from behind me. I slowly turned around, already knowing who the voice belonged to. "Hi, Zayn," I mumbled, cracking a small smile.

He nodded curtly. "What's up?"

I shrugged. "Nothing, I guess. Harry still hates me."

A smirk made its way to his face as he looked at me knowingly. "Everything is about him nowadays, isn't it?"

I shook my head, letting out a groan before walking into the classroom that was full of students. I could hear him laugh behind me, causing me to get even more frustrated than I already was.

"Morning, Mr. Tomlinson," Mr. Olsen greeted as I walked by his desk.

I raised an eyebrow, turning around to face him. "Um, morning?" Why was he greeting me? He had never greeted me before, ever.

He just chuckled, shrugging. "It looked like you needed to be cheered up."

I nodded slowly, unsure of what to say. Luckily, though, Zayn stepped into the classroom right then and pulled me with him so I didn't need to come up with a reply.

We walked by the desk Niall and Harry were sitting at, both of us noticing how Harry was leaning his head on Niall's shoulder, burying his face in it. All I wanted was to stop and ask either Niall or Harry what was wrong then because it wasn't hard to tell that something had happened, but since class had already started, I let Zayn drag me to an empty desk instead.

Throughout the entire lesson, I kept an eye on Harry, watching his every move while Zayn kept texting Perrie, who was sitting across the room next to Trisha. Although I couldn't care less about Zayn and Perrie's relationship at the moment, I found it quite cute how they simply couldn't get enough of each other, even though they were only a few feet apart.

Once the bell rang, I gathered my books and got up from my seat, ready to leave the classroom. I started walking towards the door when I noticed that Harry and Niall were still sitting in their seats. I decided to stop, shoving the thoughts of what consequences could follow of my next movement aside.

"Um, can I talk to you, Harry?" I asked hesitantly, scratching the back of my neck.

He looked up from the desk, making eye contact with me. His eyebrows were furrowed and his eyes were still red from crying. "No," he said with no emotion whatsoever.

Ouch, that hurt.

"Louis, go away," Niall sighed. "Harry's not feeling well, as you can probably see."

I ignored him, only focusing on Harry. "Please, Harry. I'm sorry for what I did yesterday. I... I didn't mean to humiliate you like that. I just... I didn't know how to react. I mean, you were about to reject--"

"Just stop, Louis. As Niall just told you, I'm not feeling well. Please don't make this any harder for me by trying to apologize right now," Harry muttered, staring back down at the desk again.

I turned to Niall, looking at him with furrowed eyebrows. "What happened?" I asked.

Niall's eyes flickered between me and Harry as if he was contemplating whether or not to tell me. Eventually, he let out a defeated sigh, looking up at me with big, honest eyes. "Harry's mom... she uh, she hit him this morning," he explained, looking at the boy who had stiffened by Niall's words.

Harry looked up at him. "Y-you promised not to tell him," he frowned, avoiding my gaze.

"I couldn't just not, Harry. He deserves to know since she practically did it because of him."

Harry let out a huff, burying his face in his arms again. I turned to Niall with a confused look on my face. "Wait, what?"

He only nodded his head. "It's true, Louis. Harry defended you even if the two of you aren't on the best terms right now. Anne - Harry's mother - told him how she didn't like how he was hanging out with someone like you, and it made Harry upset. He told her that she shouldn't judge someone before knowing them. Then when he told her that she didn't feel like a mother to him, she slapped him," he explained, looking down at Harry in concern.

My eyes widened as my mouth fell open in shock. Did Harry actually stand up for me to his mother? No, it must have been someone else he defended because he wouldn't do that for me, not after what I did to him yesterday. "What?"

Niall nodded his head again.

"But, *why*?"

Harry suddenly looked up at me then, and before I knew it, he said the words I had wanted him to say ever since I realized I had feelings for him.

"Because I like you.

CHAPTER 23 ~ SMILES & CRIES

Louis' POV

Harry's eyes widened as he slapped a hand over his mouth. "I-I didn't..." he trailed off, standing up abruptly, causing his chair to fall over.

Before I had found the ability to talk, Harry disappeared out of the classroom, leaving both me and Niall dumbfounded. What just happened?

It didn't take long until Niall's mouth formed into a small smile, and I could swear I heard him mumble the word 'finally'. "What are you doing still standing there? Follow him for God's sake!" He urged me, motioning towards the door.

I just stared at him, still shocked by Harry's words.

Niall nudged my arm. "Come on, Louis. You obviously like Harry in return. This is your chance, take it!"

I swallowed hard, blinking. "I-I, what?"

"It's really damn obvious, you know? I've never really been a fan of you, but after seeing the fondness in Harry's eyes every time he looks at you, and you at him, I've decided to accept you. He really does like you, and you like him, so what are you waiting for?"

It wasn't until then I finally managed to compose myself enough to let everything sink in. Harry liked me. He actually liked me... as more than a friend? If that was true, this was for sure the best day of my life.

I finally found the ability to move my legs, and with a quick nod to Niall, I ran off towards God knows where because I had no idea where Harry could be.

The first place that popped into my head about where he could have gone was the bathroom, but considering every student at school had a break right now, it would probably be full of people, so I doubted he would be there, after all. He was most certainly at a place where he could be alone.

I rounded a corner, running on the tips of my toes so I could see over the students' heads in the hallway. Call me short, and I'll punch you in the face.

Harry was nowhere to be seen, which caused a sudden wave of panic to wash over me. I needed to find him, and that was now.

Running through the hallway, I spotted a curly-haired guy with blonde locks standing at the lockers, talking to Tarah. Although I disliked him, I decided to walk over to him. He could know where Harry was, after all. "Hey, whatever your name is, have you seen Harry?" I asked in a rush, tapping him on the shoulder impatiently.

He spun on his heel, his features hardening at the sight of me standing in front of him. "What the fuck have you done now, Tomlinson?" He growled, gritting his teeth together.

I reached my hands up in defense, taking a few steps back. "I haven't done anything. I was just wondering if you had seen him. I have to talk to him," I explained, looking around the hallway to see if he by some miracle had shown up. Obviously, he hadn't.

"Well in that case, no I haven't."

I glared at him and let out a huff before turning on my heal, regretting I had even asked him in the first place.

I started running again, but not before hearing him mutter the words 'stupid fag' behind me. If I hadn't been looking for Harry right now, I would have stopped dead in my tracks and probably kicked him in the guts, but now I was looking for Harry, and I didn't have time for a jerk like him.

My legs carried me outside to the - for once - sunny weather. I didn't know what I was doing out there, but since my legs had control over me, I presumed there was a reason as to why I was heading in this particular direction.

The sun was shining through the almost none existent clouds, causing a warm sensation to shoot through my body where my skin was exposed. I took a right turn, almost instantly catching sight of the boy I had come to like so much sitting on a bench, his legs pulled up against his chest.

My heart sank to my stomach when I noticed he was crying. His curly hair was a mess where it was sprawled all over his knees, his face pressed against his kneecaps. It wasn't the sight of him that made me realize he was crying, it was the sobs that were escaping his mouth. They were barely audible, but if you listened carefully, you could hear them quite clearly.

My legs that had just been my compass started feeling weak, and I was soon struggling to keep myself upright. Chills were running down my spine, and I didn't know if it was due to the wind that suddenly blew up, or the fact that Harry might be crying for what he said to me. What if he didn't mean it?

Slowly, I moved my jelly-like legs forward, not daring to make any noise in case Harry would notice me and run off.

I was soon standing right in front of him, looking down at his slightly shaking body. Placing a gentle hand on his shoulder, he flinched and let out a loud gasp. "What are y-- Louis?" He said, mumbling the last part.

I sat down next to him on the bench and turned my head so I could look directly into his eyes. "The one and only," I smiled faintly.

His features suddenly hardened and he looked away from my eyes. "What are you doing here?" He asked coldly, making my heart pound in my chest.

I didn't like this, I didn't like it at all.

I took a deep breath, deciding not to care about his demeanor, and reached forward to caress his cheek lightly with the back of my index finger. "I was looking for you."

Harry swatted my hand away, looking down at his knees again. "Why?"

I ignored the tug I felt in my heart by being rejected and rolled my eyes instead. "Maybe because you just ran off after telling me you liked me?"

He bit his lip, still looking down at his knees. I waited for seconds, probably minutes for him to answer until I finally realized he wasn't going to do so. I let out a deep sigh, shifting my body so I was turned towards him. "Why are you crying, Harry?" I asked him hesitantly.

"'m not," he mumbled against his knee, still refusing eye contact.

I placed two fingers under his chin, forcing him to look at me. "I'm not blind, or deaf, you know? You have dried tear stains on your cheeks and I heard you sobbing when I got here," I told him, looking deep into those gorgeous green eyes.

He broke our eye contact, freeing himself from my grip. "I just hate everything that's going on in my life right now," he mumbled, barely audible.

"What do you mean?" I asked, furrowing my eyebrows together.

He took a deep breath, looking at me through the corner of his eye. "I'm talking about the fact that my mom and stepdad don't approve of the people I hang out with... more specifically, you. Then my mom just *hit* me this morning. I don't know if you've ever experienced it, but I can tell you that it's something you don't want to go through. I'm also talking about the fact that you humiliated me in front of all those people yesterday. It just made me feel so... worthless? I don't know, but I didn't like it," he mumbled, looking at me hesitantly while biting his bottom lip.

I swallowed hard, looking down at my feet in shame. "About that, I'm--"

"No, wait," he said, cutting me off. "Let me finish."

I nodded my head slowly, slumping back against the backrest of the bench. "I'm so sorry, though, I didn't mean to say those things, I swear--"

"Louis, please just... hear me out, okay?" He pleaded, looking at me with wide, serious eyes.

I sighed but nodded my head again.

"Last off," he said, his gaze trailing back to his knees. "I'm uh, I'm not sure if I meant what I said to you earlier in the classroom."

Now that made me stop talking for sure. I could feel how my heart literally dropped to the pit of my stomach. He didn't like me. Well, of course he didn't, why would he? I had bullied him for years, I had humiliated him in front of all those people, and I had even used him because of a bet Zayn made up. It would be strange if he actually did like me.

Despite this, I couldn't help but feel as though someone had just strapped me in the heart. Tears welled up in my eyes, but I forced them back. I couldn't cry, especially not in front of Harry. He would think I was weak, and I wasn't weak.

"Oh," was the only thing that escaped my mouth as I turned my body away from him.

Don't you dare be a pussy again, Tommo. Do something! My inner voice demanded.

And that was exactly what I decided to do.

Harry let out a deep sigh. "Look, I'm--mmph!" I cut him off by crashing my lips against his.

His hands instantly went up to my hair, trying to pull me away from him, but I pretended like I didn't know what he was trying to do, and reached up to cup his cheek in my hand instead. After a few seconds of useless struggle, he decided not to care about it anymore and just let his lips move with mine, clearly just waiting for me to stop kissing him.

I let out a frustrated groan, trailing my other hand down to the hem of his shirt. I lifted it up just enough to be able to rest my palm on his bare hip. When I still didn't get a reaction out of him, I pulled away, feeling nothing but rejected. What was I thinking? That he would actually kiss me back?

"Fuck," I muttered under my breath, letting go of him so I could run off, just like the last time.

Before I was able to do so, though, he wrapped his hand around my wrist, pulling me back. My eyes widened at the gesture, but also at the fact that my face was mere inches away from his flawless one.

Our eyes were locked for I didn't know how long. We just stared into each other's souls, and I could feel how my heart started racing in my chest. Then, our lips were suddenly connected again, only this time, they were moving together.

I let out a loud gasp, feeling fireworks explode in my body by the feeling of Harry's pink, plump lips moving against my own for the second time in my life. It was amazing. *This* was amazing. I had never experienced anything like it ever before.

The kiss was pure perfection.

I moved to swing one leg over Harry's lap so I was straddling his body. This meant I no longer had to bend my neck uncomfortably to keep kissing him. He let out a low moan, causing the hairs on my body to stand up. I had never heard anything more beautiful in my life, I was sure of it.

He curled his arms around my waist as I slowly, almost teasingly ran my tongue along his bottom lip. It didn't take long until he granted me access to his mouth, which I instantly took advantage of by slipping my tongue past his now wet lips.

A loud moan escaped my throat as my tongue touched his, swirling around it. My right hand trailed up to his hair, tugging on his curls gently as my left hand cupped the back of his neck, pulling him impossibly closer to me.

Since we were at school and not in a private place, I decided to slow things down after that. Besides, it was only our second kiss, after all. We had plenty of time to experience other stuff at another point.

I was just about to pull away when he caught me by surprise by taking my lip ring in between his lips, sucking on it.

"Shit," I moaned, feeling how my eyes rolled back behind my eyelids.

Seconds later, he released my lip ring, and we slowly pulled away from each other, our eyes fluttering open.

Blue eyes met green, and at that exact moment, I felt complete. I felt as though a hole in my heart had suddenly been sewn together again by none other than Harry Styles. The boy I had never in a million years thought I would have any feelings but pure hatred for, I now liked more than I had ever liked anyone before. And as a small smile broke out on his now swollen lips, I knew that I was in far too deep to ever back out. Harry was my life now, the only thing that mattered to me, apart from my sisters.

"Louis?" He whispered, nudging his nose with mine.

"Mm?" I smiled toothily.

"I think I might actually like you after all," he grinned, showing off his dimples, which almost had me pressing my lips back against his all over again.

"You think?"

He nodded his head cutely. "Yeah, I mean, I haven't made my mind up just yet."

I rolled my eyes. "Maybe I can help you with that?" I said, leaning in to press my lips against his once again.

Before I was able to do so, though, a firm voice interrupted me, causing my body to freeze. I could feel Harry's doing the same as I turned around to face the person who had opened his mouth.

"Mr. Tomlinson and Mr. Styles, office now."

CHAPTER 24 ~
KISS ME

Harry's POV

I stiffened at the firm voice that just called my and Louis' names. I didn't dare turn my head to look at the principal, so instead, I kept my eyes on Louis, examining the side of his face since he was facing Mr. Evans.

He was so gorgeous. How could I not have noticed this before? Like seriously, he had no flaws. His skin looked so soft with no pimples or anything of that sort, and his beautiful, blue eyes were framed by a perfect layer of eyeliner, then his thin, pink lips looked so irresistible and his piercings just topped everything off.

I should feel ashamed of myself for not realizing how much I actually liked him sooner. If my assumptions were right, he had liked me for quite a while now, and the fact that he had tried to kiss me twice only proved that they were most likely right.

The fact that he had to kiss me three times to finally make me realize that I liked him was just sick, though. I felt sorry for him, even though I hadn't forgiven him completely for humiliating me just yet. It happened yesterday, and even if I now knew why he had done it, it was still going to take some time until I would forgive him completely for it.

Oh, for heaven's sake, who was I kidding? I had forgiven Louis as soon as I had decided to press my lips against his, and I knew it pretty damn well.

I was so lost in my thoughts and Louis' flawless face that I almost didn't register what he said next.

"Excuse me sir, but why exactly do you want us in your office?" Louis asked calmly.

Mr. Evans who was standing a few feet away from us folded his arms over his chest and raised an eyebrow at Louis. "Do you not approve of my orders, Mr. Tomlinson?"

Louis' lips formed into an obvious fake smile as he shrugged his shoulders. "I haven't said anything about not approving your orders, sir. All I asked was why you wanted us to come with you," he pointed out.

The principal pressed his lips into a tight line. "What you two were doing when I came out here is not appropriate within the school grounds, especially not when there are underaged people around here," he said strictly.

Louis snorted while I just sat there, dumbfounded. "As if there haven't been people doing that kind of stuff around here before," he said, rolling his eyes.

"Well, it's another thing when it comes to two boys doing... that stuff, and not a girl and a boy," Mr. Evans snapped, causing me to get back to reality.

"You did not just say that," I could hear Louis growl under his breath as my eyes darted to the principal.

"Wait, what?" I gaped, tightening my hold on Louis' hips to keep him from getting up and possibly punch Mr. Evans in the face.

"I'm certain you heard exactly what I said. Now come with me you two, or else the punishment is going to get worse than it already is," he threatened, glaring daggers at us.

I swallowed hard, getting ready to stand up and obey him, but Louis stopped me by pressing more of his body weight on me. "We're not going to obey some sick homophobe that has something against us, if that's what you think... sir," Louis retorted, adding the 'sir' at the last second while staring back at Mr. Evans.

"Well, then I'm afraid I'm going to have to give you both detention after school *and* contact your parents about your awful behavior and actions."

I swallowed hard, knowing my mum wouldn't be too happy if she found out what Louis and I had been doing just a few minutes ago. But then again, I had basically moved out of the house this morning when she slapped me in the face because there was no way I was going to face her anytime soon after that. So, maybe it wouldn't be so bad if she found out I had kissed him since I wasn't going to be there anyway? Well, she would probably get more upset with me than she already was, but I was sure I could handle it if I just didn't have to face her.

I glanced at Louis, silently asking him what he wanted to do about the situation. What if his parents were just as homophobic and stupid as mine? Then he would probably get in a lot of trouble, and I absolutely didn't want that.

He bit his bottom lip, thinking through the options, I assumed. "Will you get hurt?" He mumbled in concern, trailing his fingertips over the fading red spot on my cheek.

I shook my head slowly.

"And you wouldn't mind getting detention?" He continued.

I shook my head again.

"Then it's settled. We are not obeying your orders, sir," he announced, looking back at Mr. Evans.

The principal creased his eyebrows together, glancing at us in surprise. "You would seriously choose to get detention and a phone call to your parents instead of coming with me to my office?"

I nodded my head slowly, looking down at the hem of Louis' black tank top. "Yeah," Louis said, shifting on my lap. "Considering what you just said about gay people, there is no chance we want to know what else you have to tell us."

Mr. Evans showed no emotion whatsoever on his face as he let out a huff and turned on his heel to walk away from us.

I let out a sigh of relief that I didn't know I had been holding in. "I don't really get it, though. Why *did* we choose to get detention and that phone call instead of just going with him to his office? I mean, how bad could it be?" I asked him, furrowing my eyebrows.

"Because," he started, cupping my cheek in his hand, caressing my soft skin with his thumb. "For one, I didn't really want him to say more sick things to us. Didn't you see his face, Harry? He thought what we did was disgusting."

I looked up at him, biting my bottom lip as I nodded my head.

"Then, I think that you and I really need to talk about everything that just happened between us before anyone else tries to get in our heads, don't you agree?" Louis smiled slightly.

I thought about what had been taking place before Mr. Evans showed up, and nodded my head in agreement. We were definitely in need of having a talk.

"So, why would we let that stupid jerk of a principal make us do anything else?" He continued, the smile never leaving his face.

I shrugged my shoulders with a grin on my lips.

"Exactly," he winked.

"But, won't we get in more trouble now? Mr. Evans is most likely going to be more upset with us now than he was before," I reminded him, furrowing my eyebrows together slightly.

"Yeah, probably, but guess what? I don't care. It's not like he can suspend us. We didn't do anything wrong," Louis shrugged, not seeming to care at all about the fact that our principal disliked us.

There was a short silence where I just let everything sink in. Mr. Evans was upset with us for not following his orders, and it couldn't possibly be a good thing to have your principal be upset with you, could it?

"Hey, Harry?" Louis said, making me snap out of my thoughts and look up at him. "I won't let him do anything to you, okay?"

He looked me deep in the eyes, searching for something. Trust? Confirmation? No matter what, my stomach erupted with butterflies and a small smile made its way to my face. "Okay," I nodded, feeling like a little child that was being looked after by their father.

He flashed me a smile. "So, how about we have that talk now, yeah?" He suggested, getting off my lap to sit beside me instead.

"Where shall we begin?" I wondered, looking at him.

"Let's start with when you decided not to let me run away... what happened?" He asked, turning his body so he was facing me fully.

I shrugged my shoulders, looking down at my lap. "I don't know... I just... I think that I deep down knew I had feelings for you, so I didn't want you to run away again?" I said almost hesitantly, biting my bottom lip.

I could see him furrowing his eyebrows together through the corner of my eye. "But if that's it, then why didn't you reciprocate my kiss when I tried to kiss you?"

I let out a deep sigh, looking up at him. "I think I have been denying my feelings for you ever since we kissed that first time in the hallway... up until now," I explained, feeling quite embarrassed to confess my feelings for him. "That's why I didn't kiss you back. I was too afraid of the fact that I would actually like it."

Louis sucked his lip ring into his mouth, thinking deeply. What he didn't know, though, was that him sucking his lip ring was a huge turn on for me, so I wasn't surprised when I could feel myself getting aroused in my pants.

Not now, Harry, this is not the right time for this.

I forced myself to think of disgusting things like people eating their own snot, and luckily, it worked.

"So what you're saying is that you were afraid of liking me?" He questioned, still seeming a bit confused.

I nodded my head. "Yeah. I mean, I have never had feelings for a guy before, so I didn't exactly know how to handle it. The best thing I could think of was to deny it, deny that I didn't have feelings for you, and it worked more or less up until now. You just had to kiss me... again. It was hard enough not to kiss you back that first time at my house. You never realized how close I was to return that kiss, did you?"

Louis shook his head slowly.

"I was. The only thing stopping me was the fact that I was shocked by your actions. I would have probably started reciprocating that kiss if you had just given me a little more time," I admitted, lowering my head a little.

Louis just gaped at me, and I took that as my cue to continue. "The fact that you were my bully didn't exactly help me admit my feelings for you either. It uh... it only made me deny them even more. I thought that it should be illegal to have feelings for someone that beats you up every time they get the chance to."

182

By now, I could see tears prickle his eyes, which almost made me stop telling him my side of the story. Louis never cried. Throughout the years I had 'known' him, I had never seen him let a single tear fall. This was something new, and for some reason, it made my heart flutter in my chest.

"Then it was my lame attempts at seducing you," I said, letting out a chuckle. "I wanted to get back at you for all those times you made me all flustered, which I've already told you. It wasn't easy, though. Throughout the years I've known you, I've always been afraid of just uttering a single word to you. And now I was going to seduce you? Yeah, right. But somehow, I succeeded. Now that I think about it, though, I only did because you liked me, and not because I was good at it, didn't I?"

Louis nodded briefly, an amused smile playing at the corners of his lips, his eyes now free from any tears.

"After a few days of being seduced, you had enough, though. We ended up in the bathroom, and there I agreed to go back to my normal self if you promised to stop bullying me. Everything seemed so great then that I couldn't stop myself from asking you to be my friend. It was a little rushed, I know, but I wanted to be able to talk to you whenever I wanted now that we finally were on good terms, so I asked for your confirmation. You said no, though, and that hurt. I don't think I've never felt so rejected before, not even when I was a little kid and my mom left me alone in the house to go out on a stupid date when I begged her to stay. I liked you, and that was like you telling me you didn't like me back."

Louis looked down at his lap in shame as he pursed his lips. "I uh... I apologized, though," he reminded me quietly.

I nodded my head. "You did, but I didn't want to forgive you as easily as I did," I mumbled.

Louis swallowed hard, fumbling with his fingers. "You know I really do like you, though, right?" he wondered, looking up at me with big, honest eyes.

Every thought left my mind then because wow, that was the first time he confessed his feelings for me. He had never said the words 'I like you' to me before. "I-I..." I trailed off, not knowing what to say.

He let out a sigh, shifting in his seat a little. "Do you remember that day when you told me you dated Liam?"

I nodded my head slowly. How could I not? I mean, I had blurted out Liam's name by accident, and there was nothing I could do about it. Louis had stormed off before I had the chance to explain myself.

"That was the day I realized I had feelings for you. Liam was right, I was jealous, beyond jealous even. One of my best friends had taken a short cut to you, while the only thing I could do was watch everything happen before my eyes. I was so frustrated that I just wanted to strangle everyone that walked by me," he admitted, biting his bottom lip.

So Liam and Niall were right all along? Louis did have feelings for me back then, and he had been jealous, so jealous that he even had considered strangling innocent people.

"So, you have known about your feelings for me since then?" I gaped in shock.

"Yeah, but I know I started liking you ever since Zayn came up with that bet. The kiss was meant to be short, only long enough for you to start kissing me back. It wasn't short, though, as you can probably remember. I just couldn't bring myself to stop kissing those soft, plump lips of yours," he admitted, a light blush covering his cheeks.

I scooted closer to him so I could press a soft kiss to his reddening skin. "If it makes you feel better, I didn't want you to stop kissing me either."

He let out a soft chuckle, nuzzling his nose into my neck. "I'm sorry," he muttered after a short while.

I pulled him away from me a little so I could look at him. "For what?" I asked, wanting him to tell me what he was referring to specifically.

"For putting you through so much pain. During all those years I have known about you, I haven't done anything but caused you pain. Not only did I bully you, but I have also humiliated you, made your mother hate you, confused you and scared you. I don't ever want to do any of those things again," he mumbled, looking me in the eyes.

My lips formed a small smile, and I pulled his face closer to mine so there were mere inches between us. "I forgive you."

Louis' eyes widened slightly. "Harry..." He trailed off. "Are you sure?"

I nodded my head, making our noses bump together. "I'm sure," I promised him.

"But I mean... I have--" I cut him off by placing a finger on his lips.

"I don't care, okay? I couldn't care less about what you have done in the past. It's the present that counts, and in the present I like you."

Louis smiled widely, lifting a hand to brush a few strands of hair away from my eyes. "I like you too."

"Could you do me a favor?" I asked him, my lips twitching up-wards.

"Of course."

"Kiss me?"

"Gladly."

And with that said, Louis leaned in to press his lips against mine for the fifth time, but it was only the third time I had returned the gesture.

CHAPTER 25 ~ HESITATIONS

Louis' POV

We sat there for a while, talking about other incidents that needed to be sorted out. Like, when I visited the bakery with Daisy and Phoebe that time a few weeks ago and Harry stood up for himself for the first time. He told me it was due to frustration, that I had annoyed him by calling him perfect when he didn't see himself as that.

I did, though. Not in the same way I meant back then, but in a more... romantic way? To me, Harry was the closest thing to perfect you could come, and I meant it.

We kept talking, and when we came to why I had humiliated him in front of the students in the hallway, I told him the truth. I told him I was afraid of getting rejected by him, but also that I was afraid of getting embarrassed in front of all those people. I felt so ashamed of myself for doing such a thing to him. Instead of getting embarrassed myself, I had embarrassed him, which was even worse.

Harry understood, though... kind of. He told me that was what he thought the reason behind my actions was, but that he didn't get why I had to practically shout it so everyone could hear. I didn't either, and that just made me feel even more guilty and upset with myself than I already was.

The next question he asked me took me by surprise, though. "Why did you kiss all those girls? First Laura, then Eleanor and to top it off Sarah?"

I scratched the back of my neck, looking everywhere but him. "Um, do you remember how I was before eh... before I started having feelings for you?"

His mouth formed the shape of an 'o'. "Wait, so you um, kissed them for fun?" He asked me, hesitation lacing his voice. He didn't really seem to like the topic, and I understood why.

I shook my head vigorously. "No, God no. I uh... I kissed them to uphold my reputation. It's always been about that, upholding my reputation, I mean. It started a few years ago when my step-dad passed away," I explained, grimacing a little. This was such a sensitive topic for me.

Harry raised his hand for me to stop talking, and I immediately obeyed him, wondering what he had to say.

"You don't have to tell me, Louis. I can tell this is a touchy thing for you talk about." He gave the hand that was in his a light squeeze.

I flashed him a small smile, shaking my head. "It's okay. It happened a long time ago," I assured him, although I wasn't so sure that I was okay after all.

It wasn't Mark's death that had caused me to feel this way, but the consequences that followed after it. My mum's refusal to move on, and the fact I had to become an adult before I had even turned fifteen. When I looked back at it now, I realized how tough it had been for me, raising my sisters and all, but I also knew I could have handled it better. Instead of getting piercings and tattoos and sleeping around with girls, I could have been there for them even more. They deserved the same upbringing I had once received from mom.

I told Harry everything, from the day Mark was in the car accident to when mom had snapped back to reality a few days ago. He listened carefully the entire time and sympathetically massaged my thigh when I told him about situations that were more touchy. The gesture only made me like him even more. Those kinds of small and caring gestures were so sweet, and they made my heart explode in my chest in a way it had never done before.

Everything good must come to an end, though, and the bell was what interrupted our good this time. However, I was pretty sure it wasn't the first time it had rung since we went out here. We had probably missed at least one of our classes... not that I cared all that much about it, though.

"We should probably head back inside, yeah?" Harry suggested, getting up from the bench.

I followed his actions after nodding my head in agreement. "Yeah, it must be lunch break or something by now," I said, taking his hand in mine.

From the corner of my eye, I could see his cheeks heating up, and for some reason, my heart swelled at this fact. *I* had the ability to make him blush.

We started walking towards the entrance in silence until Harry spoke up again. "Lou?"

My heart skipped a beat in my chest at the nickname. "Yeah?" I smiled toothily.

"Um, do you want to um... have an open relationship, or do you want to hide it?" He asked hesitantly, glancing down at our now entwined fingers. "Not that we're actually in a relationship yet. I just... Well, not that I wouldn't want to be. I mean, it would be amazing and all, and--"

"Harry, you're rambling," I chuckled, cutting him off.

He looked up at me, biting his bottom lip. "I tend to do that when I'm nervous, don't I?" He blushed.

I nodded my head, remembering when we had been in the bathroom and he asked me to be friends with him. He definitely tended to ramble when he was nervous.

"Yeah, and to answer your question; Even if we aren't exactly together... yet, I'd like to show people whatever relationship we have right now," I smiled.

Harry's cheeks went even redder, and his gaze trailed down to his feet. "But only if that's what you want too, of course," I added quickly.

He looked up at me, smiling cautiously. "Yeah, I'd like that."

My smile couldn't get any wider then. I couldn't believe how I managed to get so lucky. For once, I had actually found someone I wanted to be in a relationship one day, and it turned out that someone wanted to be with me as well.

As soon as we entered the hallway, everything went silent as everyone turned to look at us... or, more specifically, our entwined hands. I swallowed hard, looking down at the floor to avoid the intense gazes.

I could feel Harry tense up beside me, causing both of us to stop in our tracks. Slowly, I turned my head to look at him. His eyes were flicking between every student that was watching us, his bottom lip trembling a little. It was not a pleasant sight because who wanted to see their boyfriend/friend or whatever being scared of something?

It was at that second I realized that this was bullshit. Why would either Harry or I need to be afraid of some students' opinions? We were just like them and we had always been, only that we were now kind of dating. Why should we be afraid?

I looked up at the people, my jaw clenched as I squeezed Harry's hand in reassurance. "What are you looking at? Haven't you seen two guys holding hands before, huh?" I snapped, silently hating them for doing this to Harry.

Their eyes widened, and within the next second, all of them turned away to look at something else. "Come on, let's head to the cafeteria," I muttered under my breath, pulling Harry forward with the hand that was still holding his.

We were just about to step into the cafeteria when he pulled me back, surprising me. "Louis, wait," he ordered, biting his bottom lip.

I furrowed my eyebrows together. "What?"

"I just... Are you sure about this? Coming out, I mean?" He wondered, looking at me hesitantly.

I searched his face for any sign of uncertainty, but the only expression I could find was hesitation. Didn't he want to have an open relationship, after all? "Of course I am, why?"

He scratched the back of his neck. "I just don't want you to lose your reputation and be uncomfortable with having people not liking you because of um... because of you liking me," he mumbled, not looking me in the eyes.

"Harry," I said, reaching up to cup his cheek in my hand, turning his face so he was looking at me. "I don't care about that, okay? All I care about anymore is you. So, the question is, are *you* sure about this? Do *you* want to come out?"

He thought for a while before nodding his head firmly. "Yeah, I want to show people that the most beautiful guy at school is taken," he smiled, blushing a little.

My lips twitched upwards. "Well, in that case, what are you doing Friday night?" I asked him, raising an amused eyebrow.

"Nothing?" He replied uncertainly.

I caressed his cheek with my thumb. "Will you go out with me then?"

"Y-you mean like a date?" He wondered, biting his now swollen lip.

I rolled my eyes. "Yes, Harry. A date."

It didn't take long until he nodded his head, a smile breaking out on his face. "Yeah, I'd like that."

"You would?" I beamed, leaning in to rub my nose against his.

"Mhm," he hummed, fluttering his eyes closed.

"Thank you," I smiled before closing the small gap between us, pressing my lips to his plump ones.

It was only meant to be a peck, but when Harry wrapped his arms around my neck, pulling me closer to him, I forgot about everything else. Instead, I leaned in even more, curling my arms around his waist and trailing my tongue along his bottom lip.

Harry hummed, nudging his nose with mine as he changed the angle. I started licking his upper lip when his bottom one was all wet, earning a moan from him.

My hands played with the hem of his shirt until they slowly started to move up under it, his hands finding their way to my hair and pulling at my black locks almost teasingly.

Eventually, Harry granted me access to his mouth so I could slip my tongue past his sweet lips. I eagerly yet slowly and passionately explored his mouth, licking at places I had never done before. My tongue found his and swirled around it.

One of my hands found their way back from under his shirt and moved up to cup his flushed cheek. I smiled against his lips, not being able to contain myself. This was all I had ever asked for; someone who liked me just as much as I liked them. I just hadn't been aware that this was all I wanted when I slept around with different girls every night. I didn't want a one night stand with someone I barely knew, I wanted a long-lasting relationship with someone that genuinely cared for me. And, who knew that someone would be Harry Styles, my victim when it came to bullying?

After a good three minutes, I slowly pulled away, fluttering my eyes open.

I was met by the most beautiful sight ever. Harry's gorgeous, green eyes were boring into mine while he had this wide smile playing on his lips, making his dimples pop and all.

I could feel my heart skip a beat in my chest because wow, what did I ever do to deserve this perfect boy? I seriously couldn't come up with anything close to good enough. He was just too amazing for my own good.

I leaned in to peck his lips one last time before pulling away completely. What I saw behind Harry's shoulder right then, made my body go stiff.

The same guy Harry had been with yesterday was standing behind a corner, smirking mischievously at us.

CHAPTER 26 ~ SUSPICIONS

Louis' POV

"Louis, why are you pulling me forward?" Harry whined as I dragged him into the cafeteria, heading towards the table we usually sat at.

"Let's just not talk about it, yeah?" I muttered, walking past students who were looking strangely at us.

Harry then stopped dead in his tracks, causing me to do so as well. "No, we are going to talk about this, and we're going to do it right now," he said stubbornly, folding his arms over his chest after freeing himself from my grip on him.

I let out a deep sigh, running a hand through my black hair. "Shit, fine. Let's buy some food and sit down first, okay?"

He thought for a while before nodding in agreement. "Okay."

As soon as we were sitting at the table where Liam, Niall, Zayn, Harry and I usually sat, I turned to Harry with a defeated look on my face.

Was I really going to tell him about that blonde guy? I didn't even know his name. The only thing I knew was that I was fricking jealous of him yesterday when I had seen him with Harry and that he had threatened to punch me if I ever were to hurt Harry again.

"It's about the curly-haired guy you were with yesterday," I started, looking him in the eyes.

He furrowed his eyebrows. "You mean Mike?"

I shrugged. "If that's his name, then yes. I just... your perception of him is that he's a nice guy, right?" I anticipated, sucking on my lip ring.

Harry seemed utterly confused about this but nodded his head. "Yeah, of course. He was there for me when no one else was."

I mentally hit myself for that. I should have been there, but no, I just had to screw everything up and be the reason Harry had even talked to that Mike guy in the first place instead.

"I'm still sorry about that, you know?" I muttered, looking down at my lap.

He squeezed my hand under the table, nodding his head. "I know, and it's not your fault... Well, it kind of is, but I don't blame you. Not now when I know the reason behind your actions," he reassured me. "Now, keep going. What does Mike have to do with anything?"

"Oh yeah. He's uh... he's not been as nice to me as he has to you, you could say."

Harry shot me another confused look, and that was when I decided to tell him everything I knew about the blonde, curly-haired guy I had seen for the first time yesterday.

Harry had a concentrated look on his face throughout my entire speech about Mike (which was apparently his name), most likely trying to put everything together. I doubted it was possible, though. Mike was one strange man who apparently had different personalities depending on who he was around.

Once I was done with my speech, Harry leaned down so his chin was resting against the surface of the table. I reached my hand out to run my fingers through his brown curls.

"And you're sure he treated you like that?" He muttered, turning his head slightly so he was looking at me.

"I'm pretty sure you do remember such things," I said, trying to lighten the mood by smiling a little and adding sarcasm to my voice, and it worked.

The corners of Harry's lips twitched a little, and it wasn't hard to tell he was trying to hold back a small smile of his own. It didn't take long until it dropped, though, and was replaced by a frown instead. "I just... he seemed so nice and all. I mean... He really helped me out yesterday. I can't believe he would be able to do something like hurt someone," he mumbled.

I moved my hand from his hair down to his shoulder. "I know it must be hard for you to believe that Harry, I really do. There's just something about him that screams you can't trust him. Something is not right, and I'm afraid he's planning something I have no idea what."

Harry sat up straight in his seat at this, seeming more alert now than before. "What do you mean 'he's planning something'?"

I bit the inside of my cheek, looking him in the eyes. "The only reason I pulled you in here so quickly was that he was staring at us with this sick smirk on his face. It was almost scary, and it almost made me throw up in discomfort," I shivered, remembering that mischievous smile of his.

"Wait, he was staring at us? But what's that supposed to mean? Is he happy we're finally together, or what?" Harry asked me, his voice laced with panic. He made pointless gestures with his hands, making me pull them down in order to calm him.

"Harry, you need to calm down, okay? Mike's not coming anywhere near you again, so you don't have to worry. I won't let him do anything to you," I soothed him. "And I'm pretty sure the reason behind his smile wasn't because we are finally together," I explained, grimacing.

Harry slumped in his seat, looking up at me through his wild fringe of curls that had fallen in his face. "I-I'm not worried about me, Lou. He hasn't done anything bad to me. The one I'm worried about is you. You said he threatened you, and yet here you are, feeling worried about me," he said, shaking his head. "I just don't want anything bad to happen, not now when I've finally realized I like you, and you've admitted you like me too."

I let out a sigh, trailing my fingers up towards the back of his neck. "Nothing bad is going to happen, not to you or to me. I can assure you that I'm going to stop whatever Mike's planning before he does anything, okay?"

Harry hesitated for a while before nodding his head. "Alright."

He looked so fragile then that I just wanted to embrace him in a tight hug, and that was exactly what I did. I wrapped my arms around his waist, pulling him against my chest. He leaned into the touch, curling his arms around my back.

"Thank you, Louis, for being here," he hummed against my neck.

I pulled away a little so I could kiss his forehead and look into those gorgeous green eyes. "I will always be here from now on."

This made a smile form on the curly-haired boy's lips, and he nuzzled his face into the crook of my neck once again, this time hugging me even tighter.

At that very moment, Zayn decided to join us. He sat down beside me, waiting for us to pull away from our hug before raising an eyebrow.

"So, what's going on between you two, huh?"

I raised my and Harry's entwined hands in the air, smiling proudly at him. "Um, we're kind of a thing now... right Harry?" I glanced at Harry who nodded his head, smiling slightly.

"Yep."

"Wow, since when? And why didn't you tell me, Louis?" Zayn gasped, his eyes flicking between the two of us.

I rolled my eyes, rubbing circles on the back of Harry's hand with my thumb. "Since like an hour ago, so calm your tits, mate. Jeez."

Zayn pouted his lips. "Well then, I'm happy you finally confessed your love for each other. It was about time," he snorted.

From the corner of my eye, I could see Harry quirking an eyebrow.

Zayn took this as his cue to continue. "Louis here has been in love with you for ages, but he's been too afraid to admit it, even to his best friend," he chuckled, shaking his head.

I hit him on the arm, glaring at him. "Not funny, mate. And how the hell did you know? I thought I was good at hiding my feelings," I pouted, my bottom lip sticking out.

He let out a loud bark of laughter, smacking a hand over his mouth to muffle it. "Yeah, as good as you are at cooking."

"Hey, I'm not a bad cook."

This caused Zayn to burst out into another fit of laughter. "You joking with me, right? You almost burned the house down when you cooked pasta at my place once," he managed to let out in between laughs.

I ignored him, turning to Harry so I didn't have to see that jerk. I was not a bad cook, I just had a little difficulty when it came to using the stove and oven, okay? Anyway, what did this have to do with my feelings for Harry?

"Lou, I already know you've liked me for a long time. You told me earlier, remember?" Harry smiled, leaning his head on my shoulder. "And the reason I raised my eyebrow was that I was shocked that Zayn knew about your feelings for me. I thought you kept those kinds of things to yourself... which you did, only that they were too obvious," he chuckled against my shoulder.

I gasped. "Well, at least you didn't know about them, right?"

"Right," he nodded, still chuckling slightly.

"So, how's it going with Perrie then, huh?" I asked, turning back to Zayn who had now stopped laughing.

There was a smile on his face when he replied to me. "We're good. We've been on a few dates, so I guess you can call her my girlfriend now," he explained, taking a bite of his sandwich that he was holding in his hand.

"That's amazing. I'm happy you finally settled down, mate. I guess we both just needed to find the right person to do it with, huh?"

Zayn nodded, looking over at Harry. "Yeah, I'm happy for you too, mate. You finally got your prince," he winked, making me blush.

I could feel Harry burying his face even deeper into my shoulder, and I assumed he was just as embarrassed as I was by that comment. "Yeah," I mumbled, rubbing a hand up and down Harry's back.

Before we could open our mouths to say something else, Liam and Niall walked over to us, each with a sandwich in their hands. "Hi guys," Liam muttered, sitting down next to Harry.

I furrowed my eyebrows together, wondering why he was so quiet. I turned to get a better view of them, only to notice that Niall had a large bruise on his cheek. I let out a gasp at the same time as Harry and Zayn did.

"What happened?" Harry gaped, sitting up straight in his seat.

Niall sighed, sitting down next to Liam and cuddling into his side. "I... Are you feeling better now, Harry?" He asked instead, trying to change the topic.

I wanted to roll my eyes, but it wasn't exactly the best occasion to do so. "Yes, I do, but please, Niall, just tell us what happened to your face." Harry looked at Niall with pleading eyes, making the blonde-haired boy let out a defeated sigh.

"Fine, I... I was just walking in the hallways when this curly-haired lad suddenly slammed me against the wall of lockers and punched me in the face. I tried to dodge it, but he was too quick," he choked, sniffling into Liam's arm.

"Tell them why he did it," Liam said flatly, stroking his fingers through Niall's hair.

Niall looked up from Liam's arm to see our reactions when he said; "Because I'm gay."

Well, that, I was not prepared for.

CHAPTER 27 ~ REVEALING SECRETS

Harry's POV

Later that day Niall, Liam, Zayn, Louis and I hung out at Niall's place. We talked about how we were going to find out about why Mike was treating homosexuals the way he was, but also what we would to him in revenge for what he had done to Niall. I really didn't know what to think about it all. As far as I knew, Mike was a nice lad who had helped me when I needed someone the most, but according to Louis, he was the complete opposite.

It was hard to picture Mike as the bad guy, but I did believe Louis when he told me what Mike had done to him because I knew Louis wouldn't lie to me, not after everything we had been through.

Eventually, we all came to the conclusion that we should keep our eyes on Mike before doing anything stupid. So, tomorrow, Louis, Zayn and I would sneak on him while Liam and Niall would talk to other people who he had treated badly.

When everything was settled, Louis and I figured we should probably finish the project almost everyone in our class was done with except for us. The lads didn't mind and just headed downstairs to play some video games while waiting for us to join them.

"Lou, why aren't you helping me?" I pouted, crossing my arms over my chest. I was sitting on the floor across from him.

"Because I'm too fab for school projects," he said nonchalantly, avoiding my gaze.

I furrowed my eyebrows, tossing my pencil at him.

"Ouch," he whined, rubbing at the spot on his head where the pencil hit him.

"You deserved it."

He let out a gasp. "I did not."

"Did too."

"Did not."

"Did too."

"Did not."

We continued bickering until I could feel him crawling over to me. His protests turned to whispers, and soon he was breathing the words 'did not' in my ear, making me shiver involuntarily.

"Stop it. You're just trying to make me forget what we're talking about," I pouted, looking away from him.

He let out a soft chuckle, getting even closer to me. "Maybe I am," he whispered, pressing soft kisses along my neck.

I grabbed his shoulders, pushing him off me with a scowl on my face. "Nope, you don't get to touch me before we have finished this," I said with determination, avoiding the sad look he gave me.

"That's not--" I shot him a glare, making him let out a defeated sigh. "Fine, I'll help you."

"That's what I wanted to hear," I smiled, leaning in to kiss his cheek softly.

His face turned a light pink at this, and he darted his to the hands in his lap. "Um, shall we get started then?"

I nodded, picking up the pencil from the floor.

We then began working on the project again, only this time, we did it together. It took an hour until we were finally finished. It was eight in the evening by then, so it was unfortunately time for everybody to leave. Zayn shook his head sadly as Louis and I entered the living room. "You never had time to join us."

Louis flashed him a wink, telling him we could play video games some other time instead. Tomorrow, for instance. Liam, Niall and I agreed, and we quickly made plans to go to Liam's place after school the next day.

Zayn was the first one to leave while Liam and Louis lingered in the doorway. I, on the other hand, had asked Niall if I could stay the night because I didn't want to go back to my house after what had taken place this morning.

Considering the best friend Niall was, he approved of this and happily let me spend the night. It wasn't like I didn't want to go with Louis and sleep at his place - because I really did - but I didn't think we were ready for that just yet. I wanted to take things slow, and the date this Friday was a perfect start.

"Goodnight, babe. See you tomorrow," Louis smiled, reaching up to trace his fingers along my cheek.

My face turned red at the nickname, and I could feel myself leaning into his touch. "Night, Lou," I mumbled, stepping forward to close the small distance between us.

It was only a short kiss, but nevertheless, it felt as though my entire body suddenly was on fire. The way his pink, thin lips touched mine so softly and tenderly made me feel things I had never felt before, and it was right then it dawned to me that I liked this boy more than I first thought I did.

The next day, Niall and I entered the school with nervosity seeping in our bodies. We had no idea what this plan with Mike would lead to, and to be honest, we were quite scared of the answer. What if he would catch us sneaking on him? Would he suspect anything? If so, what would he do about it?

There were so many things that could go wrong with this plan, which all of us were aware of. Though, we desperately wanted to know the reason why he bullied gay people, so that was why we were going through with the plan after all.

Niall and I separated to get to our lockers, and on my way there, I started looking for the other three people who were in on the plan. I turned my head to the left, in hopes of seeing (most preferably) Louis. What I saw instead, made my body go rigid.

A few feet away, Mike was standing, smiling sweetly in my direction. I gulped, looking behind me to see if there was someone else he was looking at. When I realized it wasn't, and that Mike was in fact smiling at me, I felt goosebumps rise on my skin.

Hesitantly, I forced a smile on my face, reaching up to wave at him. What he did next though, made my eyes widen, and I had absolutely no idea what to do. Mike started walking towards me.

As soon as my mind registered this, I started moving my legs in the direction of my locker. I picked up my pace as I glanced backward, noticing he was still following me at a distance. I rounded a few corners, taking a detour to my locker in hopes of getting rid of him.

Eventually, I was standing in front of my locker with no Mike in sight. I let out a sigh of relief and shrugged off my jacket before tossing it into my locker. I was just about to pull out of my English books when I felt a pair of arms snake around my waist from behind.

I instantly tensed up and felt a wave of panic wash over me. Did Mike find me after all?

"Morning, darling," a familiar voice whispered in my ear, making my muscles relax again.

A wide smile broke out on my face as Louis pressed a kiss to my cheek before leaning his chin on my shoulder. "Good morning," I replied, turning my head a little so he could kiss my lips softly.

Gasps suddenly filled the hallway, causing my head to snap towards the sound. A mini-crowd had gathered around us, and every single student had a surprised look on their face.

In the corner of my eye, I could see Louis facing them as well, and to say he looked happy would be a lie. "What are you staring at? Haven't seen two guys kissing before? No? Well, you have now, so get out of here," he snapped, making their eyes widen in shock.

As the crowd eventually dispersed, I could see from afar how Mr. Evans was watching us with a scowl on his face. I raised an eyebrow at him, wondering why he was even watching us in the first place. With a shake of his head, he turned on his heel and walked away, leaving me shocked, to say the least. However, I decided to put it aside for now because it was probably not important anyway.

"Lou, you shouldn't have been so harsh. They were just surprised," I muttered, turning around in his arms.

He shrugged his shoulders, furrowing his eyebrows a little. "Maybe, but they shouldn't go around staring at people like that. It's creepy, and I didn't like the feeling of being watched like that."

I cocked an eyebrow. "But you didn't have anything against it when you kissed those girls in the hallway," I pointed out, shifting on my feet.

His hands squeezed my hips as he replied, "No, but that wasn't the same thing. Now they were watching us as if they were looking at something they had never seen before, while all those other times, they were just watching out of curiosity. It's not even half as creepy."

I swallowed hard, looking down at my feet. "I'm sorry."

I felt my chin being lifted by two fingers, and before I knew it, I was looking into a pair of ocean blue eyes. "What are you sorry for? You haven't done anything wrong," Louis frowned, not releasing my chin.

"I just... I'm sorry you had to feel that way when they were watching us. If I would've been one of those girls you kissed instead, then yo--"

"No, Harry," he cut me off. "Don't you ever think that way. I'm glad you're not one of them and do you want to know why?"

I shrugged my shoulders.

He let out a sigh. "Because you are the one who makes me feel something. I really do like you, and to be honest, I've never liked anyone before. All those girls... they meant nothing. Nowhere near as much as you mean to me."

A small smile made its way to my face at those sweet words. "You mean that?"

"Of course I do. I would never lie to you, Harry," he said truthfully.

I took a step closer to him and wrapped my arms around his neck, hugging him close to me. "Thank you, Lou."

"I'm just telling the truth, love."

Right then, the bell rang through the hallway. Louis and I pulled away from each other unwillingly so we could head to our first class of the day; English. On our way there, we met up with

Liam, Niall and Zayn, and decided we should put the plan into action after the first hour.

Throughout English, I kept squirming and shifting in my seat, which Louis took notice of. He wrapped an arm around my shoulders, rubbing his hand along my arm in an attempt to soothe me. It helped, but not enough for the nervousness to disappear completely.

"He followed me earlier," I choked out as the bell rang, signaling the end of first class.

"Who?" Louis asked, getting up to gather his books.

"Mike."

His head snapped up at this, his eyes meeting mine. "Wait, what?"

I sighed, running a hand through my curls. "H-he followed me when I walked to my locker this morning. I managed to get rid of him, though, so nothing really happened," I swallowed, grabbing my books from the desk.

"What do you think he w-wanted?" Louis asked hesitantly, sucking on his lip ring.

I looked away, knowing what would happen if I watched him doing so. God, I really had a hard time controlling myself when he sucked on his lip ring like that. "I don't know. All he did was smile at me. Then he all of a sudden started walking in my direction, and I panicked," I explained, leaving out the fact that I had actually smiled back *and* waved at him.

A scowl made its way to Louis' face, and he shook his head. "I don't understand that guy. He's just full of secrets."

I nodded my head in agreement and started walking towards the door with shaky legs. Thankfully, Louis caught up with me and wrapped an arm around my waist, keeping me steady. "I think we'd better find out what's going on inside Mike's head as soon as possible. This is not good for you," he sighed, shaking his head.

I didn't say anything because I knew he was right. The nervousness was killing me, and just like Louis just said, it wasn't good for me.

As if on cue, Niall, Liam and Zayn walked over to us. We started preparing for the plan together until Niall and Liam were the first to walk away, seeing as they would only talk to Mike's victims. Zayn, Louis and I, on the other hand, began searching for Mike.

It turned out to be quite difficult. We couldn't find him anywhere. Not in the bathrooms, not in the hallways, and not in any classroom in the entire school. We had almost given up when we could suddenly hear voices in an office we knew about all too well.

We all exchanged glances before Zayn decided to walk over to the door that was ajar, making sure he couldn't be seen by the two figures in the room. Louis and I followed behind, so all three of us could hear what was being said in there.

"Plan A didn't work, dad. Louis doesn't care that the entire school knows about his and Harry's relationship," an all too familiar voice spoke, and I immediately recognized it as Mike's.

Hang on for a second. Did he just call someone 'dad'?

"So I've witnessed, son. This means we'll have to stick to Plan B," a voice I knew belonged to the principal replied.

My eyes widened at what I had just heard. Mr. Evans was Mike's *dad*? And why were they talking about me and Louis?

Louis and Zayn seemed just as shocked as I was, but we all tried to contain ourselves in order to not get noticed. Moving closer to the door, we kept listening to the conversation in the office.

"And what exactly is plan B?" Mike asked hesitantly.

Mr. Evans let out a deep sigh. "You already know Louis is not good for this school. He keeps failing classes, he acts as if he thinks he owns the entire school and now he's gay as well, and you know how much I can't stand gay people, right?"

"Yeah but--"

"So, what you're going to do now is to make Louis lose his reputation by beating him up in front of the entire school. Do you think you can do that?" Mr. Evans asked with a firm voice.

"Yes, of course, dad."

"Great, and you wanted an explanation as to why you had to talk to Harry, am I correct?" The principal continued.

I couldn't hear Mike responding, but I assumed he nodded his head due to the fact Mr. Evans replied to him. "As you know, plan A was to humiliate Louis in front of the school by outing him so he would lose his reputation. To do this, we had to make sure Louis was gay in the first place. Luckily, I managed to overhear Louis mentioning something about a kiss between him and Harry when I walked through the hallway, so I sent you after Harry as soon as he had run away, in order for you to put them together. Did that answer your question?"

Mike was quiet for a while before speaking up. "So, all I had to do was to put Louis and Harry together to be sure Louis was actually gay?"

"Exactly."

"And it worked until Louis ruined your plan by coming out with Harry," Mike murmured, seeming to finally fit the puzzle pieces together.

"Yes, he's apparently not as weak as I thought he was," Mr. Evans chuckled, causing Louis to grit his teeth together beside me. I gave him a warning look, trying to get him to understand that this was absolutely not the best occasion to do anything stupid like revealing us.

"So, you want me to beat him up just like you told me to beat the other gay people at this school?" Mike pondered.

"Yeah, I knew if plan A wouldn't work, it would be better if you already had a reputation of beating up homosexuals so no one would get suspicious if you had to beat Louis."

"O-okay, and you promise I'm not going to get in trouble for this, right?"

"Right," Mr. Evans confirmed.

Suddenly, I could hear footsteps approaching us, and I instantly panicked.

Just as I thought the door would swing open at us, Mike (I presumed) stopped in his tracks and turned back. "Dad, can you promise me something?" He mumbled, and at first, I thought Mr. Evans didn't hear him.

"That depends what it is."

"Please don't hurt Harry. I... um, I really got to know him, you know? And I... I don't think he deserves it. Getting hurt, I mean," he said uncertainly, which caused me to tense up.

Mike actually cared about me? That wasn't just part of the stupid idea his sick father had come up with?

Louis grabbed my hand where it was resting on the door to intertwine our fingers. He shot me this look that I couldn't put my finger on what it meant, but it was gone the next second, which only made me want to know what it meant in the first place.

It took a while for Mr. Evans to respond, but when he did, I never expected his answer to be what it was. "Sure. I guess I don't have to do anything to him. He's actually a great student, despite the fact he's gay."

Mike was standing so close to the door now that I could see him nod his head. To say my heart was beating out of my chest would be an understatement, it was practically exploding. "Great, so when shall I do this to Louis?" He asked his father, scratching the back of his neck.

Was he uncomfortable, or maybe even *nervous*?

"Tomorrow, as soon as possible."

With a quick nod, Mike left the office and shut the door behind him, thankfully not looking back to see the three students behind it, who had heard the entire conversation he just had with his *father*.

CHAPTER 28 ~
TWO TEASES

Louis' POV

"You did what?!" Niall and Liam gasped in unison.

We were all standing at Harry's locker, trying to look normal, but after what we had just witnessed, I doubted it was possible. We had just told Liam and Niall what we had heard, and well, they didn't seem to take it all too well.

"We overheard Mike and Mr. Evans talking about what they would do to Louis tomorrow morning. Apparently, they're father and son and have planned to make Louis lose his reputation for a long time," Zayn repeated, leaving out quite a few things.

Well, I couldn't exactly blame him. There were probably more things than our brains could comprehend that Mike and Mr. Evans had talked about only a few minutes ago.

Zayn, Harry and I tried our best to repeat everything they had said, and fortunately, Liam and Niall seemed to understand most of it. When Harry finished his side of the situation, the bell rang and we all separated to go to our second class of the day.

Since Harry and I had Civics together, we were walking down the hallway, hand in hand. We were just about to turn a corner when an all too familiar voice was heard behind us, causing both of us to freeze on our spots. "Hi, Harry," Mike said with a happy voice.

We turned around to face the curly-haired boy, me with an angry look on my face and Harry with a nervous one. "Um, hi, Mike," he replied, looking down at the floor.

I released Harry's hand only to wrap my arm around his waist protectively instead. Mike wouldn't fucking dare lay a finger on him.

The blonde-haired guy furrowed his eyebrows together at my movement, but it didn't take long until his face turned into a sad expression. "I wanted to talk to you this morning, but you just ran away. Why?"

"Because you're a fuc--"

Harry cut me off by coughing awkwardly while shooting me a glare. "I just... I was in a hurry, so I didn't have time to talk. I'm sorry," he said, scratching the back of his neck.

Mike's lips twitched upwards in a small smile. "It's okay, I, um... I just... I was wondering if you were free tonight?"

Oh no, you did not, you fucking cunt. How fucking dared he, that son of a bitch. Was he actually standing there, asking Harry if he wanted to hang out with him when he could clearly see that he wasn't available? And who did he think he was, acting as if he wasn't planning to beat the crap of me up the next morning? What the hell was wrong with him?

I took a step forward, ready to beat the shit out of him when Harry grabbed my arm, pulling me back. "I um... I don't know... Where exactly are you going with this?" He asked, biting his bottom lip.

Mike shrugged his shoulders. "I... Well, it could be a date... if you want," he smiled cautiously.

I seriously wanted to burst out laughing because he was being so ridiculous. Here he was, beating up gay people at school, and yet, he was gay himself? How ironic. And having a dad being homophobic? Well, it couldn't be easy for him, but honestly, I couldn't care less about it, or him for that matter. He was trying to steal Harry away from me, so no one could blame me. He deserved it.

"Mike I..." Harry trailed off, glancing at me.

I had my hands clenched into tight fists at my sides, not being able to keep my arm around Harry's waist due to the sudden anger that was boiling up inside me. I was glaring daggers at Mike when I spat; "What the fuck is your problem?" I backed him up against the nearest wall, gripping his collar tightly.

"I... I..." he trailed off, looking quite nervous.

"Don't you dare act all shy, you piece of shit. I know everything about what you and your dad are planning," I growled, causing all the color to drain from his face. "And next time, don't you fucking dare try flirting with my soon to be boyfriend. Because if you do, I won't hesitate to beat the shit out of you." I pushed him against the wall, before turning around to join Harry again.

To my surprise, though, he didn't look angry, but instead, he was smiling slightly at me as we continued walking to Civics class. "May I ask you why you're smiling?" I asked bitterly as we walked by student after student.

Harry shrugged his shoulders, pressing himself closer to me. "I don't know, but the fact you almost beat someone up because of them trying to ask me out is quite amusing," he said, turning to face me.

I swallowed hard, avoiding his gaze. "How so?"

"Well," he mumbled, leaning in closer to my ear. "It means you were jealous."

I bit my lip as his words hit me like a slap in the face. Jealous?

That was a feeling I had only experienced a few times before, and all of them had been because of Harry. Was I really jealous now, though? Yes, there was no doubt about it. Mike had tried to take Harry away from me. Of course I had been jealous.

"And do you want to know something?" He continued, getting even closer to my ear. I didn't even have time to nod before he added; "You look really hot when you're jealous." With that said, he pressed his lips against my neck.

I literally thought I would flip right then and there. This was just too much right now. "H-Harry, please, I..." I trailed off because I was in need to let out a moan. His tongue was poking out slightly, trailing up my neck.

He backed me up against a locker, pinning me to it so I couldn't escape even if I wanted to. He closed his lips around my skin to start sucking on it, making me go weak in the knees. My hands reached up to grip his hair, pulling him even closer to me. "Just fucking kiss me," I groaned, pulling his head away from my neck, so he could press his lips against mine.

I didn't even care if people were watching us when I slipped my tongue inside his mouth, rubbing it against his because all I wanted and cared about was Harry. The rest of the world could fuck off if they thought this was wrong because this felt so right. Everything with Harry felt right.

His hands moved up my t-shirt, roaming my bare back as I sucked his tongue. A loud moan escaped his lips, and this, *every-thing* was just so *hot*. Our lips moved feverishly against each other while our noses kept nudging together every now and then. I had never experienced a kiss like this before. It just held so many emotions; Love, passion, lust, hunger, and whatnot.

Eventually, though, both of us ran out of air and had to pull away to breathe. I kept his face close to mine, though, so our noses were still brushing against each other. "That was probably the best kiss I have ever experienced," he panted, dropping his hands from under my shirt.

I reached up to cup his cheek, caressing it with my thumb. "Mine too," I smiled. "Do you remember what I said to you just after we kissed the first time?"

Harry arched an eyebrow, thinking about it. "Hum... You told me I was a great kisser, didn't you?" He grinned, showing off his dimples.

I couldn't help but dip my index finger in his left one, feeling his soft skin against the pad of my finger. "Yeah, and I meant it. You're literally a pro," I winked.

He let out a chuckle, shaking his head. "I'm not, Lou. I've only kissed like three people in my entire life, and one of them is you." He blushed a little when he said that, and I just wanted to kiss him all over again. Why did he have to be so damn cute?

I was just about to open my mouth to disagree with him, that actually yes, he was a good kisser, but I was interrupted by the bell. "We should probably..." I started, nodding in the direction of the classroom.

"Yeah," he agreed, taking my hand in his as we started walking to class again.

Harry's POV

We all hung out at Liam's place that afternoon, just as planned. We played some video games, me racing Louis in Need For Speed because he said he wanted revenge after the last time we had played it at my place. Unluckily for him, though, he lost... again.

At eight, we decided to put on a movie; The Amazing Spider-Man 2. I rested my head on Louis' shoulder throughout the whole thing, snuggling into him as he rested his head on top of mine. It was really cozy, especially when Louis draped a blanket over both of our bodies. I fell asleep like that, with my arms around his waist and my body pressed tightly against his.

The next morning, I woke up by a sudden weight landing on my lap. My eyes snapped open and darted to what was now lying on my thighs.

My lips twitched upwards in a smile at the sight of Louis' black hair sprawled all over them, his head facing my stomach. Instinctively, I reached out to tangle my fingers in his feathery locks, tugging on them lightly.

He hummed in his sleep, pressing himself even closer to my stomach. It wasn't until he lifted the thin fabric of my t-shirt and started leaving kisses along my happy trail that I realized what he was thinking. "Lou!" I gasped, swatting at his head in an attempt to pull him away. I didn't succeed very well because only tightened his grip on my t-shirt and moved his lips up to my belly button.

To say it wasn't turning me on would be a lie, but it also tickled like hell, especially when his tongue made contact with my skin, swirling around my belly button. I once again tried to push him away from me, but just like the last time, he only tightened his hold.

"L-Louis, please... W-we're going to wake u-up everyone," I moaned, closing my eyes as his fingers trailed up my shirt. By now I was extremely hard in my pants, and I knew he was aware of that.

He let out a laugh against my skin, causing shivers to run down my spine. "Nah, as long as you're quiet, no one's gon--"

"I'm awake, so don't you dare go any further," Zayn snapped from the couch he, Liam and Niall were lying on, but you could hear the smile in his voice.

Louis pulled his head back, letting my t-shirt fall as he turned to Zayn innocently. "I haven't done anything."

He rolled his eyes, shaking his head. "Yeah, and that's why Harry's got a boner at this very second," he laughed.

I turned light pink, trying to avoid his gaze the best I could. Shit, this was extremely embarrassing. Damn Louis and his ways.

Louis turned back to me, a wide smile playing on his lips. "Don't be embarrassed, love. I know I have my ways," he winked. It was as if he could read my thoughts.

I groaned, finally pushing him off of me so I could stand up from the couch. "I'm going to the bathroom," I muttered, walking out of the living room.

"Do you want my help to get rid of it?" Louis shouted after me, chuckling slightly.

I felt my cheeks burning with embarrassment as I shook my head to myself. "Shut up, Louis!"

When I had taken care of my problem, and Liam and Niall had woken up, we all ate breakfast together. It wasn't exactly planned that all of us would sleep over, so when Karen and Geoff walked in on us all sitting at the kitchen table, they were pretty shocked.

Fortunately, though, they didn't mind too much and just scolded Liam a little for being irresponsible. Well, Liam was raised well and usually didn't do stuff that his parents didn't agree with, so he squirmed a little in his seat when Karen glared at him, but Niall was quick to reassure him.

Eventually, we drove off to school in separate cars. I went with Louis and Zayn while Niall went with Liam.

It wasn't until Louis parked the car in an empty parking lot that

I remembered that today was the day. Mike would beat Louis up in front of the entire school just to humiliate him.

I just hoped no one would get hurt, especially not Louis because I was sure I wouldn't be able to handle that.

CHAPTER 29 ~ THE FIGHT

Louis' POV

Harry and I were just leaving second class when we saw the first sign of Mike the next day. He was walking with Trisha, not even glancing our way as we passed by them in the hallway. Harry squeezed my hand anxiously, pressing himself closer to me.

"Lou," he whispered. "I'm scared."

We walked to the end of the hallway where Harry's locker was, so he could get rid of his books. I pressed my body against his, so his back was against the lockers behind him. I reached up to brush a few strands of hair from his forehead. "Don't be, babe. Nothing's going to happen to you," I assured him, smiling slightly.

He furrowed his eyebrows, shaking his head. "I'm not worried about me, idiot. I'm worried about you. I don't want you to get hurt."

I trailed my fingers down to his chin, lifting it up a little so he was looking me in the eye. "I won't get hurt. I won't let Mike succeed in this plan, and you know that."

He nodded my head slowly, letting out a sigh.

I leaned forward to press my lips against his tenderly, cupping his cheek while doing so. He let out a whine as I pulled away but kept our faces close. "Harry, I... I really, really like you, you know that, right?"

His lips twitched upwards as he nodded. "And you know I really, really do like you too, yeah?"

A smile made its way to my face as I leaned in to press my lips against his for another short kiss. "Of course," I mumbled against his lips before pulling away.

We walked to third class hand in hand, swinging them back and forth between each other. It was a nice feeling, and I dared to say I had never felt this happy in years, if ever. If someone had told me three months ago I would be together with Harry Styles in the future, I would've laughed at them, if not even punched them so hard they would have gotten a bruise.

One reason was that Harry had always been my target when it came to bullying, another was just simply that he was who he was. I had always hated how perfect his life seemed to be while mine was just a total mess. It turned out his life wasn't so perfect, though, and maybe just maybe, that made me like him a little bit more because even Harry Styles had a flaw.

We entered the classroom and sat down at a table in the back. I instantly wrapped a protective arm around his waist while he leaned his head down to rest on my shoulder. We stayed like that throughout the entire hour, listening to whatever Mr. Williams had to say.

When the bell rang, I felt a knot build up in my stomach. It was lunch break. I knew for a fact that could only mean trouble. You didn't have to be smart to figure out that was the perfect time to beat someone up.

I had to stay calm, though, for Harry. I knew he would get even more nervous if he found out I was nervous as well. It wasn't that I was afraid of getting beaten up because I knew how to fight and defend myself, but I had no idea how or when Mike would perform the plan. He could jump at me any second, for all I knew.

Grabbing Harry's hand tightly, I pulled him to the cafeteria where Zayn, Liam and Niall were already sitting at a table. Without uttering a word, I glanced at Zayn's face, looking for some kind of help.

All this was stressing me out, and I was in desperate need of my best friend. We had to come up with some kind of plan because there was no way I would let Mike beat me and get away with it.

"Louis?" Zayn asked, looking at me questioningly.

I snapped my head towards him. "Yeah?"

"Tell me what's on your mind."

I swallowed hard, leaning in so only he could hear what I was about to say. "We need a plan. Now."

Zayn immediately understood what I was talking about and nodded his head, flashing me a wink. "I've already got one, mate."

I looked at him in surprise, curiosity building up inside me. "Tell me," I urged desperately.

He shook his head, an obvious smile playing on his lips. "I can't. It won't work if you know."

I glared at him before turning away, causing him to let out a laugh. Harry tilted his head to the side when I was facing him again, giving me a confused look. I shook my head, leaning in to kiss his forehead softly.

"Ew, could you at least keep it to holding hands?" A female voice snorted behind us.

I spun around in my seat, seeing none other than Sarah Hamilton standing there with her friend by her side. Harry froze beside me, gripping my hand tightly under the table.

"Shut up," I growled, which made her roll her eyes.

"And to think I dated one of you and kissed the other," she huffed, scrunching her nose up in disgust.

I could hear Harry swallow hard beside me. "You've changed," he mumbled, and I could tell by the look on Sarah's face that she'd heard him.

"I could say the same to you." She looked at our entwined hands that weren't under the table anymore pointedly.

I rolled my eyes when something suddenly hit me. "You do remember you kissed me after you witnessed me and Harry kissing in the hallway, though, right?"

All the color drained from her face, and I knew then that she hadn't thought about that. Without a single word, she stomped off with a huff, pulling her friend with her.

I laughed, shaking my head as I turned to Harry, who had a small smile playing on his lips. He leaned in to my ear. "Although I don't like hearing that your lips have been on anyone else's than mine, I will admit that was amazing."

I felt goosebumps rise on my skin and shivers run down my spine at his words. What this boy did to me, damn.

Instead of answering him immediately, I leaned in to kiss him. His lips moved with mine slowly and gently, and for a second I forgot we were in the cafeteria and that everybody could see us. It was just me and Harry.

We were interrupted by a cough I knew belonged to Zayn. In all honesty, I wanted to punch him for being a clockblock, but I was too busy staring into a pair of piercing green eyes to care about anything else.

"My lips are all yours, babe, all yours," I assured him, making him smile widely.

"And mine are yours, Lou."

"Okay, guys. As much as I love seeing you all loved up, it's getting a bit too much, isn't it? You don't think there could be a better occasion to confess this to each other, eh?" Liam asked in amusement, glancing at a smiling Niall beside him.

I rolled my eyes but pulled away from Harry a little anyway. Zayn shook his head with a smile on his face, causing Harry's cheeks to turn pink.

Once the bell rang, we all got up from our seats to exit the cafeteria, but for some reason Zayn, Niall and Liam departed from us as soon as we were out in the hallway. Shrugging it off, I pulled Harry with me to my locker.

I was just about to let go of him for a second to open it when it happened.

I felt someone grab a hold of my upper arm, yanking me away from Harry. A yelp escaped my lips as a fist connected with my stomach. My body was instantly slammed against the wall of lockers behind me with such force that my eyes rolled to the back of my head. I desperately wanted to defend myself, but I couldn't even feel my fingers at the moment.

Somewhere, I could hear Harry crying my name, begging for the person to stop hurting me. I wanted to hold him tight against me and make sure he wouldn't get hurt, but I couldn't right now.

Collecting all my willpower, I pulled myself up into a sitting position just when the person kicked me in the chest, making me slump back again. I winced, opening my eyes to see a mop of curls - and they weren't Harry's. Sudden anger boiled up inside me as my eyes met Mike's brown ones.

It was the bastard who had tried to ask Harry out in front of me but also planned on destroying me along with his sick dad.

These two facts made it easy for me to gain power and finally get up from the floor.

Mike's brown eyes widened when he saw me standing upright, and he instantly lunged at me, swinging his fist to punch me in the cheek. Before his hand could collide with my skin, though, I grabbed it and pulled it down.

I swung my fist at him instead, aiming at his left cheek when someone suddenly let out a whimper beside me. My head snapped towards the sound, and it turned out that was the worst move I could do because the next second, Mike's fist collided with my nose, and I found myself stumbling backward and towards the floor again.

The back of my head slammed into the locker behind me as my bum hit the ground, my mouth wide agape and blood running down my nose.

Feeling exhausted all of a sudden, I knew there was nothing I could do. I so badly wanted to get up and beat the shit out of him, but after all the blows my body and head had received, it was impossible.

When I felt another kick to my stomach, I slumped against the lockers, ready to close my eyes and just wake up when this was all over with. Before I could do so though, I heard an all too familiar voice shout; "What the fuck do you think you're doing?!"

It was Zayn.

Feeling a wave of relief sweep over me, I cracked an eye open, seeing Mike being slammed against the wall beside me. I had never been so happy for having a friend like Zayn as I was right now.

"Louis!" A voice cried, and the next second I could feel myself being pulled into someone's arms. "Lou, a-are you okay?" Harry sniffled in my ear.

I hugged him tighter, resting my chin on his shoulder. "Yeah," I managed to say.

I could faintly hear how Mike was gasping for air as Zayn threw punches at him, but I really couldn't care less. He deserved every bit of it, that sick bastard.

"I thought h-he was going to make y-you unconscious," Harry hiccuped in my ear.

I stroked his curly locks with my fingers, shaking my head slightly. "Even if he did, I would've been fine. I'm not a wimp, you know?" I said, cracking a small smile and leaning back so Harry could see it.

The corner of his lips twitched upwards, making his dimples appear. I reached out to caress his cheek with the back of my hand, and my stomach did a somersault when he leaned into my touch.

"I know, Lou. I was just worried about you."

I pressed a kiss to his other cheek after wiping my mouth from the blood that had left my nose. "Even though I told you not to be?" I sighed, but the smile was still playing on my lips.

He bit his lip, looking at me innocently. "Of course. I mean, I'm your boyfriend, right? I do have the right to be worried about you."

I raised my eyebrows in amusement. "So, we're together now, huh?"

His eyes widened as he realized what he had just said, his cheeks turning a bright red. "I- I mean, we have a date on F-Friday, and I--"

I cut him off by pressing my lips to his, but not before wiping my nose that wasn't bleeding as bad as I first thought it was again. "You're so cute when you're embarrassed," I smiled against his lips. "And, I wouldn't mind being your boyfriend, Harry. I'd love to, but I don't want to rush things considering we confessed our feelings for each other only two days ago. And I've never been in a relationship before, so I don't want to fuck this up."

He pulled away a little, his cheeks still a light red. "Neither do I. I don't know why I said that," he muttered.

"It's fine, trust me," I winked, leaning in for another short kiss.

"What's happening here?!" A firm voice asked, and I snapped my head towards the sound.

I could feel all the color drain from my face when my eyes settled on Mr. Evans. He was glaring at Zayn who was holding Mike by his collar.

Students were now gathering around all five of us, curious about what was going on.

Zayn swallowed hard, letting go of a bleeding Mike, who instantly slumped to the floor. Thankfully, Zayn didn't look scared for long until his eyes turned dark with anger. "You know exactly what's happening here, sir," he snapped.

Mr. Evans looked surprised for a second, but it didn't take long until his face hardened again. "What are you talking about, Mr. Malik?"

Zayn opened his mouth to reply, but right then a classroom door was slammed open, and Mr. Williams was joining us. "What in the name of God is happening here?!" He gasped, locking eyes with me.

"I- I can explain," I tried, but he just shook his head, turning to Harry.

"Explain."

Harry glanced at me before taking a deep breath. "Louis and I were standing here at his locker when Mike came over and started throwing punches at him."

I could hear a snort coming from my left. "Nonsense. Do you really think my son would do such a horrible thing?"

The mini-crowd that was watching our every move let out a round of gasps, noticing Mr. Evans' mistake. From the looks of it, Mr. Williams seemed to do so as well. "Excuse me. Did you just call that boy your son?" He asked, gesturing towards Mike, who was now clutching his bleeding nose.

Mr. Evans gulped, avoiding Mr. Williams burning gaze. If I hadn't known better, I would've thought Mr. Williams was the principal and not Mr. Evans. "Yes."

Mr. Williams pressed his lips in a thin line, turning back to Harry. "Continue, please."

Harry nodded. "Mike punched Louis so hard I thought he would get unconscious, but Zayn showed up before it was too late. He only punched Mike to make him stop beating Louis."

Mr. Williams quirked an eyebrow, turning to Mike. "Why on earth did you beat Mr. Tomlinson in the first place? I know he's not the most innocent guy, but what was your reason?"

Mike opened his mouth to answer, but Liam and Niall suddenly came running towards us, beating him to it. "We fixed it, we fixed it!" Liam yelled, slipping past the people in the crowd with a following Niall behind him. His eyes widened at the scene in front of him, flicking between me and Mike on the floor. "Shit," was the only thing he said.

Niall stopped beside him, slipping his hand in Liam's as his eyes found me and Harry.

"Excuse me. Are you two involved in this?" Mr. Williams asked, turning to the two boys.

"Well, that depends on what you mean by 'this'," Liam said,

shifting on his feet.

"I mean what was taking place here only a few minutes ago, obviously."

"No, we were not involved in that, but one thing we are involved in is the story behind it, right Niall?" He glanced at the blonde boy who was gripping something in the hand that wasn't holding Liam's.

"Yes."

"What do you mean?" Mr. Evans asked, speaking for the first time in what felt like hours.

"This," Niall said, pressing on the thing in his hand that I assumed was some kind of remote.

Suddenly, the speakers in the hallway started blaring; *"Plan A didn't work, dad. Louis doesn't care that the entire school knows about his and Harry's relationship."*

My mouth fell open as I realized this was from yesterday when we had eavesdropped on Mr. Evans and Mike's conversation. Turning my head to Zayn, who was now leaning against the wall with a smug look on his face, I knew very well that this had been his plan all along. He had actually recorded the whole thing?

"You already know Louis is not good for this school. He keeps failing classes, he acts as if he thinks he owns the entire school and now he's gay as well, and you know how much I can't stand gay people, right?"

The recording continued to blare through the speakers, and none of us in the hallway dared to move a single limb.

"So, what you're going to do now is to make Louis lose his reputation by beating him up in front of the entire school. Do you think you can do that?"

"Yes, of course, dad."

When the recording eventually ended, everyone, and then I meant *everyone* was staring at either Mike or Mr. Evans. The principal's face was beet red while Mike was staring at the floor, biting his bottom lip anxiously.

Luckily, Mr. Williams decided to break the awkward silence that had occurred after the recording only seconds later. "Mr. Evans, I'd like to have a private talk with you, and believe me, I don't think I'm the only teacher at this school who wants that after this," he said sternly.

The principal nodded his head curtly, adjusting his tie uncomfortably. Before the two men left, Mr. Williams turned to give us a smile. "I think you guys solved this situation in the best way possible. Well done."

A few minutes later, the crowd dispersed, and the only people who were still in the hallway were Mike, Liam, Niall, Zayn, Harry and I. To everyone's surprise, Mike was the first person to speak up; "Guys, I'm really sorry for what I did. I would honestly never have done any of it if it weren't for my dad," he apologized, still nibbling on his bottom lip.

I seriously wanted to walk over and slap him across the face because that apology was the most pathetic one I had ever heard. Stupid bitch.

Thankfully, Harry seemed to think just like me because his face was in a scowl while he was gritting his teeth. Liam and Niall seemed just as upset as we were since Niall had been one of Mike's targets, so the only person who didn't want to beat the shit out of Mike right now was Zayn, oddly enough.

Mike seemed to understand the vibes we gave off and pulled himself up from the floor. "I guess this is my cue to leave," he mumbled, heading towards God knows where.

Before he disappeared completely, though, he turned around to face Harry. "Before I leave, I just want you to know that I really do like you, Harry, and I have done so ever since I first laid my eyes on you. I'm not stupid, though. I do know you love Louis, and I'm not going to do anything to about that. You two deserve each other, and I'm glad I was one of the reasons you got together in the first place," he said, and with that, he spun on his heel and walked away, leaving all of us dumbfounded.

Well, what could I say? It wasn't every day you heard the person you hated the most saying something that actually wasn't so bad.

CHAPTER 30 ~ THE DATE

Harry's POV

Everything went pretty well after that. I brought Louis to the school nurse so she could clean his cuts and put bandages over them. Louis wasn't very willing to have someone taking care of him, though. He crossed his arms over his chest and desperately tried to decline all help he was offered. However, I tried my best to talk some sense into him, and eventually, he gave in and let the nurse take care of him.

I almost let out a sigh of relief. Louis could be really stubborn when there was something he absolutely didn't want to do, and it could take ages for a person to convince him before he gave in. I was just lucky this time, and I knew it.

After that day, Mike didn't so much as look at me when we walked by each other in the hallway. I usually walked with Louis, so I guess that was one of the reasons, but I had a feeling it was something else as well. It was like he didn't want to bother me anymore and just acted as if I wasn't there because of that.

To be honest, I didn't know how to feel about it. Mike and I had gotten quite close during those two days we had spent together, but I wasn't dumb. He had tried to ask me out when he knew there was something going on between me and Louis. He had also beaten Louis up right in front of me. So, I couldn't say I was exactly devastated that he didn't spare a glance at me anymore.

What he had done to Louis was unforgivable, and I would probably never forgive him for that.

Today, it was finally Friday, the day Louis and I had planned to have our date. I couldn't be happier, or more nervous either for that matter. I had no idea what Louis had planned for us. All I knew was that he was picking me up at six in the afternoon. And when I said 'picking me up' I meant at Niall's.

His place was practically my home now that I didn't speak to my mum anymore. I still hadn't talked to her since the start of the week when she had slapped me. She hadn't tried to get in touch with me since then, and I surely hadn't tried to get in touch with her either, so I guess that left us to where we were today. And actually, I didn't mind it all too much. After everything that had happened, I didn't even want to be near her, that judgemental idiot.

It was currently four in the afternoon, and Niall and I had just gotten home from school. Maura had made us a light meal that we gratefully ate... Or, I did while Niall literally shoved the food down his throat carelessly.

I rolled my eyes at that, trying not to laugh. That man and his food, I swear.

However, when our plates were empty, we headed upstairs to his room to just chill for the remaining two hours until my date.

Date, that word made the corner of my lips twitch. I had a date with Louis Tomlinson, the guy once known as my personal bully, the guy I never thought I would even be able to stand up to, and also the guy I had least expected to go out with if I ever were to date one. And guess what? I loved it. I loved it so much that I couldn't even believe I was going on a date with him.

"So, what are you going to wear?" Niall asked where he was lying on his bed, fingers intertwined on his chest.

I was sitting on the edge of the bed, looking down at him. "I have no idea," I sighed.

Yesterday, Niall and I had gone over to my place before my shift at the bakery to grab some of my clothes. Since I knew mum or Robin wouldn't be home, I didn't have to worry about them being there, thankfully.

Though, I still had a problem. None of my clothes were casual clothing. The only things I owned were black skinny jeans and different types of black and white t-shirts. I couldn't go on a date with Louis in something as casual as that.

For some reason, though, Niall had a smile playing on his lips. "I figured this problem would occur, so when you were working yesterday, I went to the mall to buy you this." He suddenly got off the bed to walk over to his closet, opening the doors.

Before I could even find the ability to talk, he had tossed me a white button-up with the price tag still on. "Now go ahead and thank me for being an awesome best friend," he smiled smugly, crossing his arms over his chest while leaning against one of the closet doors.

I shook my head in disbelief, looking down at the garment in my lap. When it finally dawned on me, a wide smile broke out on my face, and I got up to embrace him in a big bear hug. "Thank you, thank you, thank you," I repeated in his ear. "I don't know what I would've done without you."

He chuckled against my neck, his arms wrapped tightly around my back. "Life would've been so boring without me, now wouldn't it?"

I rolled my eyes, letting out a small laugh. "Yes, that's so true."

We departed after a few seconds, and I pulled off my black shirt to put on my new white button-up. "Stop eye-raping me, Horan," I accused him, smiling cheekily at the boy who was staring at me from his bed.

"Pfft, I'm not, Styles. Don't you dare accuse me of such a thing," he said with feigned anger.

"Fine, fine, but don't you dare deny the fact my body is pretty damn sexy," I winked, making him roll his eyes.

I loved it when Niall and I played around like this. It was something we had always done, and I couldn't help but hope it would stay that way between us forever.

Half an hour later, I was shifting my feet nervously as I was standing in the doorway of Niall's room. I had swept my hair backward and changed my black, skinny jeans to another pair. I was almost ready for this date... almost. The only thing that wasn't was my nerves. I wouldn't calm down no matter how many times I tried to force myself to do so.

"Harry mate, are you okay?" Niall asked, eyebrows arched.

I sucked in a deep breath, running a hand through my curls. "I actually don't know. The nervousness is killing me."

Niall strode over to pull me into a hug, bringing me close to him. "You shouldn't be nervous. It's just Louis, right? It's not like he's going to try to kill you or something," Niall chuckled in an attempt to calm me down, I assumed.

I sighed against his neck, nodding my head. "You're right, Ni. I just... I don't know where he is going take me, and I don't know how to--"

The sound of the doorbell going off interrupted me mid-sentence. My body instantly tensed up, and I tried not to collapse on my spot. However, since Niall still had his arms around me, he kept me upright.

"The boyfriend's here," Niall smiled at me.

"He's not my boyfriend," I muttered, pulling out of the hug.

"Well, maybe he is at the end of the night," he winked cheekily, causing me to roll my eyes.

"Whatever you say, Horan."

We walked downstairs together, my legs shaking so much that I stumbled on one of the steps. Thankfully, Niall was there to save me this time as well.

"Shit, man. Are you sure you don't need crutches to hold you up or something?" He chuckled, making me glare at him.

"I'm fine, thank you very much."

He shrugged with a smile on his face as we continued walking to the front door. I reached out a shaky hand to turn the handle, opening the door to reveal a very good looking Louis.

He was wearing a plain, black t-shirt topped off with a black blazer and a pair of black skinny - very skinny - jeans. The eyeliner around his eyes was applied more perfectly than ever, framing his ocean blue eyes that I loved so much.

"Hi," I said, stumbling forward because of my shaking legs.

He grabbed my arm, preventing me from falling to the floor. "Oops," he laughed, making me smile toothily.

I could see Niall roll his eyes from the corner of my eye, and it made me want to punch him, but I contained myself.

"I'll leave you two to this. Have a great night... Oh, and Louis. Make sure Harry's back at least before eleven, okay?" Niall said in a mother's tone.

Louis let out a chuckle, nodding his head. "Yes, ma'am." He reached out a hand for me to take, which I instantly did, letting his warmth fill my body.

Niall left us without another word, heading towards the living room where I could hear noises coming from the TV.

"So, shall we go?" Louis smiled, tugging lightly at my hand.

I nodded, cheeks blushing a light red at the thought of going out with Louis.

Seconds later, I had slipped on my white converse and we were walking towards his car. "So, where are we going?" I asked once we had entered the vehicle.

He turned to me, a quite nervous smile playing on his lips. "Um, I thought since you haven't met my mother... that we could eat dinner at mine?"

I nodded my head slowly. "Sure. I mean, if your mom wouldn't mind," I said, thinking about my own mother who was against gay people.

He shook his head. "She wouldn't, believe me. Actually, she's started to accept my appearance now that she has let the fact that this is the way I dress now sink in," he shrugged.

"So she's okay with..." I trailed off, nibbling my bottom lip.

"Us two dating? Yes, she's happy that I've finally settled down. Even if she wasn't aware that I um... was with different people all the time, she didn't like it when she found out, so she accepted my relationship with you right away."

"That's great," I smiled warmly because I really meant it. I was happy Louis' family was all good now. He really deserved it after all those years he had to take care of his sisters.

He nodded in agreement "And later, I thought--"

"Later?" I cut him off, furrowing my eyebrows in confusion.

"Yeah? Wait, you didn't think we would spend our entire date with my mom, now did you?" He looked pretty shocked, his eyes widened.

"No..." I scratched the back of my neck awkwardly. "Well, yeah?"

I blushed, not daring to meet his eyes.

An amused smile broke out on his face, and he let out a slight chuckle. "Well, since this is our night, I thought we could go to the movies after we've eaten dinner if that's okay with you?"

I nodded my head enthusiastically. "Yeah, that'd be great."

"Great," he said, turning on the engine before driving off towards his home.

Five minutes later, Louis parked the car in the parking lot outside his apartment, pulling the key out of the ignition. "Are you ready to meet my mom?" He winked, reaching over to squeeze my hand lightly.

My eyebrows knitted together as I felt a wave of panic wash over me. "Wait. Should I be scared?"

Louis rolled his eyes, shaking his head. "Of course not, love. Nothing bad will happen, I promise."

"If it turns out it will, I'm never going to trust you again," I muttered, unbuckling my seat belt and exiting the car.

To my surprise, I was met with a pair of ocean blue eyes only inches away from my green ones when I had closed the door behind me, and it instantly took my breath away. "Lou, wha--"

I was cut off by his finger that was suddenly pressed to my lips. Louis' other hand reached up to cup the side of my neck, bringing me even closer to him. "You're really beautiful tonight, you know that?" He whispered, making my cheeks turn a dark red.

My eyes darted to our shoes, but the only thing I could see was our chests that were pressed together. I didn't know how to answer him because I had never thought of myself as beautiful, so I decided to keep quiet instead.

The finger on my lips was suddenly removed and replaced by a soft pair of lips, kissing my own lightly. "So beautiful," he mumbled, pressing me flush against his body with the hand that was now gripping my hip.

I reciprocated the kiss, tilting my head to the side while wrapping my arms around his neck. He took a step forward, causing my back to hit the hard surface of his car, but I really couldn't care less about the pain that entered my body for only a few seconds.

His tongue traced my bottom lip, licking every inch of it. It made me let out a moan, and I gripped the hairs at the back of his neck tightly. Before his tongue could slip into my mouth, my own darted out to meet his, swirling around it. A loud moan escaped Louis' throat then, and he pressed me even harder against his car, so there was no space between the two of us whatsoever.

My tongue found his lip ring, and I sucked it into my mouth, licking and tugging on it with my teeth and tongue.

"H-Harry, shit," Louis breathed, trailing his hand up my white button-up until it was resting against my stomach, making goosebumps rise on my skin.

He trailed kisses to my jawline down my neck, poking his tongue out to lick a stripe along one of my veins. My legs almost gave out at the pleasure that filled my body by his touch. "L-Louis, I don't think I can--"

I gasped as his teeth sunk into my skin, not being able to hold back the moan that escaped my lips. Shit, this felt so *good*.

I squeezed my eyes as shut in pleasure as he pushed his hips forward, grinding against me. To say I was aroused would be an understatement. I could feel blood rushing to my lower area by the second.

He grazed his teeth up to my jaw, his tongue leaving a wet stripe of saliva behind. I was just about to let out a whine at the loss of his mouth on my neck when his lips found mine again, pressing several soft kisses to my mouth.

"Always so beautiful," he mumbled with a final kiss, leaning back to look into my eyes that had fluttered open when his lips had disconnected with my own.

I smiled, shaking my head but not enough for him to notice. "No, you are."

He rolled his eyes, taking my hand in his. "Don't you disagree with me, Styles. Only God knows what will happen if you do. Now, we should probably go inside. Mom's waiting on us."

I nodded my head, letting myself be led towards the door of the apartment. We climbed the stairs in silence, and I found myself feeling a little nervous again. What if his mother would hate me? What if she thought I wasn't good enough for Louis?

Letting out a breath, I climbed the last few steps and followed Louis to a wooden door. With a jerk of the handle, Louis opened it to reveal a small entryway. We stepped inside, his hand still holding mine in a tight grip.

"Mom?" He called, and only seconds later, a pretty short woman walked out of what I assumed was the kitchen. You could immediately tell that this was Louis' mom by the looks of her. Man, he had been gifted with so many features from his mother.

"Ah, you're here!" She walked forward and was just about to extend a hand to me when loud squeals were heard from the hallway, and only seconds later two twin girls were hugging Louis' legs.

"Hi, Lou Lou," They giggled, looking up at him. He ruffled their hair with the hand that wasn't holding mine and chuckled slightly.

"Hi girls, how are you?"

"Great! We were just playing with our barbie dolls, right

240

Phoebe?" One of the sisters said, nudging what I assumed was Phoebe in the side.

"Right," she agreed. "Who's this?" Phoebe nodded towards me before her eyes darted back to Louis.

He pulled me forward a little, smiling widely. "Daisy, Phoebe, this is Harry. Harry, this is two of my sisters, Daisy and Phoebe." He turned towards his mom, who was looking at me with a small smile on her face. "Mom, this is Harry. Harry, this is my mom, Johannah."

She successfully extended her hand this time and I took it in my own, shaking it. "Lovely to meet you."

She withdrew her hand. "It's an honor to meet you, Harry. I'm so glad you're here."

The corner of my lips curled up in a smile at her words and I could instantly feel myself relaxing because I was welcomed in the household, after all.

"Dinner's ready in a few minutes. So, Louis, why don't you show Harry around first?" Johannah suggested.

Louis nodded his head, squeezing my hand. "Sure."

Johannah left us, heading towards the kitchen, I assumed. I was just about to face Louis when I could feel someone tug on my jeans. Looking down, I saw one of the twins looking up at me with a hopeful look on her face. Before I knew it, she was holding her arms out, clearly gesturing for me to pick her up.

I glanced at Louis, looking for some kind of sign that would tell me what to do. When he nodded his head, I didn't hesitate to bend down to the girl, wrap my arms around her body, and pick her up so she was resting on my hip.

To do this, I had to let go of Louis' hand, so as soon as he had picked the other twin up, I grabbed it again. Together, we walked into the flat, Louis showing me every room of it. The place was not big, but that didn't mean it wasn't cozy. You could really feel the love surrounding the place, something you absolutely couldn't at my house.

Eventually, we were standing outside Louis' room. He opened the door slowly and we stepped inside. "So, this is my room," Louis shrugged.

The walls were painted black and didn't have so much as a poster on any of them. His small bed was in one of the corners, the covers lying in a mess on top of it. There was a closet beside the door that I could tell didn't need to be there, seeing as probably all of his clothes were scattered all over the floor. The room was literally a mess, but for some reason, I liked it.

"Lou Lou! Mum told you to clean up in here before going over to pick up Harry," the girl in my arms - that I now knew was Phoebe - scolded.

Daisy nodded in agreement, looking at Louis with a frown. "Bad Lou Lou."

Louis rolled his eyes, going over to sit on the bed, patting the spot beside him while looking at me expectantly. "Come join us, love."

I walked over to him hesitantly, watching my feet so I wouldn't stomp on any of his garments as I did so. "Gosh Lou, you've really got a mess in here," I said, shaking my head in amusement.

"I'm sorry I'm not as much of a perfectionist as you are," he winked.

I sat down beside him, looking at the CD player that was on a small table by the window beside his closet. Next to it, a few CD cases were scattered and I could see that all of them were rock music.

I wasn't surprised he listened to that music genre considering his appearance and all. It was pretty predictable, and I loved it because it was just Louis.

"I'm not a perfectionist," I mumbled, looking back at him.

"You are, though."

I dropped the topic by a shake of my head, hugging Phoebe closer to me.

"What are you to Louis?" She asked out of nowhere with a small smile on her face after a few seconds of silence.

I raised my eyebrows, surprised by the question, and looked over at Louis. He nodded his head encouragingly, adjusting Daisy on his lap.

I swallowed hard. "Uh, Louis and I are almost like boyfriends." I scratched the back of my neck because it sounded so stupid, but I didn't know how else to describe our relationship so she would understand.

Louis let out a chuckle, muffling it with the back of his hand as Phoebe raised an eyebrow at me. "Almost?"

I nodded sheepishly, not knowing what to say.

"You mean you're not together, but are getting there?"

"Yeah, you could say that," I smiled, ruffling her hair, which made her let out a high-pitched squeal.

"Stop it," she giggled, wriggling around in my lap.

I laughed at her, missing the fond look Louis gave me as I did so.

All four of us talked for about five more minutes until Johannah called from the kitchen, informing us that dinner was ready. We joined her in the kitchen and were just about to dig into the food when the front door was suddenly slammed shut.

Seconds later, two teenage girls entered the room, and it didn't take long for me to figure out they were Louis' two other sisters.

We all seven ate dinner together, talking about everything and nothing. It was so nice that I even considered asking Louis if we could stay here the entire evening, but I knew Louis had other plans.

About eight o'clock, Louis and I got up from the table so we could leave for the movies. I helped Johannah wash the dishes while Louis went to the bathroom and the girls to their rooms, which left me alone with their mother.

"I'm so happy my son found you. You're a lovely young man, and I couldn't wish for a better person for Louis," she smiled, picking up a plate from the sink to rinse it.

As she handed it to me, I put it into the dishwasher. "Thank you," I blushed, trying to hide my red cheeks by looking down at the floor. Since she was busy rinsing the plates, glasses and utensils, she luckily didn't notice it.

"You're welcome."

And it was then, when she curled her lips into that tight smile that I remembered what she had been through. She had lost her husband three years ago and had been in some kind of daze up until last week.

That really explained why she had stayed quiet when Lottie had started talking about past boyfriends and when Felicity had talked about what grades she had received a year ago. It all made sense because she hadn't been there to experience it with them.

I was about to open my mouth and comment about it when I felt a pair of muscular arms wrap around my waist from behind. "You coming, darling?" Louis mumbled, kissing my cheek.

I turned around in his arms, wrapping my arms around his neck to give him a tight hug while nodding against his shoulder. "Mhm."

He pulled out of the embrace and grabbed my hand, pulling me towards the entryway. Johannah followed us with a fond smile on her face, crossing her arms over her chest while leaning against the doorway of the kitchen. "Have fun, you two, but not too much fun if you know what I mean," she winked, making my cheeks turn an even darker shade of red than before.

Louis groaned loudly, shaking his head in disbelief. "Mom, please."

She shrugged her shoulders. "I'm just saying that you should be careful with that stuff. I mean, you don't know if--"

"Okay, mom, I think we've got it. Thank you very much for your little speech," he interrupted, tightening the hold on my hand. "It's not like we've done anything like that anyway."

She rolled her eyes. "Don't act so innocent, my son. I saw you two when you arrived here and it was pretty obvious that both of you had been up to something, aren't I correct?" She looked at us knowingly, her lips curling up in an amused smile.

I gulped, glancing at a shocked Louis beside me. "Uh... huh." Louis scratched the back of his neck awkwardly, avoiding her gaze.

"It's okay, Louis. You're both young and I am not going to stop you from doing... what you guys want to do."

He nodded slowly, looking up at her. "Uh, sure. Harry, we'd better get going now, don't you think? We don't want to be late for the movie, after all," Louis rushed out, tugging at my hand a little.

I nodded in agreement, smiling at Johannah. "It was so nice to finally meet you, Johannah, and thank you so much for dinner," I said politely.

She waved a hand in dismissal. "You'll always be welcome here, Harry. You're family now. And it was so lovely to meet you too."

We said our last goodbyes to each other, but before we could leave, all four of Louis' sisters came out to hug me before we left. A wonderful feeling filled my body then, and all I wanted was to stay there. They were everything I had always wanted in a family, even though they had a flaw in their past that had caused their relationship to falter a little. They were at least happy now, and that was all that mattered.

The first thing Louis did when we entered his car was to lean over and press his lips against mine. Our lips moved together as our tongues fought for dominance. It was all pretty steamy so when we eventually departed, heavy pants escaped our lips. "I've been wanting to do that ever since we stepped into that apartment," he muttered, although a smile made it's way to his face.

I chuckled at him, closing my eyes to savor this fantastic feeling of being so happy with Louis. Everything right now was perfect and if I were to decide, I would freeze time to be in this moment forever. Louis was here with me, and really, that was all I wanted from now on, for him to always be here.

It was right then I realized it, something I should probably have realized ages ago.

I was in love with him.

I, Harry Styles, loved the punk boy named Louis Tomlinson who had bullied me for years and made me want to stay home from school sometimes. That boy was currently staring into my eyes with this intense look on his face, and all I wanted was to melt into his body so I could be with him forever.

It was like he could sense what I was thinking because the next second, his lips were on mine again. He pressed light and soft kisses to them repeatedly before pulling away to look me in the eyes. "I love you, Harry Styles," he whispered.

"And I love you, Louis Tomlinson.

EPILOGUE

Louis' POV

~ One Month Later ~

It was now June, and the summer had finally started to roll around. About a week ago, Mr. Evans had been fired from his job and Mike had been transferred to his former school. It was back to normal you could say, and I couldn't be happier.

The sun was currently shining in the blue sky as I walked on the sidewalk with Harry by my side. Our entwined hands were swinging between us while his head was resting on my shoulder. We were on our way to my place since my family had gone shopping in London today and would stay there the entire weekend.

The reason we were walking along the streets was that we had been over at Niall's place, and since he drove us to school this morning, none of us had a car. And the reason Niall hadn't driven us home was that he was a lazy arse and had Liam over. But, it wasn't as if Harry and I minded. It was nice walking with someone you loved and could talk to for ages.

A smile made its way to my face as I thought back to our first date one month ago when we had confessed our love for each other, but also when I had asked him to be my boyfriend. It had been a great night, and it got even better when we arrived at the movies and watched 'You're Next' together. Yes, it was a horror movie, and yes, Harry had gotten a little scared, but that also meant he had crawled onto my lap and hugged me tightly, which was very nice if I do say so.

When the movie ended, I had driven to Niall's house to drop him off. On our way there, I had noticed that Harry was being quiet, though. When I asked him about it, he only shrugged, making me feel more worried than I already was. Was it something I had done wrong? Or didn't he like the date?

I had gotten my questions answered once I pulled over outside Niall's house. Apparently, he didn't want to go 'home' but wanted to stay over at mine, only that he was too afraid to ask in case it would be too much for our first date.

I had wanted to laugh at him for being so ridiculous, but of course I didn't. I didn't want him to feel more embarrassed than he already did, so I had just told him that nothing could ever be too much when it came to something that had to do with me. I loved him so much.

He had flashed me a bright smile and leaned over to kiss me on the lips cutely.

After that, we had got out of the car to tell Niall the news, and oddly enough, he had actually approved.

Nowadays, Harry usually stayed over at mine. It was becoming more and more common for each week that went by, and I knew it wouldn't be long until he moved in with us permanently. I really couldn't wait for that to happen because I always wanted to be as close to him as possible.

During the month we had now been together, we had never been alone, meaning that we hadn't done anything besides sharing kisses every now and then, and I was very quickly becoming needy of more. It wasn't exactly hard to tell that Harry felt the same way.

At school, we occasionally locked ourselves up in one of the stalls in the bathroom to either suck each other off or exchange handjobs to get rid of our sexual frustrations. We had never gone all the way, though, because neither of us wanted our first time to be in the toilets.

Today - unlike all the other days - we had the flat to ourselves, and I was pretty certain both of us wanted to take advantage of that opportunity.

"So, what do you wanna do when we get home?" I asked tentatively, sneaking a glance at him.

A cheeky smile made its way to his face, and I knew right then that yes, we were definitely thinking the same thing. But, when the smile suddenly disappeared just as fast as it had shown in the first place, I wasn't so sure anymore. Had my mind only been playing a trick on me or had the smile actually been there?

"I was thinking we could watch a movie now that we're alone and all," he beamed.

I nodded in agreement. Movie. That meant cuddling, and cuddling meant being close to Harry. "That sounds like a great idea."

We walked the rest of the way to my place, taking the elevator as soon as we stepped into the building. To my surprise, a pair of lips connected with my own just as the doors closed, and before I knew it, I was being pinned to the wall by an all too familiar body.

I moved my lips against Harry's, humming at the wonderful feeling of his fingers roaming the exposed skin on my neck. My arms went around his waist, flipping us around so I was the one pressing him against the wall. "You can try, but I will always be the one in charge," I winked with a glint in my eye.

He rolled his eyes, leaning in to capture my lips with his again. He slipped his tongue out to trail along my bottom lip, making sure not to miss a single inch of it. Feeling very impatient, I flicked my own tongue out to meet his.

The elevator dinged, signaling us that we were on the right floor. We pulled away from each other reluctantly, and I let out an annoyed groan while Harry just leaned in to peck my lips quickly.

"We'll have plenty of time to do that later," he winked, walking out of the elevator, leaving me gaping after him.

I eventually composed myself and hurried after him towards the front door of my apartment. Fishing the key up from my jean pocket, Harry drummed his fingers against the surface of the wooden door impatiently. I unlocked it, stepping into the flat that I had lived in since I was fifteen. Harry followed suit, slipping his shoes off and shaking his curls out of his face.

I went into the living room and flopped down on the couch. "Since you were the one who insisted, I think it'd be most fair if you turn on the movie," I smiled as he entered the room, shifting until I was comfortable.

Harry didn't protest, but actually obeyed my orders... on one condition; He got to choose which movie we would watch, and I guess that was fair enough.

A few minutes later, Harry plopped down beside me, snuggling into my side as I wrapped my arms around his waist. He pressed his face into my neck, rubbing his nose against my skin softly before turning to the TV. I sighed in content, tracing small patterns on the skin of Harry's bare hip with my fingers. He turned his face to give me a quick kiss on the lips, causing a smile to break out on my face. I loved this guy way too much for my own good, but hey, I was definitely not complaining.

The movie Harry had decided to put on was a cliché one about a geeky girl who fell in love with the most popular guy at school. Apparently, Harry was into those kinds of movies, which I wasn't, but since we had agreed that he got to choose today, I couldn't exactly tell him that I would rather watch something else.

Two-thirds into the movie, the two teenagers shared their first kiss. It didn't last very long, but it was enough for me to get the urge to press my lips against Harry's too, and who was I not to fulfill my urges when I could?

I reached up to place a hand on Harry's cheek, tilting his head a little so he was turned to me and very slowly leaned in to seal our lips together. It was just meant to be a short kiss, but when Harry's soft lips started moving more eagerly against mine, I grabbed his face with both of my hands and pulled him down so I was lying on top of him.

His hands trailed up the back of my black t-shirt, roaming my bare skin carefully. I let out a loud moan as he sucked my lip ring into his mouth, tugging on it lightly with his teeth.

Grinding down on him, I slipped my tongue through his parted lips, licking the roof of his mouth before meeting his own wet tongue. Harry's nails clawed down my back, probably creating red marks, judging by the slight pain that was suddenly going up my spine.

I pulled back a little, looking into his sparkling green eyes that now were now dark with lust. His usually pink, plump lips were a dark shade of red and slightly swollen. He looked so gorgeous that I just wanted to ravish him right there and then, but I restrained myself because really, I couldn't do that.

Smiling slightly, I leaned down to connect our lips again, wanting to feel them move against mine forever. The feeling I got when we kissed was incredible. There was nothing that could even begin to compete with it because I was sure the fact I felt fireworks, butterflies and somersaults whenever our lips moved together would beat any other contestant by far.

"Forget the stupid movie and bring me to your bedroom," Harry growled against my lips, causing goosebumps to rise on my skin.

"Yes, sir," I chuckled, hoisting myself off of him so I could pick him up bridal style.

He wrapped his arms around my neck, leaning up to my ear, taking the lobe between his lips and sucking on my earring. My legs almost turned to jelly by the sensation that went through my body, but I luckily kept myself upright with both of my feet still on the floor.

I bent down a little to pick up the remote from the coffee table and switched off the television.

Harry hummed against my ear, and I knew if I didn't make my way to the bedroom now, I would end up in a pile on the floor with a curly-haired boy on top of me.

Following my thoughts, I carried him out of the room and into my bedroom that was on the other side of the flat. As soon as I had closed the door behind us, I walked over to my bed and laid him down on the soft mattress. His arms that were still around my neck, pulled me down so I was hovering over him again. Our lips met in a hot and passionate kiss, tongues and teeth clashing together.

I was just about to pull his shirt up when he leaned back a little, fluttering his eyes open just when I did. "I really do love your lip ring," he said with a husky voice. "But it is quite hard to kiss you properly when it's in the way."

I couldn't help but let out a loud chuckle. "You're definitely something else, Harry." I rolled my eyes but obeyed him and took it out, placing it on my nightstand before going back to kissing my boyfriend.

"Hmm, much easier," he mumbled against my lips, and I wanted to roll my eyes again, but since my eyes were now closed, that was unfortunately impossible.

Instead, I moved my lips down to his neck, my tongue sliding over his skin, leaving a stripe of saliva behind. I started sucking on a certain spot on his neck, slowly creating a purplish love bite. My tongue swirled around the now sensitive skin, earning a filthy moan from Harry.

His hands went to the hem of my t-shirt, tugging on it before pulling it over my head and tossing it somewhere on the floor.

"Someone's eager, hmm?" I smirked, reaching up to flick his nose with my finger just because I could.

He scrunched it up cutely, rubbing it with one of his hands. "I was going to say yes, but after what you just did, that would be a lie," he grumbled. "Plus, you're a mood killer."

I ground down on him, brushing our hard-ons together. Judging by the way his eyes squeezed shut, I wasn't so sure I was a mood killer, after all. "Mood killer, huh?" I chuckled, earning a swat to the back of my head.

"Just get me out of these stupid clothes already," he groaned in frustration.

I lifted an amused eyebrow at him but obeyed anyway, and reached down to pop the button of his jeans open. Unzipping them, I examined his face closely, wanting to see his reaction to what I was doing.

He had pulled his bottom lip between his teeth and his eyebrows were raised while his eyes were squeezed shut. It was a beautiful sight, and I literally couldn't wait to see what he would look like when I was inside him.

Finally sliding his pants down his legs and tossing them to the floor where my shirt already was, I quickly got rid of his t-shirt, pulling it over his head. My mouth worked its way down his chest, stopping by his left nipple to suck on it. Harry's back arched up, causing our erections to rub against each other.

"My G-God Louis, shit," he moaned, wrapping his arms around my lower back and pulling me flush against his almost naked body.

I hummed around his nipple, releasing it to leave a kiss to his other three ones before moving down to his navel and v-line. Leaving wet open-mouthed kisses all over his skin, I finally reached the waistband of his boxers.

My tongue darted out to lick the skin just above it as I slipped my fingers under the material and wrapped them around his semi-hard dick. A loud grunt escaped Harry's lips as he curled his fingers in my hair, gripping my locks roughly. "Feels good, hmm?" I muttered against his v-line as I worked my hand up and down his shaft.

"Ungghh, yes, so good Louis, s-shit."

I flicked my wrist, moving my hand up and down his length a few more times before I pulled my hand out of his boxers. He whined at the sudden loss and opened his eyes to look at me with a pout. Before he could say anything, though, I leaned up to give him a quick kiss on the lips. "I'm just going to get out of these uncomfortable skinny jeans," I winked, causing him to roll his eyes.

I reached down to unbutton them but was interrupted when two other hands slapped them away. "I'll do it."

A wide smile was playing on his lips as he said this, and I couldn't help but let out a small chuckle. He was just too adorable and cute for my own good. "Go ahead then."

He quickly popped the button open but slowed down when he unzipped my pants, teasing the hell out of me by brushing his fingers against my erection. "Just get them off, Harry. Or else I'm doing it myself," I warned, already moving my hands towards his.

He actually listened to me and pulled down the zipper all the way before my hands could come in contact with his. He slid my pants and boxers off in one go, surprising me a little because I didn't think he had the confidence to do so.

"Why are you so shocked?" He asked, glancing down at my lower region, licking his lips as he did so.

My mouth dropped open, but I quickly closed it again, giving him a mischievous smile. "You're a filthy little slut," I murmured, dipping down to take his bottom lip between my teeth, tugging on it lightly.

He hummed a reply, trailing his fingers up the back of my thighs until they were resting on my butt cheeks. "Just get inside me already," he slurred as soon as I had released his lip, pulling me down by a squeeze of my cheeks so my bare erection could rub against his clothed one.

I let out another moan, restraining myself from ripping his boxers off and pounding into him already. It was so damn tempting. "As you please, my love," I breathed, leaning down to connect my lips with his as my hands fumbled with the waistband of his boxers, finally getting rid of them.

Once the two of us were fully naked, I opened the drawer next to my bed and pulled out a bottle of lube along with a condom. I ground my hips down against his, creating friction between the two of us. I was just about to tear the condom open when Harry took it away from me, tossing it somewhere in the room. "You're clean, right?"

I raised my eyebrows but nodded slowly. "Of course, I always use protection."

"Me too, but I want to feel you, so how about an exception?" He twitched his lips up in an innocent smile, which made me want to smack him on the back of his head right then and there because what we were doing right now was not innocent whatsoever. Neither was what he just asked me.

"Fine, but only because you asked so politely," I said sarcastically, making him roll his eyes.

"My innocent smiles always work, just admit it."

"Never," I mumbled, leaning down to kiss him on the nose, his forehead, his cheeks then finally his mouth. I moved my hands to his hips, trailing my fingers up and down his sides.

"You sure about this?" I asked slowly, looking up at him.

Harry stared into my eyes, nodding with a small smile on his face.

"Good, but I wanna warn you that I've never done this with a guy before, so I may be shitty." I bit down on my bottom lip, feeling a little nervous all of a sudden.

What if I really was shitty at doing it with a boy? What if Harry wouldn't even enjoy it? And what if it was an entirely different thing doing it with a guy? Oh, come on. There couldn't be too much of a difference, now could it?

Harry took my head in his hands, looking me deep in the eyes. "Don't worry about that, Louis. I'm sure you'll be great. Moreover, we're doing it together, right?"

I let out a deep sigh, nodding my head. "Together," I agreed, dipping my head down to capture his lips with mine in a kiss full of love and passion.

Popping the cap of the lube open, I coated three of my fingers with the substance and started circling my index one around his rim. "You ready?"

He nodded vigorously, glancing down at me with a small smile on his face. I slid my finger inside him, stopping when I was knuckle-deep due to the fact he let out a whimper. "You alright?" I reached up to caress his cheek lovingly as I looked at him carefully.

His eyes were squeezed shut and he had scrunched his nose up a little. "I'm okay, Louis. Just, go o-on." His voice cracked in the end, causing me to start contemplating if this was such a good idea, after all. I didn't want him to suffer like this.

"Harry, I'm--"

"No, Louis. I want you to continue, please?" His eyes were now open, and he was staring at me with this pleading look on his face. It was impossible for me not to listen to him. Damn him and his ways.

I let out another sigh, pushing my finger a little deeper before pulling it out and thrusting it back in again. I proceeded to do this a couple of times until a loud moan escaped my boyfriend's lips, making my eyes widen.

"Add another finger."

Doing as he said, I started scissoring him, opening him up the best I could. Once he was finished being prepped, I pulled my fingers out and coated my dick with lube. I lined up at his entrance, my forearms on either side of his head as I pushed in, bit by bit. Harry's face was scrunched up in the sexiest way possible, his bottom lip stuck between his teeth and eyes clenched shut.

"Tell me if it hurts," I ordered once I was halfway in, searching his face for any sign of discomfort or pain.

He only shook his head, gripping my hips so he had a firm hold of them. His fingers dug into my skin, and I took that as a sign to thrust all the way inside him, pushing my hips forward slowly as I did so.

I leaned down to press my lips against his neck, littering his skin with red marks. My mouth soon found his lips, and together, they met in a wet kiss with teeth and tongues clashing and swirling together. I eventually moved my hands to his hips, gripping them tightly as I pulled out almost all the way before pushing back in with a snap of my hips.

He let out a deep, filthy moan, gripping my ass cheeks roughly. I picked up a rather quick pace, thrusting in and out of Harry, hard.

"S-shit, Lou, you're so f-fucking amazing... unghh," Harry moaned, arching his back from the mattress to meet my deep thrusts.

We tried to have our mouths connected, but as my movements only increased even more, it was almost impossible. The only things you could hear in the room were the sound of skin slapping against each other, the sound of the headboard hitting the wall with my every thrust, and our loud moans that escaped our lips every now and then.

"You feel so good a-around me, gosh," I breathed, changing the angle a little, in search of his prostate.

When Harry let out the loudest moan yet, I knew I had found it. Hitting the same spot over and over again, he became a whimpering mess under me, clawing his hands up my back towards my nape. He pulled at the roots of my dyed black locks, breathing deeply in my ear. "I'm gonna c-come."

I hooked his legs over my shoulders, determined to go even deeper and harder into him. This apparently became too much for Harry because the next second, he came undone between us, squirting his liquids onto his stomach. The feeling of him clenching around me drove me over the edge and before I knew it, I was releasing my own load deep inside him.

As soon as I had ridden out of my orgasm, I collapsed on top of Harry, hugging him close to me. We didn't say anything for a while, just letting ourselves catch our breaths.

Once our hearts were beating at a normal speed in our chests again, I pulled out of him and rolled off of his torso so I was lying on my back beside him instead.

"That," he said, scooting closer to me so he could nuzzle his face into the crook of my neck and wrap his arms around my waist. "Was the best sex I've ever had. By far."

I snaked my arms around him and placed a soft kiss on his forehead. "Same here," I mumbled against his skin.

I suddenly felt my eyelids get heavy by the second, but I forced my eyes to stay open because this was a moment I knew I would remember for the rest of my life, and I didn't want it to end this soon. "I love you," I mumbled, carding my hands through his dark curls.

He looked up at me with a smile on his face. "I love you too," he said, leaning up to kiss me on the lips tenderly.

I smiled into the kiss, loving every second and millisecond of it. Truth be told, I loved absolutely everything that had to do with Harry, and I wasn't planning on changing that anytime soon... if ever.

A few months ago, I could never picture myself being here today, doing this with Harry - the boy I had hated more than anyone else. Everything had changed since then, and I now couldn't picture myself not being here, doing this with him this exact day.

It was all pretty insane how so much had happened in so little time. I had gone from hating a person to loving them to bits in just a matter of months, and the best part of it all was that I didn't regret one thing. I mean, how could I when the best person in the world was lying here beside me, tracing one of my many tattoos on my chest while kissing my neck?

"I can't believe it all started with a kiss," I breathed in disbelief, making Harry stop his movements and look up at me.

He shook his head while staring at me with big, green eyes, a small smile prominent on his lips. "No, Lou. It all started with *the* kiss."

And with that said, I pulled him in for another of the many kisses we had and would share, just like I had done that one time in the hallway.

THE END!

Printed in Great Britain
by Amazon